TRADITION

TRADITION

BRENDAN KIELY

MARGARET K. MCELDERRY BOOKS

NEW YORK   LONDON   TORONTO   SYDNEY   NEW DELHI

MARGARET K. McELDERRY BOOKS

An imprint of Simon & Schuster Children's Publishing Division

1230 Avenue of the Americas, New York, New York 10020

MARGARET K. McELDERRY BOOKS is a trademark of Simon & Schuster, Inc.

For information about special discounts for bulk purchases, please contact Simon & Schuster Special Sales at 1-866-506-1949 or business@simonandschuster.com.

The Simon & Schuster Speakers Bureau can bring authors to your live event. For more information or to book an event, contact the Simon & Schuster Speakers Bureau at 1-866-248-3049 or visit our website at www.simonspeakers.com.

Jacket design by Russell Gordon, interior design by Brad Mead

The text for this book was set in Adobe Caslon Pro.

Manufactured in the United States of America

First Edition

2 4 6 8 10 9 7 5 3 1

Library of Congress Cataloging-in-Publication Data

Names: Kiely, Brendan, 1977- author.

Title: Tradition / Brendan Kiely.

Description: First edition. | New York : Margaret K. McElderry Books, [2018] | Summary: At Fullbrook Academy, where tradition reigns supreme, James Baxter and Jules Devereux take on privilege, sexism, and the importance of consent.

Identifiers: LCCN 2017026455 (print) | LCCN 2017039364 (eBook)

ISBN 9781481480345 (hardcover) | ISBN 9781481480369 (eBook)

Subjects: | CYAC: Conduct of life—Fiction. | High schools—Fiction. | Schools—Fiction. | Wealth—Fiction. | Rape—Fiction. | Sexism—Fiction.

Classification: LCC PZ7.K5398 (eBook) | LCC PZ7.K5398 Tr 2018 (print) | DDC [Fic]—dc23

LC record available at https://lccn.loc.gov/2017026455

For my mother and father,
who continue to remind me that all love begins with listening,
and for Jessie and her listening heart

THERE'S REALLY NO SUCH THING AS THE "VOICELESS."
THERE ARE ONLY THE DELIBERATELY SILENCED, OR THE
PREFERABLY UNHEARD.

—ARUNDHATI ROY

THEY HAND IN HAND WITH WAND'RING STEPS AND SLOW
THROUGH EDEN TOOK THEIR SOLITARY WAY.

—MILTON, *PARADISE LOST*

For the record . . .

JAMES BAXTER

Most people don't get second chances. I wasn't sure I deserved one. I wasn't sure I even wanted one. But I got one: Fullbrook Academy. This is what I did with it.

JULES DEVEREUX

I once heard another girl put it like this: This is a boys' school and they accept girls here too. At Fullbrook, they told us to be ready to take on the world, but then they told us to do it quietly. What if I wanted to be loud? What if I needed to be?

The night everything changed . . .

JULES DEVEREUX

I'm fighting for breath and all I can do is look up and see the white flame of moonlight outlining each branch, every leaf. I'm in the dirt, again, shoulder against the tree, the shock of air so cold it seizes my bones. I can still feel his grip on my arm, as if he's still here, shackling me to the trunk with his hands and his weight, but he's not. He's gone. I'm so cold. I'm shaking, but it feels like it's this tree and the sky above that are shaking, that are blurry, unreal, no longer what they were. It's as if I'm naked, but I'm not. It's as if the ground is swinging up to slap me, but it's not. I collapse by the edge of the bluff. There are still voices in the woods behind me. Voices down along the far end of the bluff. Voices in the night air like invisible birds screeching in the wind.

There's a voice inside me, too. It's mine, I think, but it doesn't sound like me. It's me and it's not me. It grows louder and louder, barking, bellowing up from somewhere and squeezing my head with noise. It's me and it isn't, or it's me splitting in two, and this other voice, this new voice, keeps shouting. *Run*, it says. *Run, run, run.*

I'm so close to the cliff edge, I could crawl forward and drop, crouch on one knee by the side of the pool like I did when I first learned to dive, but I'm hundreds of feet in the air, and the voice tells me to back up. I obey. It tells me to stand, and I use the tree to help me to my feet. *Run,* it says again, and I do, into the woods, down the far path, away from the party, away from the other voices, away from everyone. I know where I'm going, but I still feel lost. Alone. I just want to get home, though the word means nothing now. Just because I live there doesn't mean it's somewhere safe.

JAMES BAXTER

I can't believe this, but I'm so out of breath I have to crouch down and lean against the back wall of the girls' dorm, just to put some air in my lungs. Damn, it hurts. But you can't lug a passed-out person through the woods, across campus, get her up through the bathroom window, and not want to collapse. Even if you're me. And even if I did get some help.

I know she thinks I'm an asshole, and I didn't do it to change her mind. I just did it because it was the right thing to do and I knew it was the right thing to do, and it was the first time in a year I'd felt so certain I knew right from wrong—that I had to do the right thing and forget all the rest.

If you care about a person, my ex-girlfriend used to tell me, don't just tell her. Show her. Show up, listen, and act so she knows you heard her. Seems so simple the way she put it, but it's never that simple. An avalanche of other pressures buries that wisdom most days, all days, except this night, when, for some reason, I heard that advice strong and true, like a wind through the eaves of the old wooden rooftop above me.

Way up in the sky the man in the moon has something like sad eyes, as if his pale face gazes down with pity, as if he wishes something better for us, or maybe wishes we ourselves were the ones who were better. I'm sure I'm sober, not drunk, just going a little crazy to think like that, but I think it anyway, because I feel that way. Sad. Like this whole stupid paradise, this very good school, is nothing but a fancy promise, a broken one, a big lie. And worse, that I'm actually a part of it.

PART ONE

BEFORE

CHAPTER 1

JAMES BAXTER

n the mess of my first day at Fullbrook I had one clear
thought: *I do not belong here.* I didn't have the right clothes,
the right hairstyle, the right way to speak. I didn't even know
I had no clue about any of those things until I stood on the sidewalk outside my new home, boys' dorm number 3, Tapper Hall,
and watched the families swirling around the residential quad.
The seniors managing Move-In Day strolled around in their
soft-toed loafers, their linen jackets and ties, relaxed and carefree,
putting parents at ease with the smiles they tossed to each other
across the walkways and grass. I watched, amazed, as some of the
freshmen plucked those smiles out of the air and tried them on
for themselves. They were naturals.

Not me. I was the eighteen-year-old moron starting all over
again at a new high school. A fifth year—postgraduate, they call
it, to be kind.

"Hey," one of the linen jackets said, approaching me. "You must
be the Buckeye." All I wanted to do was hide, but the sun was a

spotlight burning down through the leaves of the tree above me. When I didn't respond, he continued. "They told me you were an athlete from Ohio." He grinned. "Just look at you. You got to be the Buckeye. Hey, Hackett," he yelled over his shoulder. "Found the Buckeye."

I tried to look natural but I never knew what to do with my hands. That's why I'd grown up holding a stick or a ball or a dumbbell. I clasped my fingers behind my back, and ended up looking like some keyed-up military man. I even had the stupid buzz cut.

All these guys had hair they had to style. Especially the guy walking up to us, the one called Hackett. These guys looked like they flossed their teeth with the kind of money I'd make in a summer working Uncle Earl's farm. The short guy with a pit bull's bulging shoulders and flat-faced grin, and his taller friend, the shaggy-haired pretty boy, the one called Hackett.

"What's up?" I didn't mean to sound standoffish, but I did. It comes too easy. I'm the kind of guy people expect to punch holes through walls—not because I want to, just because I can.

"Freddie." The pit bull stuck out his hand. I took it.

The pretty boy looked on, sleepy eyed. "Hackett," he said, without taking his hands from his pockets. "Ethan Hackett."

"Hackett and I," Freddie continued, "we've been assigned to you. All the new guys get a mentor to show them the ropes. Mostly freshmen, of course, but there are a couple PGs this year. So whatever, you're one of the new guys."

"We actually picked you, Buckeye," Hackett went on.

"Ha!" Freddie barked. "No, I got assigned to you because I

play real sports too. Hackett thinks skiing is a sport."

"Ignore him," Hackett said. "He has a limited vocabulary."

Freddie pushed Hackett, who stumbled, but balanced himself quickly. "See," Hackett said, smiling. "Guy talks with his fists."

"Back home everyone called me Jamie," I said, trying to say something.

"Yeah, great," Freddie said. "Drop those last two bags in your room, Buckeye." He wiped a broad arc in the air. "We'll show you around."

Freddie urged me on, slapping me on the shoulder, pushing me through the dorm. He and Hackett walked down the hall throwing those smiles, shaking hands with parents and freshmen along the way. "Welcome to Fullbrook!"

They could have been running for office.

Once we'd dumped the bags and were back outside, Freddie led us up the street between the dorms. "Girls," he pointed. "Girls. Boys." He grinned. "We'll get to the girls themselves later."

"Cool," I said, trying to follow him. I was taking in the sweep of scenery, the narrow, zigzagging paths winding through clusters of trees, connecting one brick mansion to another. The blue day—even the watery reflections in the stained-glass windows seemed curated, cultivated, perfected. History was everywhere, looming over me like the long, leafy branches casting shadows over the walkway.

"Hear you're a football player."

A sliver of pain sliced through me. "Was." Football was out. That life was over. One play and it was as if I'd ripped a hole in the ground and pulled my whole town down into the darkness below. "I'm here for hockey."

My second sport. The one my family, Coach Drucker, and the handful of people who still talked to me back home all told me was my ticket up and out. Kid like you deserves a second chance, I'd been told.

"Yeah, yeah. I know," Freddie went on. "You're the new secret weapon. But this is fall. Football, football, football." He stutter-stepped, threw a fake left, and rolled around Hackett. He got a few paces ahead of us, stopped, and turned back. "What I mean is, Coach O would give his left nut to have you on the football team. What'd you play?"

"Linebacker."

"Damn. That's what we need, man! A defensive line. Blitz pressure. Sacks."

He rambled on, setting nerves on fire beneath my skin. I hadn't been on campus for an hour, and already I could hear the echoes from back home. *What the hell's the matter with you, Jamie?*

"Look at you. Must have racked up a hell of a hit count. We scratch ours in rows on our lockers." He bumped me with his shoulder. "Hit, hit, hit." He nodded. "You know wassup."

"That's right."

"Why aren't you playing?"

I searched for something that wouldn't sound as awful as the truth. "Grades," I lied.

"For real?" Freddie said. "You have to do it all here, Buckeye. Do it all. Be it all."

We crossed another street and Hackett pointed to a tree in

front of the administration building. "Oldest tree on campus," he said. "I don't know, 250 years old, something like that." He pointed to a break between branches. From where we stood looking up, the branches perfectly framed the engraved lettering in the arch above the front door of the administration building. It was Latin, which I only guessed because of the weird *V* for a *U*.

"School motto?"

"That's right," Hackett said. " *'Ut parati in mundo.'* Ready to take on the world, we say." He grinned at Freddie.

"Are you screwing with me?"

"No," Freddie said. He rolled his eyes.

"Yeah, it's corny as hell," Hackett continued. "They'll take the whole freshman class here and show them this. They'll talk about the tree, its deep roots, its soaring branches," he said, dropping his voice cartoonishly. "They'll point to the school motto and remind them what it means to join the Fullbrook legacy."

"Corny," Freddie echoed. "Now let's get to the real shit."

Ready to take on the world? I'd seen the motto when I'd visited the previous spring. Everybody at Fullbrook seemed like a genius to me, already worldly, already honing their special skill, building robots, singing arias, starting their own tech company. I wasn't ready to do one night's homework. I wasn't ready to tie a tie. What did I do? I could stop a puck from passing between the pipes—but I had to make it all the way to winter before anybody would care about that.

They swung me around the administration building and into the academic quad. The lawn in the center was as long and wide as three football fields combined. In fact, Fullbrook might as well have been a college campus. It had the multimillion-dollar sports complex, physics lab, arts center, and global studies buildings to prove it, not to mention the two-hundred-year-old redbrick mansions and halls housing all the other classrooms and offices. At the far end of the lawn, at the edge of the forest that surrounded the campus, were the baseball and football fields. But next to the sports complex, set slightly apart, as if to show off that it was there in the first place, was the hockey rink.

"That's it," Freddie said, pointing to the small stadium. "That's where it's all going down this year. I swear we're making it to States." The roof over the rink was concave, and because the great lawn sloped toward it, the entire building seemed sunk into the ground, the forest rising above it in the distance. The gleaming roof caught and threw back the light of the sun.

"Yeah, right," Hackett said.

"Not football, maybe," Freddie conceded. "We're too small." He eyed me. "But hockey? Hell, yes." He clamped down on my shoulder. "We got our new secret weapon, right here. New goalie. My man, the Midwestern Monster."

That nickname stuck like a fishbone in my throat. I was speechless.

He laughed and I forced a weak smile in return. "I know Coach O's got to be talking to you about playing football, too," he continued. "We need a line, man."

Coach O'Leary wasn't. He wasn't supposed to. Football was out. Instead, we were supposed to meet the next day to begin planning my off-season training. I had to get decent grades, show the college world I was worth its time. I had to be ready to show my stuff this winter. I'd been All-State junior year, but I hadn't played senior year, so everybody needed to see that I was the goalie they all believed me to be. Coach O was counting on me. Back home, my folks were counting on me, and Coach Drucker. My old principal, too. Even Uncle Earl. This winter, everything was on the line.

CHAPTER 2

JULES DEVEREUX

I'd been sitting behind the folding table for nearly two hours before I realized that if I was going to give away any pamphlets at all, I was going to have to get off my butt and start handing them out. It had been a battle to get my request taken seriously in the first place and an even bigger one to get it approved. When it finally was, I was hopeful enough to think it might be a smash hit. I was wrong.

At first, a few people took pamphlets from me without even looking. I didn't mind that. As long as they had them—that was the point. But others were more hostile.

"Please. We don't need that," a mother of a first year said to me, using her forearm to block me from handing her daughter one of my pamphlets.

I offered her my *hey, I'm just saying* half smile, but she pushed past me. "I'm trying to be helpful," I called after her, but they hurried toward the dorm. I shook my head and turned back to the street. There was a line of cars parked haphazardly along the curb.

Parents fumbling with bags and plastic storage bins. Girls with their heads bent toward their phones, which wouldn't last long at Fullbrook—they were pretty strict about no phone usage, when they could enforce it. Move-In Day was an exception, of course.

I tried another first year by her family's car. "There's a lot of important info in here," I told her.

She took it and thanked me.

"You excited?" I asked her.

She nodded. "Yeah," she eventually got out. She did look excited—but also nervous. I could see the sweat already wrinkling the pamphlet I'd just given her.

"HPV vaccines, Plan B, body image counseling," I said. "Better to know than not know."

The girl's face went fifty shades of red and, as if she had a sixth sense for that kind of thing, her mother poked her head over her daughter's shoulder. She glanced down at the pamphlet and read the bright pink header: WOMEN'S HEALTH. She gently pulled the pamphlet from her daughter's fingers, looked at it briefly, then cocked her head and glared at me.

"Excuse me," she said. "Do you think this is appropriate?"

"Our health?" I asked. "Of course, right?"

"Birth control? Condoms?"

"Well, that's part of it. We have to be safe and stay protected. But there's so much else in the pamphlet. The health center has a dedicated specialist for women's health, and she's a resource for—"

"What's your name?" she snapped.

"Jules Devereux. I'm a senior and I run the—"

"I'm going to get to the bottom of this immediately." She grabbed her daughter's hand and yanked her down the walkway toward Mary Lyon Hall.

I'd suspected the first day back at Fullbrook was going to be tough, so I'd made a plan to give the day a boost from the jump: I'd gotten in an early swim and I'd made a serious dent in my paper on the summer reading, and with all that forward momentum, I'd psyched myself up for pamphleting. I'd wanted to do it the last two years, but nobody would agree to do it with me. Finally, I decided I'd just have to do it myself. I didn't realize how much it was going to suck doing it alone.

I'd gone to the trouble of donning what I called my 1950s Catholic school outfit, because I knew Mrs. Attison would appreciate the "attitude and decorum," as she'd say, even though it was sunny and warm, the kind of day that made you wonder why wool sweaters had ever been invented. So while maybe Mrs. Attison looked on with a dash of approval—hard to tell with her; she always held herself like one of those stone-faced people in a nineteenth-century daguerreotype—I wasn't sure it was worth it. I needed to get some of my classmates to join me so I didn't look like some fringe radical—which I wasn't. All I was doing was passing out health center flyers, not trying to induct first years into some hedonistic, druggy sex cult.

"Want to help?" I asked Shriya, as she approached. I'd seen her at the pool earlier too, training hard. I wasn't on the team like she was, so I hadn't wanted to bother her there. Now she was dressed like she was going to an interview: a gray pencil skirt and heels and a blouse as black as her hair. I held the bundle in the air and waved it at her—almost making fun of myself with mock extra enthusiasm.

She glanced ahead, over my shoulder to the dorm. "I can't." She hesitated and avoided looking at me. "I'm already helping with the tours." She flashed a fake smile. "With Gillian, obviously."

And of course there was that, too. Last year I'd told Shriya there didn't have to be a split. She didn't have to choose sides. But that was dumb. Of course there were sides. There are always sides, and she didn't choose mine.

I took a deep breath. I wanted to show her it didn't hurt as much as it did—or maybe I just wanted to fool myself. "It's cool," I said, as she was walking away. I shrugged and didn't know why. It's not like anybody had made me come out here to pass out the pamphlets. I just wanted to do something good for the community.

It took all of no time for the mother who was pissed at me to find Mrs. Attison on the front steps of Mary Lyon. They'd barely said hello to one another before the mother turned and pointed to me. I knew exactly what was coming.

Mrs. Attison walked with her hands bouncing slightly on either side, a kind of sped-up sway. When she got to me, sweat glistened above her eyebrows. "Julianna, I think it's time to wrap it up."

"Oh, I'm happy to stay out here to the end of the day. It's important, you know."

"I know." Her mouth folded into a tight, wrinkled stamp. "I'd appreciate if you stopped all the same." She took a step back, as if that was the end of it.

"I'm just passing out health center pamphlets," I added. "It's like passing out pamphlets about the gym or the arts center. What's the difference?"

"Julianna, I'm on your side. It's one thing to provide help. It's another to shove parents' worst fears in their faces as they're dropping off their kids."

"It's all available at the health center. What's the big deal?"

"You always have to push it one step further, don't you?"

"That's not how I see it."

"Of course not."

"I'll sit behind the table if that is somehow better, but—"

"Julianna, this isn't a discussion."

"Mrs. Attison."

"Julianna." She rubbed her thumb and forefinger like she was balling wax. "For once, try not to make a scene. Try to take a step back and be a team player." When I shook my head, she continued before I could make my argument. "This is your senior year. The last thing you want to do is make this year difficult for yourself. The politicking is done for the day."

This shut me up. I was stunned. I simply nodded.

"Thank you," she said, collecting herself. "I have to get the tour leaders prepped."

Prepped. Now *there* was a familiar word at Fullbrook. Make sure you are prepped. Prep this, prep that. So much prep. Sometimes I wondered if "prepped" was actually the right word. There were a lot of rules at Fullbrook, written and otherwise. Unspoken codes. Codes Mom had embraced and still lived by. This was her school, not mine. If she'd sent me elsewhere, what would that have said about Fullbrook? Or her, really? She'd been in the first class to admit women, and the codes had stuck with her. Or maybe they'd been a part of her all along?

A stone of sadness plunged deep within me. The lemonade pitcher sat mostly full on my folding table, and I pictured myself knocking back shots of lemonade all afternoon on my own, pamphlets leaving the table only when a breeze lifted them into the air and blew them like whispers across the quad.

CHAPTER 3

JAMES BAXTER

Freddie and Hackett walked me to the far edge of campus. When we got to the tree line beside the baseball field, they glanced around, then leapt over the metal gate in front of the access road and bolted down the dirt road. I followed, uneasy and wary, but it felt good to run, to get out of the sun and the feeling that people were watching, waiting for me to say something stupid or incorrect and prove to them that I really was the dumbass from corn country they all thought I was.

Once we'd turned a bend and the campus was out of sight, we slowed. "Not supposed to be down this way without supervision, of course," Freddie said.

"Cray-Cray might come zooming out of nowhere in his security cart," Hackett added. "But I doubt it."

The path bent around the base of a hill rising in the woods. The further we walked, the steeper and steeper the side of the hill became, until the path opened up to a narrow beach, where the cliff edge hundreds of feet above us was a sheer drop to the water. The river was a bright sheen of sunlight disappearing into the thick woods beyond.

Freddie pointed to the boathouse next to the beach. "Home to another one of Hackett's non-sports."

Hackett shook his head.

"Rowing isn't a sport, dude," Freddie continued.

"It's a race."

"Yeah, but not like a real race."

"It's in the Olympics," I added.

"Hell, yeah!" Hackett said, pointing two fingers at Freddie. "The Buckeye doesn't say much, but when he does—he gets you."

Hackett and I slapped hands, but it occurred to me that I'd never known anyone who played either of his sports, skiing or crew. Still, I liked the banter. Liked being a part of it all. There was something familiar—not the words, just being part of the conversation.

Mom, in her way, had given me only one mandate for my year at Fullbrook: *Make friends, James; you deserve them too.* Dad's had been another one entirely: *Don't screw this up. You have one more shot. Make it count.* Then he added *buddy*, as if that somehow softened it.

Freddie sprang over the rubble at the base of the cliff like a mountain goat. Hackett and I followed more slowly, to a rock that rose out of the water. We all wobbled at the top, trying to keep our balance and not flop forward into the river.

Hackett pulled out a Zippo. "Well," he said, putting his hand on my back. "Welcome to your first real Fullbrook tradition."

For a second I thought he was going to make me dive into the river, but he kept dancing the lighter through his fingers, rolling it around his knuckles. Freddie reached behind his back and pulled out a padded envelope he'd hidden beneath his blazer in his waistband. "Out with the old, in with the new," he said.

He pulled a framed photo from the padded envelope and held it in front of me. "But you're going to do it."

"That's right," Hackett said, pointing the lighter at me. "Come on, man. You weren't here last year. You haven't been here. You want to be a part of all this or what?"

"Yeah," I said, hoping I sounded as confident and carefree as he did.

Freddie nodded. "We stole it from the admin building."

"Why?" I didn't want it, but I found the package in my hand. Then the lighter.

"Tradition," Hackett said. "Seniors have been doing this since my father went here. We take one thing from the admin building to start the year."

"But no one has ever taken something directly from the headmaster's office," Freddie added. He nodded, trying to egg me on. "You're with us now, man. You got to jump in. We stole it. You burn it."

"Last year's graduating class," Hackett added, pointing to the photo.

"Burn it! Burn it!" Freddie chanted. "Out with the old, in with the new. This is our year! Come on, man. Do it! Do it!"

Hackett reached into his pocket and pulled out a flask. "Hold up," he said. "Take one down and pass it around." He swigged down a mouthful and passed the flask to Freddie, who did the same and passed it to me. I sniffed it. Hackett laughed. "That's Macallan 25. Bottle's in my room. Only break it out for the real occasions." He loosened half a smile. "It's the good stuff, man. You've probably never had it before, but trust me, this is what the big boys drink."

"Come on," Freddie said. "We don't have all day!"

"You're one of us now, Buckeye," Hackett said. "Drain it!"

It smelled like fire, woodsmoke in a can, and it seared my throat as it went down. I coughed and wiped my mouth. My eyes stung. "Holy crap," I said. "That's awful."

Hackett laughed. "So much to teach you, man." He put his arm around me, and even though I thought this was all stupid as hell, at least I wasn't sitting in my room staring at the wall, trying to figure out if my Pink Floyd poster was as out of place at Fullbrook as I was. Instead, I was out with Freddie and Hackett, with people—which was more than I could say for the last ten months.

I held the frame, turned it so the glass threw little spears of sunlight, and quickly smashed it against the rocks at our feet. Glass shattered, the frame splintered and snapped, and I pulled the photo loose from the mess. Freddie and I kicked what we could into the river.

"All right," I said, trying my damnedest to sound like them. "Out with the old, in with the new."

"Hell, yeah!" Freddie shouted again.

There was that butterfly feeling jumping in my gut, because ever since last fall I'd become overly hesitant and anxious, and every time I had to make a decision, I was stunned into wide-eyed inaction. I just wanted to do the right thing, but I had the hardest time knowing what that was. Something bugged me about what we were up to along the river, but it seemed worse not to just go with the flow with the guys. Freddie and Hacket weren't worried at all, so why should I have been a stick in the mud?

All right, Mom, here's me making friends. I held the photo and the envelope together, flipped open the Zippo, and set the flame to a corner. At first they smoked, blue-green veins burning and melting the bubble lining and photo paper, but they gathered, ignited more, and I held what seemed like a ball of fire in my hands for as long as I could, before dropping it into the river below me. *Don't worry, Dad—it's just tradition, they do it every year.*

"Woooo-hoooo!" Freddie hollered, tipping back, roaring at the sky.

"Last year's gone," Hackett said. His voice was steady, but he had some of Freddie's mania in his eyes too. "Last year's classes, gone. Last year's records, gone. Sports seasons, gone. A quarter of those Fullbrookers are gone too."

"And the new prospects have arrived," Freddie said.

Hackett shook his head but smiled.

"What?" Freddie asked, already bounding back down the rocks. "Come on, Buckeye. Let's see what these prospects look like. Little looking ahead to the Senior Send-Off, baby!" He waved to me over his shoulder.

At first I thought he was talking about the other athletes like me. "Gillian and Shriya probably have them down by the student center by now," he called back. Then it dawned on me what he really meant.

"Guy's an animal," Hackett said, as we climbed down the rocks after Freddie. "Tie a piece of meat to a string. Hang it out in front of him. He'll chase it for miles."

CHAPTER 4

JULES DEVEREUX

I t was so strange, starting senior year like that, feeling as if the ground was opening up beneath me, I was slowly sinking into it, and it might swallow me up for good. I was trying to figure out how to shake that feeling when I saw Javi strolling toward me.

Tie loose, collar unbuttoned, he wasn't wearing any socks either. Sunglasses. New. Versace, of course. I glared at him to let him know I was judging him. But not really.

"What?" he asked, playing along. "I'm not leading any tours today. I almost stayed in my room, but then I saw little old you fluttering across the quad all on your own."

"If you call me 'little' one more time . . ." I shook a finger at him.

He took off his sunglasses and faked a sad face, those green eyes of his dipping toward me. I held my glare for about half a second more, then walked straight into him, nose to his chest, arms at my side, expecting a hug, which he delivered immediately, closing me in. Even on a hot day he smelled so fresh, so clean, as he always did, which, to me at least, was part of what made him seem so strong.

"This sucks," I mumbled.

"Senior year? How is that possible? We can finally stand on the senior carpet outside the dining hall. We can finally sit in the senior couches in the library. Come on. We've been given the keys to the kingdom."

He couldn't stop himself from laughing, a boom I felt all around my head until he let me go and I stepped back to look at him—his perennial south Florida tan richer than when I'd seen him last, as if he were still at the beach, smiling up at the sun. He always looked more relaxed than I did, even when he wasn't. "It's good to see you, Javi."

"This was my biggest fear, this year. You."

"Thanks."

"No, seriously." He began pacing around me. There was something radiant about Javi; he danced when he walked, like a boy unable to hold back his enthusiasm. I loved him more now than I did then. All the kissing was behind us. It was something much deeper now.

"I have to get out of here," I said, waving at the bustle in front of Mary Lyon.

"Out of Fullbrook?"

I frowned. "I wish. No, but seriously. Take me away from here."

"Want to go for a walk?" he asked. He smiled, and I knew exactly what he was thinking.

"Sure. But remember I have rules this year."

"Rules? Julianna Devereux." He raised an eyebrow. "To quote

one of my absolute best friends in the world, 'Rules were made to be broken.'"

If I had to go to my mother's world for high school, I was determined to go to mine for college. I just had to get in first. Hence, the plan: my exit strategy. Senior year. I was going to be on top of all my shit. *One more year, one more year.* That was my mantra. Do everything I needed to do and more and skip everything that would get in the way. Stay focused. *One more year, one more year.* I looped my arm through his and tugged him back toward the table. "Help me clean up first."

He made me drag him down the path. "Jules, forget it. Mrs. Attison had her fit. You're done. Let's jet. It'll get cleaned up."

That was another phrase I heard all too often at Fullbrook, and it annoyed the hell out of me. As if it was magic. As if there wasn't a *someone* who would have to clean it up. As if it wasn't expected that those who made the mess had to clean it up.

"Come on," I insisted.

He rolled his eyes but followed me.

We broke the table down and propped it up beside the front steps—I didn't know where it belonged—and we bundled the pamphlets and brought them and everything else back to my room. By the time we'd finished and were heading out the front door, a campus tour was gathering near the front steps. Gillian and Shriya stood with their heads held high above the group of first years, explaining the route they were all about to take.

"Don't worry," Gillian explained. "You can always ask for help." She had changed her look. Gone was the preppy athlete of her first three years. The Gillian addressing the crowd was styled and polished like a TV pundit. Her blond was even whiter.

She glanced toward the steps and found me and Javi try-ing to squeeze behind the last lingering parents who'd already overstayed their welcome for Move-In Day. I looked up and, for some sick, Pavlovian reason, flashed her a quick smile.

Gillian and Shriya had been chipping away at me ever since Ethan and I had broken up the year before. They'd made it seem like I was breaking up with them, not him. Gillian especially. I was out. Out of their inner circle, the clutch of kids at the top of the social scene. I'd been one of them once without even trying, but Gillian and Shriya were the queens of Fullbrook this year, and I wasn't a part of it.

All I ran was my one-woman club. Gillian was the captain of the field hockey team, president of the Winter Ball committee. And if the guys ever had to vote, all the ones who weren't numb-nut racists would vote Shriya hottest girl on campus—since that was the dumbass kind of vote boys took the time to com-plete. And that was what it was, she was beautiful—but more important to me was that she had an air of authority, the poise of someone ten years older than me. It wasn't only Mrs. Attison who loved her. It was every single adult on campus. "A star is born," Headmaster Patterson said to a couple of other teachers, after Shriya's speech at our final all-community sit-down dinner last year, like they were taking credit for having molded her—as if she hadn't been brilliant before she'd come to Fullbrook.

But now that Gillian and Shriya had dropped me, I won-dered if we'd ever really been friends at all, or if the boys had been the center all along and we'd just orbited them, hoping to get pulled in closer. It pissed me off. We should have been our own center.

Now Gillian was with Ethan.

Javi grabbed my hand. "Can we please get out of here?"

"Please," I said, more demoralized than I wanted to sound.

We waved to the crowd, offered a few vague welcomes and hellos, and hurried across the quad. Once we were out of earshot, I leaned into him again. "So you're not going to abandon me this year?" I asked. I hated myself for sounding so pathetic, but I just needed to hear what I knew he was going to say.

"Yes," he teased. "Starting now." He spun out of my grip and skipped ahead. "Get away from me, crazy lady," he mocked. "I don't want to catch your crazy!" When I didn't run after him and sock him, he doubled back and looped his arm through mine. "No. I'm friends with everyone—I don't care. But if they are going to make me pick sides? Shoot."

It was true. Javi and I had always rolled around the edge of that inner circle.

"Besides. You know how I feel about Ethan."

He's not that bad, I'd told Javi a million times last year—until I'd finally broken up with him. At least Javi hadn't said, I told you so.

"Whatever," he said, as if he was reading my mind. "Let them have Fullofit. The rest of the world is ours."

We crossed Old Main, swung around the admin building, and took the road to the gym and student center. Just as we got near the side door, it swung open violently. Aileen had kicked it open with so much force, it hit the brick wall, bounced back, and tagged her shoulder as it closed. She spilled the coffee she was holding down her leg, and screamed.

"Are you okay?" I asked, running over.

"Can we get you a towel or something?" Javi said. He stepped past her into the stairwell without waiting for an answer.

I held her coffee and she brushed her skirt and tights. "The one frigging day I wear this shit." She glared at me, knowingly, because she and I were both pants girls. None of the cocktail dress attire so many of the other girls around Fullbrook wore. The school had abandoned uniforms a while back, but the dress code was still pretty strict. Aileen and I were the kind of girls who pushed it to the limit.

"At least it's black," I said. Because of course it was. Almost everything she wore was black, and if it was one of those times we could dress down, it was just a hoodie, or some T-shirt of a band that looked like it practiced Satanic rituals on stage during a show. Everything was black—except her hair, which she often wore in two long, thick blond braids that hung on either side of her head.

I tried to smile as I said it, but she gave me her hard glare back. "At least."

Aileen and I weren't friends, exactly; we'd only partnered on a few art projects together over the years, which I'd been grateful for, because she was the real artist, and I was more of a paint-by-numbers kind of girl. I'd always wondered why she hadn't joined the Social Consciousness Club, because I knew she cared about all the things I did, and it would have made it so much easier to be friends, but she roamed mostly as a loner, only jumping into the mix at parties here and there.

Javi rushed back out with napkins from the center, which he handed to Aileen. She dabbed at the coffee. "Goddamn, that was hot," she said.

"Are you burned?" I asked. "We can walk you to the health center."

Javi nodded along.

"I'm fine," she said. "Besides, I'm supposed to be introducing the arts center to the tour groups."

"Really?" As soon as I said it, I wished I hadn't spoken my first thought out loud. I hadn't meant it the way it came out.

"Yeah, really."

"Skip it," Javi said. "We're heading to Horn Rock. Want to come?"

"Right now? No." She stuffed the napkin wads in the barrel next to the door. "I'm a host."

"Yeah, but others will be there. Come have some fun."

"I'm not getting stoned with you two in the woods." She made it sound like it had never happened before—which it had, a few times, but always at night, always at one of the parties where everyone slipped through the shadows until the earliest hours of morning. "Too bad, huh?" she added. "Gillian and Shriya wouldn't let you lead the tours with them."

That stung. I wanted to say more, but I couldn't find the words. She had no reason to be extra nice to me, but I'd never been outright mean to her. I thought back, though. I guess I hadn't said anything when I'd seen others be that way to her. Collateral damage is real. What about collateral accountability? I hadn't thought about that.

Aileen walked off with a curt good-bye, and Javi and I didn't linger. The bluffs were off-limits, and it was one thing to sneak up there under the cover of night, but it was another altogether to go there during the day. We hustled to a narrow clearing at the far end of the bluff. Most of the late-night parties happened at the other end, at the wide patch of dirt around Horn Rock, but here, a slim pale elm clung to the edge, its roots fingering into the sandy rock, its trunk leaning out over the precipice. My tree. My favorite spot at Fullbrook. I'd discovered it my first year.

Javi pulled his vaporizer from his pocket and, as he'd done so many times before, pointed it at me.

"No."

"All right." He shrugged. "Whatever you say."

He took a hit and smiled. "Aaaand," he said, exhaling. "Let me tell you what happened this summer. This boy. I just wanted to climb up and down and all around him."

Javi was probably the most attractive guy at Fullbrook: a man's head of hair, thick and full, not curly, always groomed, and he was built like a man in his twenties too—not in some cartoonish way, just enough so you could see the lines of muscles slipping around his body. He'd always looked like that. He'd always had a smile that everybody bent toward like the sun. We'd made out on my very first night at Fullbrook. "No parents around?" we'd both said to each other. "Is this a dream?" And we snuck around that whole first year, finding places to make out every chance we got, until later, when he told me he was gay. We'd been sneaking around ever since, just hooking up with different people.

Javi unloaded about the clubs his older sister had gotten him into back home in Miami. E11even, Blackbird Ordinary, Bâoli, bars with swimming pools and fountains, beautiful men, lights flashing everywhere overhead, beneath your feet, in the corner of your eye. I loved Javi, and he loved that scene, but the endless party wasn't the be-all-end-all for me. There was something more. Hence, the rules. Like no smoking pot. I had to be sharp. Everything mattered. *One more year. One more year.*

While Javi smoked and talked, I looked out over the river and the dense, undulating carpet of trees rolling over the hills and the low, blue peaks beyond, as if there was nothing but wilderness out there, a vast and endless unknown, and Fullbrook, behind us, was the school that sat on the edge of the world.

Javi interrupted himself and nudged me. "Is someone down there?" he asked.

He pointed toward the river. Boys hollered from below, their yelps leaping up the cliff face. The boys shouted again. Loud whoops. Howling.

Javi and I crept toward the cliff edge. Below, and far to the right, closer to the boathouse, three boys stood on the rocks at the foot of the bluff, one of them holding what looked like a ball of fire.

"Insane," Javi said.

"It's Ethan."

"What?"

I could recognize him, even from that distance. His silhouette, long hair, the timbre of his voice echoing up to me. I knew I'd see Ethan as soon as I was back, but I didn't realize how much seeing him again would sting. I didn't miss him. It was almost like seeing him reminded me of a part of me I'd shed and no longer wanted but that still clung to me, not completely shakable, too close to be forgotten.

"How can you even tell from all the way up here?"

"I just can."

He poked me. "Don't you dare tell me you're still thinking about him."

"No."

"You don't miss him?"

"Good God, no."

"I'm telling you. I always said, 'That guy? He's a snake.'"

The fire flared for an instant and then dropped, smoke and steam rising and disappearing in the air above the river, and the boys quieted, scrambling off the rocks toward the beach. Javi and I crawled away from the edge.

I whacked the dust off my skirt. "We should probably get out of here," I said. "All the fuss down there might get people looking toward the woods."

"No weed, girl, and you're still as paranoid as ever."

"Ha and ha."

He threw his arm around me.

"I'm not paranoid," I said. "I'm observant. Quick-witted. Quick-footed." I ducked out from beneath his embrace, sprang into a Superman pose, and beamed a ridiculous cartoon smile.

"Nice try," he teased.

Instead of scrambling back through the brush, we decided we'd take the narrow path behind Horn Rock down to the main boathouse road. Javi pulled me along, almost a skip in his step as he explained why he was so excited about everything coming out of Ultra and Electric Zoo this year, and I nodded along, just so incredibly glad to ride the wave of someone else's enthusiasm, because it was only the first full day back and I was already feeling exhausted and overwhelmed, and I hadn't realized how much I needed someone else to breathe a little joy into me.

But Javi stopped us when we reached the top of the downhill path. "What the hell?" he said.

He pointed into the trees off the path. A bra hung from the stub of a broken branch on an old fallen log. I stepped over and inspected the area around it. I couldn't find anything else. No other clothes. No other signs that someone had been there. Thin lines of moss and mold threaded through the cloth so the bra clung to the dead wood more than hung from it.

"Wait, do you think someone's already had sex on the first day of school?" Javi laughed. "Oh my God, I think I'm actually jealous."

"It's too dirty." It was. The mold and grime had stitched a kind of camouflage over the fabric. I was surprised he'd even seen it. "How long has this been here? Since last year?"

"How does that even happen?" Javi asked. He stifled a giggle, poorly. "Like whoops, where are my pants?"

"Are you serious?" I shot him a look. "Nobody just leaves this behind on purpose." I had the strangest urge to take it, and try to find out who'd lost it. Was she still here? Had she graduated? But I wasn't really going to touch it. Only the underwire and the plastic clasps were keeping the fabric from tearing apart altogether.

He cocked his head. "Jules, just leave it. Who knows what the hell happened."

"Might be from one of the parties at the bluffs last year. But I can't believe I didn't hear about the girl who lost her bra," I said. Last year, at least before I called it off with Ethan, I had assumed I'd been plugged into everything.

"Oh, really?" Javi cracked. "Like you think you know every little thing that happens at every party?"

"Don't you?"

He laughed and extended a hand to help me step back out onto the path. "I don't want to know it all."

He was right. We walked back down the path together, and Javi, because he was Javi, just instinctively knew I needed a hug, so he looped his arm through mine and squeezed me close as we walked. He could sense it. I didn't know why I was so shaken, but I was, just imagining all that I didn't know.

CHAPTER 5

JAMES BAXTER

Hackett held us up on the way back to look through the windows of the boathouse and point out the single sculls and the eight-man longboats. I tried to act excited, but I was with Freddie on this one. These sleek boats seemed worlds away from me.

Hackett put his arm around me. "All right, I get it. The finer things in life are lost on you." He laughed it off like he meant nothing by it. He steered me around so we faced Freddie. "We have to get this guy back," he continued, tugging at the yellow eye of my sweaty Cleveland Monsters T-shirt. "So he can get dressed for dinner."

What a school. The idea that I would change clothes for dinner. It freaked me out thinking about the vast number of formalities I'd have no clue about.

As we walked back, Freddie kept nagging Hackett, asking him to have Gillian put in a good word for him with Shriya. We were only a hundred yards down the road when I heard a branch snap up the hill. A boy and girl stood still on the path that went down the back side of the cliff. They stared at us. Freddie and Hackett hadn't noticed, so I stopped them.

"Hey," I said. "Who's that?"

They looked toward where I pointed. Hackett took a deep breath. "Oh, man," Freddie said. He waved, and when it seemed like they weren't moving or coming down, he shouted back up: "It's all good. We'll just wait for you here."

They said something to each other and then began to make their way down the hill, and when they got to us, the girl looked right at me for a moment, and I had the strangest jolt of homesickness. It had nothing to do with the way she was dressed, or what she looked like—it was the way she looked at me that reminded me so suddenly and powerfully of home. Everybody I'd met or seen at Fullbrook had had an air of knowing confidence, or if not that, then a loud, bright, electric joy, that made me want to pull back and get some space. Not her. She held her face tight, stared at me with a kind of intense skepticism, and I didn't mind it at all. It felt familiar.

"What's up, guys?" she said. It wasn't husky or low, but her voice broke occasionally, as if her throat was dry, or she didn't want to let the whole word out.

"Hey," Hackett said. He hesitated; then, as if he was going in for a hug, he leaned toward her, but she stepped closer to the guy next to her.

"This is like one of those moments where two people are walking alone on two different sidewalks, but they are approaching the same point, so then they have to suddenly walk side by side, even if they don't want to, right?" the guy with her said.

"Yeah, exactly," she replied.

"Relax, Javi," Hackett said.

"Oh, I'm relaxed," Javi said.

Hackett laughed. "I bet. Javier Alvarez. Day one and the dude is already stoned. I should have joined you two."

"Whatever," the girl said, glaring at Javi. She reached for his hand and started to pull him forward. "We'll just run ahead."

"Hey," Hackett said again, this time more forcefully. He stepped in front of her. "Jules." She wouldn't look at him. "How're you doing?"

"I'm busy," she shot back. "I have a college to get into."

Freddie belted out a laugh. "Oh, yeah. Like you won't get in everywhere."

"Easy, Freddie," Javi said. His face suddenly got still.

Freddie just shook his head and shuffled his feet, grinning at Javi.

She glanced at me again, obviously trying to ignore Freddie and Hackett. "You new?"

"Why don't you join our tour?" Freddie said. "We've been showing the Buckeye around." His face lit up. "We're his mentors."

"Lucky you," Jules said to me.

"Why are you acting so cold?" Hackett said. "I'm just trying to say hello. I can't even get a hello back?" He stepped away to let her pass. "So intense."

Jules grabbed Javi's hand again and pulled him past us. "Seriously," Hackett called after her. "That's how it's going to be this year? We can't even have a normal, everyday conversation?"

"It's not personal," Jules said over her shoulder. "Get over yourself, Ethan."

"What the hell?" Hackett said quietly. He looked stunned and hurt.

"Nice to meet you," I shouted after them.

Jules didn't turn around, but she shot a peace sign in the air as she kept marching them forward. "Thanks, Buckeye," she yelled.

Hackett and Freddie gave me a look.

"What?" I asked.

"Don't be an ass." Hackett glared at me.

"Who's being an ass?" I asked, but he ignored me. "Who was that?"

"Jules?" Freddie said. "Don't mind her. She thinks she runs the school."

"Yeah, but seriously."

"She and Hackett?" Freddie said. "They were scoring last year." He slapped my back and pushed us forward, but Hackett kept us moving slowly. Jules and her friend were walking so quickly, they disappeared behind the bend in the path back to campus.

"Scoring?"

"Yeah." Freddie grinned.

Hackett threw me another one of those lazy smiles. "You know."

"Gotcha," I said, picking up Freddie-speak. Everything was happening so quickly. I needed to stick my finger in a socket just to keep up with these guys. "Hooking up or whatever. You're a thing with someone."

Hackett laughed through his nose. "A thing. Yeah. Just like that." He dropped a hand on Freddie's shoulder. "Well, no longer.

Me and Jules, we're no longer a thing." He grinned. "She's all yours," he said to me.

I nodded, as if I agreed. No one said anything else for a bit, but as we got closer to campus, Freddie turned to me, frowning.

"But seriously. Buckeye, you gotta be thinking about it."

"What?"

"Girls, right? You're the new guy. Girls love that shit."

Actually, no. That wasn't the first thing on my mind. At that moment, I was mostly worried about what the hell I was doing at this school. I hadn't thought about girls since Heather and I had broken up. But now, at the thought of her, I couldn't help but remember the language of her drawn up knee, so dark and beautiful and brown, rising and falling as it rested on the shocking paleness of my belly. And how that was gone. How I'd lost her.

"Yeah, man," I said. The words just fell out of my mouth automatically. "Always."

"See," Freddie told Hackett, "Buckeye's going to fit right in. We just have to introduce him to the right people first." He grinned. "Like the Viking."

"Oh God," Hackett said. "Although?" He paused and raised an eyebrow. "Hell of a way to start the year." He and Freddie laughed.

"For real," Freddie said.

"Who's the Viking?"

"We'll introduce you," Hackett said.

"And first party we get you to," Freddie continued, "we'll find a way to get the two of you alone somewhere."

"The Viking?" I repeated, trying to sound as interested as they were. "All right."

"Oh, yeah." Freddie cupped the air in front of his chest. "Good times."

He and Hackett went on about how parties worked at Fullbrook. Nothing like home. There were no older brothers buying kegs and there were no empty houses. Curfew was taken seriously, and the faculty lived in the dorms. Security patrolled campus every night. Parties were harder to throw. But they had them all the same. They just had to be subtle and clever about it. "We have our ways," they said.

"Where there's a will, there's a way," Freddie said.

"Where there's a wallet, there's a way," Hackett echoed.

"Where there's a window, there's a way." Freddie and Hackett slapped hands.

Everything about life at Fullbrook was different. Different language. Different way of walking, of shaking hands, of holding yourself when you spoke to other people. I felt like a goddamn alien. Like I'd crash-landed on another planet and I was too far away from home to ever get back. And I couldn't go back. There was no way I could go home, and it felt like there was no home anymore anyway. Home was only home when it had still made sense, the home where I'd floated through school not worrying about a damn thing, because I didn't have to. Everything so familiar I could get from here to there with my eyes closed and talk to everybody I knew with my ears closed, so to speak, because I already knew what they were going to say. The home where I knew all the traditions and didn't have to slam scotch I'd never heard of, where I didn't have to wear a tie to dinner, home where girls wore jeans around school, just like I did, not dresses and skirts.

That home was lost and gone—and I was the one who'd ruined it.

Back in my room, before jumping in the shower, I pushed the bed over to the corner of the room and sticky-tacked Coach Drucker's little sign on the wall next to my pillow, so I'd have to see it every morning when I woke up: THERE'S NO SUCH THING AS FAILURE, THERE'S ONLY TRY AGAIN.

The previous spring, I'd been at a particularly low point of feeling lousy. I was out behind the house, staring at the old tire swing, when Coach Drucker pushed open the screen door and sat down next to me on the tiny back porch Dad had built the year before and still hadn't gotten around to painting. We were on the steps and he stuck his feet down into the high grass right next to mine. He'd obviously spoken to Mom in the kitchen for a while first.

"You don't deserve this, Jamie," he said.

I didn't answer because I disagreed. I wasn't sure what I deserved, exactly.

"Kid like you. You're supposed to go places."

I nodded. I'd been hearing the same line for months—ever since I'd dodged and avoided the hockey recruiters and thrown away my chances for a scholarship to college. I couldn't get in anywhere without hockey. What was the point?

When I didn't say anything, he continued. "There aren't many kids out there who have your talent. You owe it to the game."

You're just that good, Jamie, everybody said. But was I? It had all started when I was in fifth grade and we were looking for something to do. We wrapped duct tape around a few Wiffle Ball bats, tipped over a dumpster next to the old Kroger loading dock and called it a goal, and I stood in front of it as the guys whacked tennis balls at me. By the time I was sixteen I didn't really care, except it felt good to actually be good at something. *You're a goddamn phenomenon, Jamie.* They say Babe Ruth could see the seams on the baseball as it gunned toward him. It sounds crazy, but I believe it. For me it's the puck. I can see where it's going no matter how fast it's coming at me.

"I'm sorry," I said to Coach. It was the one clear thing I'd been able to say for months.

"Nope. I'm not hearing that," Coach said. "Things happen, Jamie. You got to accept that. You got to man up and move on."

"I'm not sure."

"Well, I am," he said, getting off the step and pacing out into the yard. He walked back. "My sister-in-law runs admissions for this boarding school in New England. Fullbrook. Hell of a place. I've never done this before, but I'm doing it for you. I'm calling in a favor. You didn't get your shot this year, and you were supposed to." He lifted his hat and wiped his brow. "Boys like you need exposure. You'll get national attention there, Jamie. Big league." He nodded and looked off across the yard. "Just think, I'll be able to say I knew you when. I'll be the guy who gave you your start." He spun back to me. "I can only call this in once. You're it. Gloria will understand."

Who you knew, where you went to school, where your family went to school, who they knew—those things just mattered in life, they unlocked doors and flung open heavy gates, even for an overweight farm boy like me. I was grateful, but I also felt like a spoiled piece of garbage, since I knew folks back home whose parents had been out of work so long the family could only pay for their groceries with their EBT cards. I was just a jerk who'd been given a second chance.

CHAPTER 6

JULES DEVEREUX

Headmaster Patterson stood beside the podium in the dining hall, resting one elbow on the edge as if casually leaning, except he wasn't, because he never did anything casually. It was still almost eighty degrees outside, the sun hadn't even set, and he stood in his dark three-piece suit, smiling his stiff, press-on smile, gesturing to everybody and nobody like the Queen of England.

Javi was already there, all the way across the room, near the podium, and already holding court with a few underclass students. He had them giggling like kids at the circus. He needed his fill of attention, and I didn't want to bring my cloud over there and rain on all the fun. Aileen stood by one of the tables closer to the door, and there were still a few empty seats, so I shot over to one next to her. "Mind if I take this one?"

"I don't care," she said.

The room filled quickly around me, and Headmaster Patterson cleared his throat in front of the microphone. "Please, everyone. Seats, please."

He cleared his throat again and was about to repeat himself, when Freddie burst into the dining hall holding a hockey stick above his head. He leapt up onto the closest chair and held the stick above his head with two hands. "This year!" he shouted. "Number one! Red Hawks number one!" Other guys on the team roared into the room behind him.

Cheers erupted. Applause. My shoulders cinched around my neck. I don't know why, but I laughed, almost painfully, as if it was kicked out of me.

Aileen gave me one of her irritated glares. "Animals," I said into her ear as the room got louder around us.

"Feral, hungry beasts," she replied. I laughed, honestly this time. She seemed to smile too, if only with her eyes.

Something I knew about her I wished I didn't: the boys called her the Viking. Not only was it mean and stupid, it was so patronizing. They meant it as a joke, but I thought the joke was on them. There was something steely and indomitable deep down inside her.

"Mr. Watts," Headmaster Patterson said without disapproval. "Okay, Mr. Watts." He chuckled as he said Freddie's name.

The mammoth I'd met earlier, the Buckeye, began a slow clap, and the other guys from the team joined him. They kept at it until more and more of the room clapped and stomped with them. "Red Hawks. Red Hawks," Freddie yelled, egging everyone on.

"Okay," Patterson said, backing away from the microphone. He didn't clap, but he couldn't keep his bald head from nodding along in rhythm with the clap and cheer.

"Red Hawks. Red Hawks. Red-Hawks. RedHawks, RedHawks, RedHawksRedHawksRedHawks!"

It was mostly guys stomping, cheering, hooting, thundering through the room, but some of the girls joined in too. Gillian and Shriya rallied a few of the younger girls.

Ethan stepped out behind Freddie, slapped him on the butt, and laughed. Freddie hopped off the chair and together they swung around the table and wove through the crowd until they found their tables on the other side of the room. The Buckeye looked around the hall, a little lost, then saw us. People cleared the way for him as he came over.

"Hey," he said to me and Aileen. Then he stood there silently, waiting for something to happen. He put his big hands on the back of the chair next to me. He smiled at Aileen, but kept looking at me from the corner of his eye. I frowned and stared back.

"Please, everyone," Patterson said into the microphone again. "Take your seats now."

The Buckeye plopped down. He nodded as if I should too.

"James Baxter," he said, sticking out his hand. "But Jamie is good."

"Look, Bucky," I said, taking his hand and squeezing it— none of that dainty *my hand's nearly weightless* kind of crap. "You guys just busted in here like a pack of frothy-faced hyenas. It's annoying."

"Just fun and games," he said. He had the look of a guy who was about to tuck his napkin into the collar of his shirt. "I think if I stood on one of those chairs," he continued, "it'd break beneath me. And I wouldn't want to make a mess on my first day." The

Buckeye might be built like a bear, but there was something soft in his smile, hypnotizing, and I knew why immediately. It was a rare thing at Fullbrook. It was honesty.

I realized I was one of the few people still standing in the room. I must have looked like I was about to make my own announcement. The Buckeye kept that smile aimed right at me, though—as if I amused him. "What?" I said, taking a seat. I could have made a speech—I'd done it plenty of times—but for some reason I found my cheeks burning. Even Aileen raised her eyebrows when I glanced at her, and that bothered me.

"Nothing," he said.

"What?"

"No, I've got nothing to say." He pulled the napkin out from underneath the silverware, unfolded part of it, and threw it over his thigh.

"I thought for sure you were going to tuck that into your collar," I told him.

"Why?" he asked. "We eating meatballs tonight?"

And that's when I surprised myself with my own honest laugh.

"Besides," he said, tugging at the collar, "I don't think I can get another thing in here."

It was true. Most people don't have actual neck muscles, but he did. The thing was enormous, just like every other part of him. I could have taken a walk around that neck.

"I welcome you all to the new school year." Patterson paused briefly, before launching into his standard convocation address, the one where he used the word "august" with all three of its meanings, just because he could. Around the room, some people looked up at him, nodding along, but many didn't. Most of us had heard a version of the address too many times before, and he droned on, killing time with his well-rehearsed nod toward earnestness. His voice only shifted as he began to wrap it up. "People say you raise yourselves when you attend a school like ours, or better, that you raise each other." He lifted his hand into the air as he spoke, giving it his best to reach the aspirational, as he neared the end of the speech. "Do that, as students have been doing here since 1801, raising themselves, raising each other. This life, here at Fullbrook, provides you with tremendous advantage. Take your advantage. Run with it."

Some people began to clap, but he gestured for everyone to quiet down. "We're proud of our traditions at Fullbrook." He leaned one arm on the lectern again and grinned. "Though some traditions might be more important to a few of you than they are to the rest of us. Starting the year by taking a photo from my office, for example?" He paused for dramatic effect. "Was that necessary?" He tried to look stern, but as giggles bubbled around the hall, he had a hard time keeping a straight face. "With all I have going on, you're going to make me start an investigation?" He waved to his secretary, who stood a few feet behind him, and she handed him a bag. "We take this kind of behavior very seriously."

I glanced at the Buckeye, who looked ashen. The guilt read all over his face, and I was certain that was what he and Ethan and Freddie had been burning by the river. Of course they'd been behind the annual convocation senior prank. "Don't worry," I said, leaning close to him. "They're not really going to do anything about it. They never do."

"Now we're going to have to search high and low," Mr. Patterson continued, holding up the bag. He pulled out a framed photo. "For this exact same photo." He nodded along conspiratorially as a low mumble rumbled through the room. "Am I going to have to bolt this one to the wall, guys?" He laughed, and many of the students and teachers laughed along with him.

"See what I mean?" I told the Buckeye.

"Now that we've had our fun, let's get down to business. Make this year the best year of your life so far," he bellowed. " '*Ut parati in mundo.* ' Ready to take on the world!" He stepped back from the lectern, and there was a burst of applause. Then he clapped along with the crowd, his hands echoing in the microphone. But unable to resist one more line, he leaned closer. "First, let's eat!" He smiled to himself as he stepped away from the lectern and the clatter of silverware on china rang out around the room.

While we ate, the Buckeye asked a few *get to know you* questions, mostly to me, but I was trying harder to talk to Aileen. She didn't add much. "You heading to Mary Lyon?" I asked her when people started pushing back their chairs and getting up. She was down the hall from me this year—which I was starting to look forward to. Of course, Shriya's room was between ours.

The Buckeye stood too. "I'd walk with you," he said, "but I think I have clean-up duty. What do I do?"

I couldn't help myself. "Well, you clean up," I said. I felt a little mean, but there'd be a bunch of people doing it with him, so he'd figure it out. I just wanted out of there. The day had already exhausted me.

"I'll show you," Aileen said to the Buckeye. "I have clean-up duty too."

Nobody ever wants that job, but suddenly I found myself wishing I had it. "'Kay," I said to her, way too chipper. "I'll just see you back there."

She shrugged. "Maybe." She couldn't have cared less, I realized, but now that I'd said it, I had to make sure I did it.

Out in the foyer, the senior carpet was packed—everyone taking advantage of their first day of being able to stand on it. I'd been pulled onto it a couple of times last year, and it had weirdly felt good, as if I'd been given a prize, but now that I could stand on it without a senior invite, it felt like the stupidest thing in the world. A land grab of a rug. Most of the guys leaned against the wall, scanning the crowd of students as they passed by on their way to the door. I knew exactly what they were doing. Their eyes floated from one body to the next like flies, landing, sticking briefly, and drifting on. They elbowed each other as they whispered into each other's ears. The two guys closest to me were on the football team. "Nice," one of them said loud enough for me to hear. I realized they were both staring at my bare legs.

One more year, one more year, I kept saying in my head. Spring couldn't come soon enough. By then I'd be accepted into college. Lands where trans-friendly bathrooms were the norm and mannequins weren't seen as the ideal body shape.

Headmaster Patterson stood by the door, laughing along with Freddie, who was telling him a story, gesturing with his hockey stick as if it was a scepter, and I decided I'd take the long way home: head out the basement door, loop around the other side of campus, and come up to the dorms from behind. I'd avoid everyone that way. It was the darkest side of campus, and unless Cray-Cray came zooming up the path for no reason at all, nobody would see me and I could let the night air blow all the Fullbrook intensity out of me—just let it get lost in the wind.

That was the plan. I waited until I was sure no one was looking, made a beeline across the foyer, popped open the basement door, slipped in, closed it softly behind me, and took the stairs down one flight as quickly as I could, until I wound around to the second flight—and nearly jumped right into Ethan and Gillian's laps. They were locked together in an open-mouth kiss, both half-sitting on the radiator against the wall on the landing. Of course they were here. It was another place I'd shown Ethan.

I spun around to run back up the stairs, but they'd already seen me. "Jules?"

Why did he have to say my name? Why couldn't he just let me slip away and deal with the embarrassment, not add to it by saying something? "Sorry," I said dumbly. "I didn't know."

"Are you spying on us?" Gillian asked. She said it with a laugh, though. She said it as if it didn't bother her at all.

"No," I snapped. This made Ethan laugh too, of course. "Sooo. Never mind." I began to make my way back up the stairs. "I'm just leaving."

"Oh, don't be all weird about it," Ethan said. "Stop."

For some reason, I did. I turned and looked down the stairs at him.

"Can this just not be weird, please?" he said. I wasn't sure, but

I thought he was asking both of us, me and Gillian. It confused her, too.

"What?" she said. "Nothing's weird."

"We can all just be cool, right?" he went on. "I mean, we were all cool with each other last year. Nobody had to get all worked up and crazy. Remember?" He smiled. He knew what he was saying, he knew what he was asking, but his voice—he was pleading. He sounded so much younger than he was.

"Oh, for God's sake, of course we're all cool," I said, realizing I'd been clenching the hem of my sweater. I let go. "Everything's cool. I just don't need to bust this whole thing up," I said, waving my hand at them. "I mean, you don't need an audience, right?"

"Ooooh," Ethan said, cocking his eyebrows at Gillian. "I mean, we could film it, right?"

Gillian forced a short, fake laugh, and I knew why. He must not have remembered, or maybe he didn't even know, because he was more idiotic than mean. A video of Gillian had gotten around our sophomore year. Another girl had taken it, of Gillian in the locker room. I'd thought Gillian was going to die from embarrassment. But she didn't. Time passed. Eventually, people stopped caring; other dramas flared up and attracted the flutter of gossip.

"Don't be stupid," I told him. "Nobody wants to watch you. But seriously," I continued, looking at Gillian. "Everything really is cool. We don't have to be weird around each other." Just to prove my point, I walked back down the stairs, right up to them, and put a hand on each of them. "Now, let me get out of here so you can get back to whatever you were doing."

I didn't let them say anything else, because I hurried down

the rest of the stairs and outside. I couldn't be sure if Gillian and Ethan had been screwing around behind my back when Ethan and I were together, but whatever, they didn't hide it after we broke up. She was all over him—he was all over her, too—and for some reason, every crazy story of their sex life came back to me. Did you hear Ethan and Gillian went skinny-dipping in the river? Did you hear Ethan and Gillian watched the sunrise from Horn Rock? Did you hear Ethan and Gillian snuck up to the roof of the arts center?

That last one pissed me off the most because I'd been the one to show him how to get there. I'd taken photos from the roof, and he'd liked the photos, supposedly, and wanted to see how I'd taken them, but we'd barely been up there two minutes before we were on our backs, rolling over each other, making out. In fact, I could have swapped Gillian's name out of any of those stories, because Ethan and I had already done all those things together, we just hadn't told anybody about it—or, I hadn't.

But that's how a place like this works. Rumors become stories. Stories become the truth. And we live by the lies we believe—at least until the *actual* reality becomes overwhelming. Then what?

CHAPTER 7

JAMES BAXTER

Even though the football season had already started and it was clear to the rest of the world I wasn't going to join the team, Freddie wouldn't stop. *For real, Buckeye, get your ass in action. You were born for this shit. You'd be out here crushing people.* Thing is, he had no idea how much he sounded like all the guys back home. Coach Drucker, too. My dad. *Get out there, boy. Hit-hit-hit—nice hit!*

"Hey," Freddie said, pulling me aside in the mathematics building after classes ended. It was only a week into school, and I was still blinded by the fog of equations from class. I was half walking, half stumbling down the hall. Freddie steadied me at the elbow. "We don't have practice today," he said, talking about football again. "Come by the bleachers at four."

I rolled my eyes. "You won't give up."

"Nope." He grinned. "But it's better than you think. I have a surprise for you."

A guy like me, a guy my size, isn't supposed to be scared, but

I was. I didn't want to be down by the field, but I didn't want to keep avoiding it either. Coach O'Leary had been bugging me that I should meet with him once a week, make a plan for getting in shape and being ready for hockey season, and I'd already begged off my first meeting, claiming I needed time to adjust to my classes. That wasn't a lie. I wasn't sure how the hell I was going to pass any of my courses, but also, I just couldn't get into the swing of training yet. It had been so long.

So I should have known, when Freddie told me he had a surprise, that Coach O'Leary would be a part of it. They stood side by side against the fence between the track and the sidelines of the football field. "Got to hand it to the Buckeye," Freddie said to Coach when I reached them. "The guy's punctual."

Coach O nodded. "The Buckeye. I like it." He dropped a hand on my shoulder and walked all three of us down the track, away from the football field. "Look," he told me. "We don't normally do this, but I talked to Patterson, and we just have to make an exception this year." Freddie bobbed his head enthusiastically. "The rink is operational year-round anyway, just have to adjust a few things here and there to keep other parts of the building open. So here's the plan." He pointed up the low rise toward the hockey rink. "Twice a week I want Freddie working you on the ice. We'll get you on a weights-and-cardio schedule too, maybe loop you in with the football team's schedule, we'll see, but first and foremost, let's get you back on the ice." He cocked an eyebrow. "After all, it's been a while."

Freddie held up a hand. A set of keys dangled from his forefinger. "And I have this," he said.

Coach turned to him. "And if you abuse this privilege in any way, I'll break your fingers." He liked to talk like that, adopting a slight shift in his voice, as if he was a gangster in a movie and wearing a three-piece suit, not a windbreaker over a shirt and tie.

He ushered us on without me saying much to agree. What was I going to say anyway? That was the whole point of me being there. I knew I was supposed to feel grateful, and I did, but I also couldn't help feeling like they'd bought me and I owed them. Scholarship kid. Full-ride kid. I owed them fifty thousand dollars or a trophy.

Freddie let us in the back door that led straight to the locker rooms, dug out some practice equipment, and we were out on the ice in no time. I got my bearings zipping around the rink for a while, picking up speed, cutting left and right, short hops, pivots. I didn't have my pads on at first, only the skates, helmet, and gloves, and Freddie came up behind me and leveled me against the boards.

He laughed as I picked myself up. "You have a long way to go," he said.

"Damn." I looked around, and even though the arena was dim and only half-lit, the seats empty, and I was chilled to the bone without the full uniform and pads, I couldn't help but smile. I took a deep breath. "Damn," I repeated. "It feels so good to be out here."

"I knew you'd love this," he said. "Come on, man, let's get you suited up. I'll drag out a net."

A couple minutes later, I was clipped into a full suit of goalie pads and hunched down in the net. Freddie took shot after shot. I missed the first few.

"Thought you were supposed to be a secret weapon," he teased. He kept at it, lining up the pucks and slapping them at me, faster and faster, and it didn't take long for the muscle memory to kick in. After the first few misses, it took him a while to sneak one by me.

"That's what I'm talking about, Buckeye."

He rushed the net with the last puck on his line, and I swiveled into position for the hit. He faked and crept closer, and just as he was about to take the shot, I sprang at him and took him out. He didn't have any pads on at all, not even a mask, and he slid across the ice on his back. For a second he said nothing, and my stomach dropped. A thousand nightmares rained through my mind and I was about to shout his name, when I heard him start to laugh.

"The hell?" He crouched on his knees. "Yes!" he yelled. "Yes, yes, yes!" He bounced back up onto his skates and zipped over. He threw an arm around me. "Dude," he said. "Twice a week. Fuck football." He knocked his forehead against my mask. He knocked again. I tore off my helmet and pressed my forehead against his. "You and me," he went on. "We're taking home the cup. You and me, man." He tipped his head to the ceiling, and roared. "Hell, yes!"

I growled along with him, feeling the warm rumble explode within me. Even if it was only for a minute, it felt like I was home, or the closest thing to it, the thing I missed most, a sense of peace and belonging.

But it didn't take long for the feeling to pass, for the worry to creep back in, for me to remember that I was the fifty-thousand-dollar kid and I didn't belong. It wasn't just that hockey was the only reason I'd been given a chance at Fullbrook. I didn't understand why I'd been given the life there at all—I didn't know why I should have been.

The previous year, near the end of the football season, we had had only three games left to play. Vinny Dawson had been averaging 250 passing yards a game. He had all the looks from Oklahoma State, USC, Alabama, and the Fighting Irish. He could run, find his way out of the pocket and not lose yardage, but mostly, he could throw. We had a Friday night game that week, away at Bucksfield. We were all confident we could maintain our perfect season. We just had to keep our offensive line sharp. Bucksfield had a terrible offense, but they had the best defense in the league. Except for me. I led the league in sacks.

My job, mostly, was to break the opposing team's line and scare the living hell out of their QB. Attack, attack, attack. *Breakfast!* I yelled all game, calling over the line to the QB. *Breakfast, you ready?* I did it every game. I had my target, and I knew my job was to keep his ass in the dirt where it belonged. *Breakfast!* I shouted. *I'm coming for you. Eat you up and shit you out right back in the grass. Come on! One more time, baby!* Coach Ellerly loved it. *Hit-hit-hit, Jamie!* he yelled from the sidelines. *Hit-hit-hit,* everyone yelled, cheering me on. *Hit-hit-hit* was the mantra shouting in the back of my mind, a deafening roar.

At practice on Thursday, before the Bucksfield game, I was

doing my game-time routine. This time scaring the hell out of my own teammates. "Come on, now," I shouted at the offensive line. "You better stop me. Bucksfield's coming for you tomorrow."

Time and again they didn't. I broke free and got two clean hits on Vinny in a row. On the third one, Vinny just slid into the dirt so I'd only tag him. "Christ, Jamie," he said when I rolled off him.

"Don't get pissed at me," I said. "Bucksfield's coming for you."

Vinny ran over to Coach, and after they talked, they made some adjustments to the line. They stopped me a few times in a row. Vinny made two completions. They got a run by me, and then another. "Come on, Jamie!" Coach yelled from the sidelines. "Keep on them. Keep on them. Nobody holds you back. Keep on them. Hit-hit-hit."

"We got this," Vinny said in the huddle. I could hear him from where I was. "We got this. Hell, yeah!" someone else shouted.

But I chanted my own phrase in my head. *I got this.* Something in me just knew. *I got this. I got this!* I was so pumped I was hopping on the balls of my feet. I clapped along with everyone else when they broke from the huddle with a roar. Back on the line, knuckles in the grass, I looked at the two guys in front of me and let them know I was going to beat them both.

"We got this," Paul Sikes said to me, his grill inches from mine.

"I'm about to chew the fuck out of you," I growled back. I spat a litany of things I'll never repeat for the rest of my life, and he cowered and stared down into the dirt. When Vinny called for the ball, I smashed Sikes so hard and plowed him so far to the left, he lost his footing and flipped backward. I couldn't hear anything except my own deafening roar blaring in my ears. I shouldered someone else to the side and gunned it for Vinny with such ferocity, my whole mind went blank, like a flash of lightning ignited behind my eyes.

I climbed up off the grass and looked around. The sound poured back into my brain, and I heard a few shouts. Whistles blew. I heard my name. And Vinny's. Screams.

For some reason, I didn't look down. I just saw Heather and the cheerleaders on the track, looking at me over the chain-link fence. Heather had her hands up to her mouth. Other girls were yelling around her, but she was silent, staring at me in a way I'd never seen.

Vinny wasn't getting up. He was a few feet away from me, face-first in the grass, not moving, not twitching. His body was twisted like a doll's, his waist and legs bent improbably to the side. For a moment, in a hushed lull, as he lay alone, with everyone else scattered across the field, he looked dead. He nearly was.

But then the whistles blew again and people started screaming from the sidelines. Coach Ellerly stormed the field with his team of assistants, and a swarm of players surrounded him. "What the hell is the matter with you?" Coach shouted, shaking my shoulder.

Vinny was out cold, but breathing. When the paramedics arrived, they were careful getting him onto the stretcher. As the ambulance pulled away, I kept thinking it was a dream, that it wasn't happening, because I'd always thought Vinny was invincible, that we all were, actually. That every time Coach yelled Hit, and every time the crowd cheered when I stuffed somebody in the dirt, and every time my teammates roared when we sacked another quarterback, it was all just a part of the game and the game was everything, but also only a game.

The ambulance, the people yelling in my face, none of it seemed real.

"What the hell were you doing?"

"What's the matter with you?"

"You could have killed him."

Vinny lived, but I'd broken his back, and delivered such a serious concussion, Vinny didn't return to school. His football career was over. Nobody held back. Not Coach, not our friends, not my teachers, not Vinny, not his family. It was unanimous. I'd ruined his life.

When Heather and I had been dating, she'd always reminded me of the many things in her life a white boy like me couldn't understand, and I'd always been a little worried it was going to be something I was ignorant about that would do us in—not something I actually excelled at instead. Because even before Heather stopped returning my texts, there'd been that day in the hall, the week after that practice. I'd walked toward her, hoping she'd hold me like she used to. But instead, she'd backed away. "I don't even know," she said, her voice shaky. I reached for her. "Don't touch me," she snapped. She pointed to my hands. "I don't understand how you can just break a person like that."

I didn't know how or why either—I just knew I could.

I kept going to school, kept trying to find a way to graduate, until the day I was walking into the pharmacy to get Mom some medicine, because she was laid out at home with the flu. I wandered up and down the aisle for a bit, but since I was never the one to actually buy the stuff, I had no clue what the best one was for her. It dawned on me the pharmacist would know, but as I went around the last aisle to wait in line for him, I nearly bumped into Vinny's mom. The little plastic bag in her hand was loaded with orange pill bottles. I went rigid and silent, unable to meet her eye. "I'm sorry," I said, but it was nothing more than a whisper of dust, lost in the air between us.

She caught me gawking at the bag of bottles. "Don't you dare," she mumbled. Trembling, she stuck a finger out toward me. "You shouldn't be here," she said. "I shouldn't have to see you—ever again." She braced herself with a breath, then leaned closer. "You're a monster."

I didn't know what to say; she was right.

That was it. I barely made it to school from then on. I skipped hockey. I closed all my accounts. No Insta, Snap. Nothing. I couldn't look at them. Here's me in the park—skipping class. Here's me in the mall, mugging behind a security guard. Here's me standing upside down on someone else's mattress. No. What was I going to do? Here's me at the hospital, looking through the window at the guy whose life I ruined. Here's me on the toilet at school. Not using it, just sitting in the only room where no one will stare at you as if you are a criminal. That was exactly how I felt that fall—criminal, and worse, one who'd gotten away with it.

Only Coach Drucker, my hockey coach, came back around. Months later, after I'd missed the whole season. I was special, so I got another chance. Vinny wasn't dead, but he wasn't living the life he'd set out for. He was improvising, trying to make the most of it back home, working the cash register at a Papa John's, where they'd lowered the counter to make it easier for him to work in a wheelchair. I was picking up where I'd left off. I'd gotten a do-over, as if what I'd done had never happened at all.

But it had.

And now I was out there in the world, going to class again, hanging out with people again, laying down the foundation for the future I was told I was supposed to have. But really, deep down, all I wanted was to be a guy who knew how to do the right thing.

CHAPTER 8

JULES DEVEREUX

I felt pretty on top of my college applications. I had my list. I was powering through the essays. I'd have drafts of everything finished by the end of the week, and it was only mid-September. So it was all worth celebrating over a huge mound of ice cream in the student center.

Vanilla with chocolate sprinkles and crushed Oreos, chocolate syrup, whipped cream, and that nasty cherry on top, which looks better than it tastes. I ate that first to get it out of the way. But I hadn't been sitting for five minutes when a group of guys sat down at the long table against the back wall and started talking over each other. They made so much noise I had to keep cranking my headphones, until it just wasn't worth it anymore because the volume was making my own ears hum with pain. I turned off the music and tried to hurry through my ice cream instead. No peace.

Freddie was in the center, and I realized he had the most recent student handbook in front of him. He pointed to it and looked up, over his shoulder, to the Buckeye. "Now, that is a good page." The other guys behind them laughed along in agreement. The Buckeye too.

"Am I right, though?" Freddie asked him.

"Yeah, yeah, I guess so," he said, more enthusiastically, nodding, mouth open like a Venus flytrap. He glanced toward me, and I burned him with a glare.

Freddie had a pen in one hand. "What do we think? 7?" He pointed to the page with his pen. "An 8? And another 8? And definitely a 9 or 10 here, right?" The guys continued to argue over the numbers: They were rating the first-year girls by their head shots in the student handbook. These assholes rubbed me the wrong way so bad, it actually hurt my body—like the sting of skin burning.

Every year Fullbrook issued each student a new and updated handbook. A binder full of rules and regulations that nobody read or even looked at. But at the back, on the last ten pages, were high-gloss black-and-white photographs of all the first years. The idea was that the rest of us would look at the photos and get to know the students' names, get to know who they were, so when we passed them on the walkway or in the student center, or wherever, we could say hi, and maybe even say their names. Make them feel at home.

Freddie shouted, "Oh, yes! Definite 10! Look at her!"

I was incensed. Filled with rage, yes, but the word "incensed" has a deeper meaning. It was first used to describe fire-breathing animals on medieval coats of arms—and that's exactly how I felt right then, like I wanted to breathe fire and burn their aggressive laughter right up in smoke.

I remembered my own photo in the student handbook when I was a first year. I had had my picture taken on the first day, wearing something my mother had put together for me, something between *Little House on the Prairie* and British manor attire. Whatever it was, it was definitely dour and of a previous century, and only made worse with doily lace. I beamed with wide-eyed terror up and off the page. I hadn't looked at the student handbook photos this year, but I could imagine so many of the girls, and the boys, for that matter, looking up at Freddie and his crew with the same expression.

Freddie wrote the scores next to the photos as the guys shouted them out to him. "No way," he argued. "Not even a 3." He laughed. "Fair is fair and all, but reality is also reality. I'm putting down a 2."

I let out a breath, not one of fire, as much as I wished I could. I knew I had to get up and say something, because no one else would. As soon as the guys saw me coming, they knew what I was going to say. That was the part that pissed me off the most—they already knew. Somewhere in their minds they heard my voice before I spoke. Maybe it was their mothers' voice, maybe their sisters'. Maybe it was a teacher's. Or maybe it was even their own voice, too soft to be heard in the rumble and roar of the mob. But none of them looked nervous as they watched me approach. Only the Buckeye cracked a crooked, embarrassed smile.

"Guys," I said in my best guyish tone. "Isn't this a little childish?"

"Ha!" Freddie laughed. "You want in? You can rate the boys."

"No thanks."

"Come on," he went on. "You're the one always talking about

equity this and equity that. Here's your chance. Start a new tradition. Rate the boys."

Some of the guys laughed, and I realized there were a few other student handbooks from years past on the table in front of him. He pushed aside two of the student handbooks and held the third one up. "Jules," he said, "let's see what they gave you!" He handed it to the Buckeye and told him to find my picture.

I'd been ready to give them a lecture, but I felt muted, not by Freddie exactly, but by the fact that some other group of guys had been sitting here doing the same thing when I was a first year. By the fact that before they really knew my name, they knew my number.

"Find it?" Freddie asked the Buckeye.

"Yeah."

"Well?"

"An 8," the Buckeye said. He looked at me hopefully, as if he thought the higher number would make me feel better about it all. I smoldered deep inside.

Freddie grabbed the book and held it high for all to see. There I was. Hair curled in a way I never would otherwise. But mostly, it was freaky to look back into the eyes of the younger me. *Run,* I wanted to tell her. *Run for your life.*

"Hey," Freddie said. "An 8. Not bad!" Some of the guys cheered along. Freddie grinned at me. "Yeah," he continued. "But what happened?"

"Aww, man," Lou Anastasos said. He was a skinny guy who shaved his head at the beginning of every soccer, hockey, and baseball season. His head gleamed as he swung it around while looking for more support from the other guys. "That's not right." He turned to me with what I think he thought was pity. "You're still an 8, Jules. All the way!"

It was like they weren't even really talking to me, but rather, right at my body, wrenching the two apart. That seemed so dangerous, to think of me and my body as two separate things—as if one could be sacrificed to protect the other.

I found it hard to speak, and what finally came out didn't have the force I wanted it to. "I want to be there the day you get cancer, or the day you lose a child. The day your wife tells you she's getting a divorce and she's taking the house with her. I want to see that look on your face when something turns your world upside down."

Freddie brushed it off. "Oh, man, so dramatic." He held up the pen. "You know what your problem is, Jules? You just don't want people to be people. You want to suck all the fun out of life until we're all dead and boring and politically correct. Lighten up. You used to be fun. What happened to you?"

My sundae sat mostly melted in my cup, and I plopped the cup down and slid it across the table at him. He bounced backward, but the behemoth Buckeye stood too close, Freddie had nowhere to go, and the ice cream soup dropped right into his lap. He shouted at me, but I was already walking away. Already trying to ignore them, or really, trying not to show them how choked up I was, or how close to screaming.

Because right then, I almost wished I could go back to living the lie that everyone else embraced so wholeheartedly. Reality *was* reality, Freddie-goddamn-Watts. But for some of us, reality was too painful.

Once, in middle school, back when I played soccer, I was stretching with three other girls, and a boy walked by with his friend. "Best legs," he said, pointing at one girl. "Best boobs." He pointed to another. "Best butt," he said to me. We were all shocked into silence, like he'd struck us with invisible bolts of lightning. "What if you could smash them all together?" his friend said as they walked away. "Ooooh," the first boy said. I felt so grossed out, like I'd been cut apart, and I looked at the girl who he'd said nothing about and wondered how she felt. She stared at the ground and ignored us.

Too many days felt like that day on the soccer field. This was my reality: having to deal with the Franken-dream fantasies of people like Freddie Watts. All the damn time. I guess I had known all this last year, and the year before, even earlier, but I'd just accepted it before. Not anymore. It was like I'd put on a pair of glasses and could see it all so much clearer, and now that I had, I couldn't ignore it.

Still, what the heck could I do about it?

At many colleges there are large groups of students who volunteer at the campus health center. I knew because I'd looked it up at all the schools on my list. But at Fullbrook, there was only one: me. And truthfully, I didn't get to do all that much. It was just somewhere I could go when I didn't know how to settle all the rage swirling and smoking within me.

I walked over to Ms. Taggart's office and tried to manage what was going on inside me by doing something useful for someone else. She sat in a chair in the receiving room, using her tea mug to warm her hands. She'd tucked her legs up onto the seat like a little kid, and she peered at me over her knees as she directed me.

I'd ordered a poster for the office, and she'd waited for me to hang it up. I pressed one thumbtack to hold it in place, and Ms. Taggart got up to help me fix the rest of it. It was a magnificent, life-size illustration of the female body, with the skin missing so you could see the muscles and tendons and organs and all that. Something to occupy your mind while you waited in the receiving room.

"It's beautiful," she said, patting my back like a proud mom. Ms. Taggart looked so young, it was sometimes hard to remember she had a child of her own—a little boy I'd seen running around campus like a Jack Russell terrier. She collected her mug from the end table.

"I love it," I told her. I ran my finger down the long, winding sartorius muscle, which looped around the thigh.

"Have you figured out your list?"

I sighed and spoke to her over my shoulder. "It's such bullshit." Sometimes I thought of her as the older sister I never had but always wanted. Sometimes I remembered she was an adult and I had to think of boundaries. I turned back to her. "What I mean is, why can't I study science *and* humanities? Like, I know I'm really good in English and history, but I love bio. I love environmental science. Why isn't there a major called science in literature?"

"That would be cool." She sipped her tea. "Also, you don't have to choose and limit yourself."

"Ugh. Yes, I know I can double major and all that, but I want it all together, all mushed together."

Ms. Taggart glanced at her watch and then at the door to her office. She was letting a first year take a nap on the couch inside. I knew girls who'd taken advantage of Ms. Taggart's couch—Gillian, for instance, for so much of sophomore year, after the video—because even though we could always go back to our rooms, napping in Ms. Taggart's office just felt somehow more protected. It wasn't something I'd ever done, but I understood that. I didn't nap here, but I volunteered, and somehow it was the same thing.

"Time's almost up." She'd have to go back in, and when she did, she'd probably talk to the first year for a bit. Find out what was stressing her out.

"Yup." I pulled a paper cup from the water cooler and filled it.

"And think about this, Jules. William Carlos Williams was a doctor and a poet. Carl Sagan wrote about the universe, beautifully."

"How about women?"

My mother was the first woman to join the board of directors at her firm. There'd been a first woman to teach at Fullbrook at some point. The first woman to get elected senator was Hattie Caraway. One of the first recorded women in the US Army was Deborah Sampson Gannett, who enlisted under a man's name in 1782, and who cut out a musket ball from her own leg so a doctor wouldn't reveal her big secret. Stories of first women stuck with me. Sally Ride was the first American woman in space. Cosmonaut Valentina Tereshkova the first woman ever in space. No woman had walked on the moon. And when she did, because surely that would happen one day—wouldn't it?—there would be all the jokes, because that was also inevitable.

For every achievement, there was always the joke intended to take it away.

She smiled. "I can't think of one off the top of my head, but maybe a few years from now, when another student comes to me with this question, I'll say, 'Julianna Devereux, of course.'" She held up her wrist. "Heading back in. See you soon."

She'd done it, even if only a little, quelled my rage by giving me a little hope. I heard my name in Ms. Taggart's voice. I loved how that sounded: *Julianna Devereux, a young woman who did a thing.*

CHAPTER 9

JAMES BAXTER

I don't know why they put a dumb kid like me in British lit. It wasn't AP, it was just an elective, but I was in a class with AP students like Gillian, Jules, and Aileen. Why couldn't I take a crime fiction course? Or better yet, sports writing? Nope. Mr. Hale paced the room, talking to us about the opening moments of *Paradise Lost*.

"When Lucifer wakes up in hell, it's not sorrow he feels, is it?"

He looked around the room, and had to wait all of two milliseconds for hands to shoot up. Not mine. I never raised my hand. Mr. Hale knew that. He stared at me, not hoping I'd raise my hand, more like he was taunting me. *No idea, Baxter?* No. I didn't even know what all the words in the damn stanza meant.

Mr. Hale's classroom was smaller than some, and he leaned back against one of the dark wooden panels on the wall. It was mostly girls who had their hands up, but this hockey guy, Ryan Tucker, had his up too, in his own way, his elbow on the desk in front of him, one finger pointing toward the ceiling.

"Go ahead." Mr. Hale nodded to Tucker. "Why don't you take a stab at it? Get us started."

I don't know what Tucker began talking about, but he went on forever. I leaned back in my chair and glanced out the door of the classroom. We were only a few weeks into the school year and I was already struggling significantly. It wasn't just the papers I couldn't write—I'd been assigned two, one in each English class—it was the hour I could spend on one pre-calc equation, the reading for history class that would take me all night to finish, if I tried to finish it. I couldn't for the life of me understand how all these people at Fullbrook did it—and without breaking out in hives.

"James?" Mr. Hale said.

"Huh?"

"Care to elaborate on Ryan's comments?"

"Huh?"

"You looked deep in thought. Maybe you have something to add. About the setup for Adam and Eve?"

Jules blew out a long sigh. I'm sure she knew as well as I did that I hadn't caught a single word of what Tucker had said, but all eyes were on me, and one thing I'd learned at Fullbrook in the short amount of time I'd been there was that it was better to fake it than to keep showing your ignorance. "Of course," I said. Someone laughed under her breath. "It's all about rules and order and it doesn't make sense to Lucifer, just like it won't make sense to Adam and Eve."

The room was quiet. Mr. Hale nodded. "Not bad," he said. "Better to reign in hell than serve in heaven. We'll talk about that."

I was as shocked as anyone else in the class that I had some sense of what was going on. I didn't. I'd just said the first thing that popped into my head. And weirdly, I felt more embarrassed that I'd said something meaningful than if I'd just mumbled my usual line: "I don't know."

There were still a few hands up, including Jules's and Aileen's, but Mr. Hale went on about the battle in Milton's mind between individualism and the moral order of a Christian universe. Jules shook her head. She reached down into her backpack, rustled for a minute, then pulled out a tampon and placed it next to the pen and highlighter beside her book.

Mr. Hale didn't see it at first, but as he looked around the table, he could see all the uncomfortable faces glancing back and forth from Jules to him. He finally noticed. "Excuse me," he said.

No one said anything, including Jules, who he was looking at. Slowly, she raised her hand. Because he was still looking at her, she assumed she'd been called on. "I wanted to get back to this question of reigning in hell being better than serving in heaven."

"No." Mr. Hale cut her off. "Julianna, please try to have a little decency in class."

"Excuse me?"

He pointed to the tampon. "Enough with the stunts."

She picked it up and waved it as she talked. "If you are referring to this, it's no big deal. I was going to go to the bathroom, but then I realized I didn't want to miss class at the moment, and really, I'm so sick of secretly slipping it up my sleeve and hiding it every time I walk to the bathroom."

"Honestly," Mr. Hale said.

"What? That's what I do. That's what most of us do," she said, looking around the room. "I'm sick of pretending it doesn't exist, just to make other people feel more comfortable. How about they just get comfortable with my reality?"

"Oh, man," Tucker whined. "Here it comes."

Just seeing the tampon kind of put me out of place too. It didn't bother me as much as make me think of the last time I'd seen one, back when Heather and I were still a couple and she pulled one out of her backpack in her living room after school. She'd pulled it out with a bottle of extra-strength Advil, complaining about her cramps. "You have no idea," she'd told me.

"Can't we just act like ladies and gentlemen?" Mr. Hale asked. He wasn't really talking to anyone else, though.

"A lady?" Jules said.

Gillian leaned forward, around Tucker, and added, "Exactly, Jules. Come on. Put it away. I don't want to see that out on the table either."

"What's the big deal?" Jules said. "Why are we all pretending like this isn't a part of our everyday lives?"

"It probably is every day for you," one of the other guys said.

"Okay," Mr. Hale said. "Let's try to have a little decency." He waved out over all of us. "Jules, put that away. Everybody else, let's get back to work. We have more important things to concentrate on."

"Actually," Jules continued, "this is relevant. I mean, we're talking about a poem that's based on the whole Adam and Eve story, and how it basically blames women for all the problems in the world—like if only we'd just done what we were told." She wagged her finger in emphasis at people across the table from her, including me.

"Oh, classic," Tucker said, leaning back so his chair tilted away from the table. "Classic Jules."

"God," Gillian said.

Mr. Hale had clearly lost patience; his face was flushed to the base of his neck. "Well, if you'd just do what you're told right now," he said, "we could get back to talking about what we need to. All of you," he added, even though he was still looking right at Jules.

"But we are," Jules went on. "I mean, you haven't called on me or Aileen, or even you, Gillian," she said, leaning down and staring at her. "You pass by us all the time. And by the way, we've all done the reading, and we aren't BS-ing like Ryan always is."

As soon as she called him out, Tucker dropped the front legs of the chair to the floor, and shot back. "You need to get a boyfriend or something and chill out."

He glanced to me, nodding, looking for approval, and something sank in my gut. Because truthfully, no matter how good it felt to be back on the ice, I was starting to feel hollowed out sometimes when I was around the guys. The way he said that, *get a boyfriend*, reminded me of Heather saying it wasn't fair, why did she have to put on a happy face and pretend like she wasn't in pain. All guys wanted to do was get in her pants, she'd said, but they didn't actually want to know anything about what was in her pants.

"See what I mean?" Jules said. "If I talk about tampons or menstrual cups or pads, suddenly it's my fault the guys don't do their homework?"

Mr. Hale was about to speak, but Jules was looking at me when she said that, and something in me clicked.

I found myself leaping out of my seat, leaning over the table, and grabbing the tampon. "All right," I said, louder than I meant to. I slammed the tampon down in front of me. "Now I have one too."

Jules didn't miss a beat. She pulled another one out of her bag and slipped it where the other one had been, beside her book. Tucker laughed. "I'm not kidding," I said. "It's not a big deal. It's a tampon. Let's move on." He stopped laughing and stared at me, completely confused.

The whole class was. Even Mr. Hale. I hoped to hell I didn't look as insanely nervous as I felt, but nobody said anything, until Jules broke the silence. "Welp," she said, "if we're taking a break, now's probably a good time to go to the bathroom." She kind of smiled at me, although not like a laugh, more like she was looking at me like I was kind of nuts, and maybe I was, but I was pretty sick of everyone around the room giving her a hard time. She seemed comfortable being on her own, but I didn't like that everyone was just as comfortable ganging up on her.

Jules stepped away, class fell into its dull rhythm again, and when she returned, she slipped another tampon onto the desk in front of her and nobody said anything.

I couldn't calm the nerves jumping through me, so at the end of class, I gathered my things in a rush and bolted out the door, but I got stuck in a crush of other people coming out of Mr. Wilson's room, so I didn't get far at all. Jules tapped me on the shoulder, and she and Aileen followed me outside, cornering me on the back steps of Childon Hall.

"That was a surprise," Jules said to me. "I thought for sure you were going to have your buddy Ryan's back."

"He's not my buddy."

"He's on the football team."

"I'm not."

"And the hockey team."

I didn't say anything.

"Seriously," Aileen said. "Somebody had to shut all that down, and nobody was going to listen to me if I tried."

"Well." Jules hesitated, then drew a slow, conspiratorial smile. "What if I start doing this every class? All class, every class, all day, every day. Normalize that shit."

Aileen laughed. "Sounds good. After all, it is normal."

"Seriously," Jules went on. "Walk into any drugstore. Makeup and candy up front, tampons and condoms in the back, by the pharmacy, close to the allergy and flu medications."

"Stupid," Aileen said.

"Well, here's the question," Jules continued. "Will you join me?"

"Hell, yeah," Aileen said immediately.

They both turned to me, Jules cocking her eyebrow, almost daring me, but Aileen taking me in differently, almost patiently. I knew that look, and it warmed me. I shrugged. "All right. Sure," I told them. "Normalize that shit."

Jules looked so determined, more than I'd ever seen her before, eyes narrowed, brows pinched, goal oriented. Focused. It was inspiring. She stood there with her hands on her hips, so certain she knew what the right thing to do was. Heather was gone—off at OSU, she was the real Buckeye, for God's sake—but what she'd told me about listening had really stuck. *Are you listening to what I'm saying? I need you to hear me.* Heather had told me I didn't have a clue sometimes. *You need to be a better listener,* she'd said.

Looking at Jules, I realized she was the kind of person who just knew deep down what the right thing to do was, even if everyone else didn't. If I gave a damn about listening, it seemed like I should start by paying more attention to her.

Aileen too. The guys at Fullbrook made fun of her, called her the Viking, with those long braids. They always called her dumb and easy, chasing after guys' attention, but she didn't feel that way to me. She seemed older and wiser than the rest of us.

"Hey," Aileen said to me. "Don't say you're going to do a thing and then not do it."

"I hear you."

She nodded. She kept her hands at her side, she didn't touch me, but the way she curled a slight smile, it felt like she'd brushed me with her fingertips and stirred a little scattershot of sparks in my stomach. I gulped to keep my voice from cracking. "I'm with you," I told them both.

CHAPTER 10

JULES DEVEREUX

"You are so disgusting, it actually hurts me," Aileen said.

I was taking tight close-ups of a scab on her leg, and I had her flat up against the very brick wall that had scraped her. "I mean it," she continued. "From deep inside. Not like this stupid cut. Like a deep 'oh my God you are nuts' kind of throb in my belly."

Aileen and I were in a couple of the same classes, and I'd found a way to partner with her in them. It wasn't easy, but the time we were spending together was starting to feel more natural. There was something like warmth in the way she glared at me now. And when the class rotation put photo at the end of the day, Aileen and I usually ran off together somewhere so it was just the two of us.

"This is a work of art," I said. "Hold still. The light keeps shifting."

"That's because I'm balancing on one leg and I'm no gymnast." Her other leg was lifted away from her body to catch more of the sunlight, and as soon as I let her know I was done, she dropped her leg and backed away from the wall. "I'll always remember you," she said, tapping it with her fingers, the black nails bouncing up and down like flies. "You turned me into a model. Who knew?"

"Exactly," I said. "Pain. If Diane Arbus can capture it, why can't we?"

"Yeah, well, I'm after something else for this project."

I rolled my eyes. "All right, I'm weird. I admit it."

She laughed. "But so am I." She picked up her camera from on top of the wall. "And I need your help. I want to do something pretty risky for my project."

"Oh, no," I said. "Don't tell me you're doing nudes."

"Oh, for God's sake." She started walking away. I guessed I was supposed to follow. "Nudes?" She dismissed this with a sniff. "That's not risky." She shot me the most skeptical glare. It was better than anything I could give anyone. "You're telling me no one has ever seen you naked?"

"What? No. I mean, I'm not saying that."

"Please," she said. "Only the boys are going to try something like that and argue that it's art. Nudes. I can just hear the way they'll justify that. Simpleminded clichés—all of them."

I laughed. The best thing about class had nothing to do with the work and everything to do with Aileen. I wished I'd realized it years earlier—I wished I'd made more of an effort to get to know her. Why had I put all my effort into Gillian and Shriya, who'd so quickly dropped me and were probably actively conspiring against me now? The younger girls were already glancing away from me too, hoping to avoid eye contact so I wouldn't come talk to them. Gillian and Shriya were everywhere, parading from one moment to the next as if they'd started the tour on that first day of school and were still on it together. I didn't want to be a part of it, but I didn't want to be quite so isolated, either. Spending all this time with Aileen, I admired her even more. It took a certain kind of strength to navigate Fullbrook mostly on her own all these years.

"No, I'm talking really risky," she continued. "Like, I need your help taking photos inside Cray-Cray's shed."

She nodded, her eyes wide and taunting, like, *How tough are you really, Jules?* And I had to admit, I kind of liked it.

"I'm in."

Aileen led me around the back of the arts building and down along the edge of the woods toward the pep rally field and then down the slope to the football field. Cray-Cray's shed was behind the stands, and it was more of a small garage than a shed. He parked one of his two security golf carts there and I had no idea what else. I was impressed. I was so sure I'd been everywhere on campus, that I'd discovered every little hidden corner and crevice. But not this one.

"Damn," I said. "I've never been here." I walked ahead of her and tried the door. It was locked. Inside, the garage was two walls of floor-to-ceiling tools, oil cans, carpentry and electrician materials. He wasn't part of the maintenance staff, but he obviously was enamored with their work. The spot where he usually parked one of his carts was empty; a huge amoeba of oil stained the concrete floor.

"This is so horror film," I said, pointing to the rusty saw hanging on the wall in the back. "Does that thing actually work?"

"I don't know, but it's cool. There's something so creepy about it all. One time I was walking by and I just looked through the window and I saw the way the light cut across the shadows, the way it fell in strips across all that metal. It was pretty cool."

"It is."

She pulled out her phone and flipped through some other pictures. Black-and-white photos of naked men, light and shadow swirling around their contorted poses. "So Mapplethorpe gave these dudes a kind of noir feel, right? Well, I want to do that with dude-like things. Cray-Cray's shed seems like the most badass dude-cave at the whole school."

I couldn't hold back. "This is awesome." I tried the door again. "But it's locked."

She smiled. "I was walking by, looking for some place to shoot down by the football field, thought that might work, you know how boys love their balls, when I saw Cray-Cray bend down and lift this rock." She demonstrated with her foot, turning over the rock beside the door. The key was right there. She dipped and grabbed it quickly.

Once the door was closed, we took it all in. Sunlight cut through the window and sent rhombuses of light knifing across the garage space. "This is amazing," I said. "But what do you need me for?"

"To hold things."

She went about picking tools off the shelf, holding them in the air so the sunlight bisected them. She passed them to me, tested a few, and kept at it. I watched her work, amazed. "Oh, oh, yes," she said, digging a canister out of the back of the garage. I recognized it as the strange watering can tool that Cray-Cray used every year at the pep rally. Somehow, instead of water, he slowly dripped fire from this can. He'd built a funeral pyre. Someone had designed an effigy of our rival, Hodges's mountain lion, and Cray-Cray had burned the whole thing down, ringing the bonfire with narrow trenches of fire in the ground around it, like some Celtic solstice festival from two thousand years ago. He'd used this drip torch to do it all. I'd never forgotten that image of Cray-Cray getting to the end of the circuit and turning back to the screaming student body, grinning wildly in the firelight.

That's what Aileen was after. Taking that kind of glory from him for her photo. She gestured for me to hold it up. "That is perfect. That's the one. Hold it higher."

I stood in the light too. I looked back at her through the space between the nozzle and heavy middle cylinder. She took a shot.

"Whoa," she said, looking at the photo on her camera. "Okay, now squat. Hold it right there, but disappear so I can't see you."

I liked Aileen's idea of taking photos of the things that were usually forgotten, the beauty of light resting on bent metal. A can of fire making it into the light, everything else a shadow—it was just like my plan for senior year: focusing on getting into college, and keeping the rest of Fullbrook in the background.

When we were finished, Aileen wanted to do some more work in the darkroom, a different photo project for another class, so I was on my own. It was late afternoon, and not all that long before we had to get dressed for sit-down dinner in the dining hall, that hour when the teachers seem to disappear and the campus feels quiet and uninhabited, and because the sunlight was warming a golden pool around the base of the old elm outside the admin building, I almost plopped down to lean against it and read for homework, but I didn't have *Paradise Lost* with me and I had zero interest in tackling calc, so I went back to my room.

I found Mary Lyon nearly empty. The first floor was absolutely quiet, and since it felt like I might be missing some meeting I was supposed to attend, I swung downstairs to the common room. When I got there, I found a kind of meeting. Shriya and Gillian were holding court. They stood on one side of the card table, flanked by two other seniors. Their backs were to me, and I saw the horrified faces of twenty girls staring in my direction as I entered the room. I didn't have to be a psychic to know something weird was going on.

Gillian noticed some of the girls looking my way, and she turned with a nonchalant grace. She dropped the innocence act as soon as she saw me. "Oh, perfect," she said. "Jules can help us."

We weren't getting along. Fine. It didn't matter that we were at odds—I didn't like how intensely she was making me feel like a disposable rag, to be picked up, used, and thrown away whenever she felt like it.

"With what?" I said, as if I could jump right back in and assume my place in the hierarchy.

"Our lesson." She stepped aside. A bowl with two bunches of bananas sat in the middle of the card table. I immediately regretted feeling left out. I wished I'd stayed back at the tree and just stared up into the sky through the branches. "Every year,"

Gillian continued, turning back to the girls, "someone holds this little seminar."

I could taste the bitter rind from across the room. I remembered it from my own first year. I hadn't cried, but some of the girls had. Shriya, for instance. The seniors at the time had picked on her first—the only brown girl in the room. I remembered handing her a paper towel from a dispenser by the sink. Now she was the senior squinting across the room at the younger girls.

Gillian ticked off her instructions. "And it's really for your own good." All four seniors laughed. "I mean, nobody wants to feel bad about it later."

Most of the girls sat on the couches or in chairs, but one first year stood in front of all of them, holding a banana. Her name was Lianne and I'd seen her around. She was strikingly pretty, American, but raised somewhere in Europe, and she'd already been caught in the older boys' hungry gazes—I'd seen them huddled around her, vying for her attention. But in this moment, her usual carefree confidence was gone. She glanced at me, terrified.

"Go on," Shriya told her.

"Do it," Gillian commanded.

Lianne closed her eyes for a second and her face lost all expression, as if she'd aged three or four years in an instant. When she opened her eyes again, she gave a slight, frightened smile. She brought the banana up to her lips.

If Gillian and Shriya and I had still been friends, if I'd still been part of the royalty, parading through my days at Fullbrook, would I have egged Lianne on too? Gillian hadn't even done it our first year. I'd done it for her—that's how we'd become friends, really. Simple as that. It scared me—I couldn't understand why—that she might have forgotten that. Or that she just ignored it and chose to live life in the lie instead. Not me. First the student handbook, then this crap—even in a room full of girls it was all about the guys. It was infuriating. I didn't know how much longer I could take this shit.

"Hey, wait," I said. "You demonstrated, right?" I said to Gillian and Shriya, as I looped around the card table. "Did I miss that already?"

"What?" Shriya said. She didn't say anything else. She just stood there blinking at me, disgusted.

Gillian cleared her throat. "That's the point," she said to me. "I mean, I know what I'm doing," she said, more to the girls than to me. She screwed a smile into her cheeks. "Come on, Lianne. Make it dirty."

A couple of the bolder first years laughed, although nervously, and they almost leaned forward, probably grateful it was Lianne up there, not them. I wondered, how did Lianne get picked?

"Hey," I said again, interrupting. "Let me show you all how it's done."

Lianne dropped the banana immediately. The sigh that escaped her could have filled a balloon.

I grabbed another banana from the bowl, cocked my hip to one side, made a duck face at the girls, waited for a couple of laughs, threw Gillian and Shriya the death glare, and then proceeded to peel the banana. "First of all, nobody eats the rind, silly," I said in my best Betty Boop voice. "Then you just have to enjoy!" I made my eyes wide, then shut them tight as I stuffed as much of the banana into my mouth as I could. I moaned briefly. "Oh my God," I said with my mouth full. "I just love bananas." I forced myself to swallow as much as I could and I pushed the rest of the banana into the front of my teeth, banana mush dripping onto my chin and shirt. "Oh my God," I said again. "You have more!" I grabbed another two bananas and slowly spun them around in front of my mouth. In the worst fake-sexy voice ever, I said, "I love bananas." I moaned and spit up some and moaned more.

Most of the girls now laughed, maybe at me, maybe with me. Only Shriya and Gillian stared at me in disgust. "Lianne probably would have been better," Gillian said. "What happened to you?"

I ignored her and peeled another banana and stuffed what I could into my already full mouth. "Oooohhh," I moaned again. "Buh-naw-naaaw."

"That's right," Gillian said. "Ethan dumped you and now you can't get any guy to like you."

"Wha?" I sort of mumbled. I stopped writhing and stared at her. "I dumped him," I tried to say, but who knows if anyone could hear me. I started to cough. Banana bits flew out onto the floor. I sniffed for air as my throat began to burn. Nobody helped. They all just watched.

I ran to the sink beside one of the refrigerators and began to spit up what was in my mouth, but the food wouldn't come fast enough. I gagged. I stamped my foot, and then the rest of the banana and whatever else I'd had that day just shot up out of me, spraying the sink, my face, my shirt, and all down the side of the cupboard beneath the sink.

Someone screamed. "Gross!" Then everyone started screaming and laughing, or they weren't sure which, but letting loose all the same. "That's disgusting!"

"Well," I heard Shriya say. "Now we know who we don't want to be like."

I wiped banana mush from my face. I was crying, from vomiting, and through my tears I watched a few of the first years circle around Lianne and lead her out of the room, as if she'd been the one to go through all that. There was a smile somewhere deep down inside but I couldn't call it up. Lianne glanced back at me once as she was led out of the room, but she didn't say anything.

Gillian shook her head. She and Shriya walked off together, leaving the rest of the bananas behind for someone else to clean up, and I tried to wash the banana off me wherever I could. At least a couple of the first-year girls waited for me and asked if I was okay. I wasn't, but of course I said I was. I thanked them as best I could.

Farah, one of the other seniors, asked me if I wanted her to go get Mrs. Attison, or if I wanted her to call the counseling center, see if someone would come over and talk to me.

"For real?" I barked. "I work at the damn center."

"No kidding," Farah said, straightening. "Well, maybe you need to check yourself in as a patient."

She stormed off and I felt like shit for being such a shit. I just wanted to be alone. But then when I was, and I was wiping up the banana mush everywhere around the sink, I realized I didn't want to be alone. I couldn't get out of here fast enough— *one more year, one more year.* But before I did, I wanted to do something. *Julianna Devereux, a young woman who did a thing.* I wanted to make Fullbrook Academy women-first for once. The tampon normalization campaign was a start. It was small, and it shouldn't have even been a big deal, but it was at least something I could look forward to doing.

CHAPTER 11

JAMES BAXTER

As promised, we put tampons out on the desks and tables in classes for an entire week. I only had Brit lit with Jules and Aileen, but I did what she did: I put a tampon next to my pen and highlighter in every class. Word got around quickly, and the teachers all ignored it, which was a bummer for Jules. "It's not having the effect I want," she'd said. "It's not normalizing anything if everyone just pretends they don't see it or that the tampons don't exist."

"Might as well hide them in our sleeves again," Aileen had said.

Tucker and some of the other guys had just assumed I was doing it because I was trying to get in good with Jules. "Dude," they teased. "Duuuuude. She isn't worth it."

Yeah, I did look forward to seeing Jules, but it wasn't like that. I could still fake it with all the guys, or try to, but hanging out with Jules made me feel for the first time since Vinny that I could do something right, something good. She just had to tell me what it was. Like this new project. She wanted to put up posters all around school that said, THIS IS WHAT A FEMINIST LOOKS LIKE. She'd already mocked up one picturing the former NFL star Donald McPherson wearing a T-shirt with that slogan. "I tell you what," she'd said, grinning. "You help me with this new normalization campaign, and I'll help you with that paper you almost failed."

We'd taken over half a table at the library, my nine-page paper laid out in a square of columns and rows and all my note cards fanned out in a messy pile beside it. Jules kept staring at the note cards and blinking, as if they might magically disappear while her eyes were closed.

"They help," I said. "This is how I gather my quotes for an essay."

"It looks a little like you're collecting recipes the old-fashioned way."

I deflated, sank my head into my hand. "You're supposed to be helping, not making it worse."

She put her hand on my shoulder. "All right, Bax, I'm only teasing." She pointed to the papers in front of me. "It's just easier for me to edit in here."

And just like that, she'd named me, or renamed me, and I liked it. Bax. It almost felt like I was becoming someone new. I'd gotten a little more than I bargained for when I'd agreed to join Jules's campaign for normalization. Since that day in class, I'd been hunkering down in some corner of the library with her, and sometimes Aileen, too, flipping through old books and magazine articles and searching online about civil rights marches, bra-burning rallies,

Stonewall. It wasn't the kind of thing I was used to, or thought I'd even like, but I could see why taking the spirit of those past campaigns and applying it to the design of the posters she wanted to create lit a fire behind her eyes.

"Look," she said, gathering up the sheets of paper. "Can I just read through this, make some notes, and we can talk about it later? I need some time to figure out what you are trying to say."

"Yeah, me too. I'd love to know what the heck I'm trying to say."

She laughed. "It's not that bad."

"Oh, it is." I pushed the note cards into a stack. "Need these, too?"

She shook her head. "I'm going to stick with the complete sentences, here," she said, waving the essay at me. "Flipping through those might get me a little too far into your head. I don't want to get lost in there."

"There's not much to see in there, so it'd be hard to get lost."

"Come on," she said. "Don't be like that." She pulled out her laptop and flipped it open. "Have you seen this before?"

This was one of the things I'd already come to like about Jules. She moved at a relentless pace. Nothing seemed to slow her down. She was like one of those remote control cars that zip around a room, and if she hit a wall, she simply backed up, like nothing had happened, and screeched off in another direction. I felt alive, getting pulled along in the rush she left trailing behind her.

"Images like this," she said, pointing to a photo of James Baldwin arm in arm with Marlon Brando, "these are the kinds of things that get people excited." In her faux-bro voice, she continued, "'No way! The Godfather was a civil rights activist?' It's powerful. Brando might have appeal for people who wouldn't usually think about inclusivity."

I nodded. "Makes sense."

"It does, but it's also sad. Why do men need to see other men talking about all this in order to feel like they can talk about it too? Why can't they just listen to women in the first place?"

I was about to say something, but then I thought better of it. I just nodded in agreement, and finally said, "You're right."

"Yeah." She paused for a moment. Then shook her head. "But still. Right now? I need help. I want to find some images like this that work for my *This is what a feminist looks like* campaign."

"That'd be cool."

She laughed. "See, this is the part where you say, 'Hey, I'm on it.'"

"Yeah," I said, rolling my eyes. "That's exactly what I was going to say, if you'd given me a sec to say it."

Jules bounced her shoulder into mine. "Thought so."

I reached across her and grabbed the laptop. "Don't disturb my concentration," I told in her in my worst fake-serious voice. "This is important business."

She let out one loud bark of a laugh, and covered her mouth. Then she attacked my paper with her pen. Just like that. Stop on a dime and get into something else. It was like the skating drills. Race forward. Cut around a cone. Hard stop. Sidestep backward around the other side of the cone. Charge. Hanging out with Jules was just like hanging out with one of the guys, but so much better. It was all the fun without all the competition. It was like we were actually talking. Like neither one of us was threatened.

But also, there was the class stuff. Mr. Hale had pulled me aside the day before to tell me that I would need to do a lot better. "You can't turn in first drafts," he told me, giving me back my first paper. "This would be an F." He sighed. "But I'm not going to give you an F. I'm going to ask you to write it again." He paused. "I know you're in preseason training, but I'm going to talk to Coach about scheduling in some tutoring time. I'm not going to be the guy who gave you an F and made you ineligible."

Searching for images for Jules, I typed "inclusive women's rights" into the Google bar, using her words, hoping I'd find images of the Marlon Brandos of the world, holding signs or whatever. I didn't find that, though. Instead, I saw women in hijabs. A WE ALL CAN DO IT sign with a black woman as the figurehead of a trio of women doing the Rosie the Riveter pose. Latinas, Asian women, women in wheelchairs. Another poster for Trans-Inclusive Feminism Always. I sat up and looked around the library space, looked at all the white faces like mine in the room.

"Hey," I said to Jules. "Fullbrook is super white."

"News flash."

"No, seriously. Back home. Public school? It wasn't like this."

"It's a problem. Javi and I tried to get a Black Lives Matter vigil going last year."

"What happened?"

"At Fullbrook? Give me a break. This place is *way* too white for that."

I nodded again, but that bugged me. "Yeah," I said. "But it's just like what you were saying before, except different."

"Wow. Profound," she teased.

"No," I went on. "It's like Black Lives Matter. All these white people who can't bring themselves to say it, actually say *Black Lives Matter*, and then they wonder why there are protests in the street? It's sad some white people need to see other white people marching to start thinking about it more. To start listening to people of color more."

Jules swallowed and took a second before she spoke. "When the vigils flopped. Well, I let all my energy for them slip away too. I shouldn't have."

"I'm not even sure I know what I'm saying," I said quietly, struggling to find the words. "I've never really said something like that out loud."

Jules was quiet for a moment.

"It's just, well. I've thought about it, though. Or, someone asked me to." I paused. "Heather's black," I said.

"Heather?"

"My ex-girlfriend." I smiled at her sheepishly. "She was a cheerleader."

"Football star and cheerleader. Just how I pictured you," Jules said. "What happened? College?"

"Yeah," I said, turning back to her computer. "Something like that."

I could feel her eyes on me as she waited for me to say more, but nothing else was coming. Staring at the computer, I felt my vision narrow, no longer seeing all the faces in the photos, just a blur of glowing color. "Whatever," I said, almost whispering.

"Heather is the first thing you've really told me about your life back in Ohio," Jules said. "You know you can talk about it with me. Or I hope you know." She put her hand on my shoulder again, and it wasn't flirty. It was none of that. It was more like half a hug from a sister I'd never known I had.

But no matter how it felt on the inside, it must have looked like something else on the outside.

"Oh, hey there, you two!" Freddie hollered from behind us. His voice made me jump.

"Oh God," Jules said.

"Oh shit," I said. "I forgot."

"I heard that," Freddie said, pulling up a chair beside me. "Dude. Coach O doesn't play. Don't think he won't notice you skipping. That's just stupid."

Jules looked at me, but said nothing. Her guard was back up, the skepticism tightening her face. I blew out a sigh, and she knew exactly what I was going to say next.

"Come on," Freddie said, grabbing my arm. "You're already late." He stood and pulled me with him.

"I'm sorry," I said to Jules. "I have to go."

"Obviously," she said, turning away. She pushed my essay aside and tapped a key on her computer to make the screen brighten again.

"Hey," I said, a little sharper than I meant. "I'm scholarship. It's not like I have a choice here."

She nodded without looking back. She tapped my essay with her finger. "We'll talk about it later. It's due tomorrow, right?"

My heart sank. "Jules," I said. "I'll help with the photo research. Tonight. After practice."

"Come on, Romeo," Freddie said, tugging me.

I spun out of his grip and whacked his hand away. "Jules," I said again. "I promise." She flashed the peace sign over her head, and I took my cue.

Freddie led me around the tables, beanbag chairs, reading pods, and down the hall to the back door of the library. "Bro. Jules?" I tried to ignore him, but it was impossible to ignore Freddie. He wouldn't let you. "She's batshit."

"Come on, man. Let it go."

"Oh, damn," he said, bringing his fist up to his mouth. "You're really into her."

"Pick up the pace," I told him. We got out onto the path along the quad. "We're heading to the rink, I assume."

"No, man," he said. "It's weight-training day. You're joining me and the rest of the football team."

I'd been avoiding thinking about it. Almost seemed cruel, I thought. Making me join the team I couldn't be on for a practice. Didn't matter that it wasn't on the field. It was too close.

Freddie eyed me, thinking he knew what was on my mind. He didn't. "And hell, no, by the way," he said. "You and Jules. She's nuts, bro. Like, super nuts." He paused. Let his eyes get all huge and melodramatic. "Unless you think that kind of crazy translates to the other kind of crazy. I mean, Hackett used to talk about how she was wild, into all kinds of stuff."

"It's not like that."

Freddie blew past me. "Wait till I tell Hackett. He's going to flip. Hilarious."

I chased after him and grabbed him by the collar. "Don't be

an ass, man. She's helping me with Brit lit so I don't fail out of school before the season starts. That clear?"

Freddie shook out of my grip as I eased up on him. "Yeah," he said. I'd shaken him, and it took him a second to find that smarmy smile, but he found it. "I got it." He walked a pace away from me. "Well, if it isn't Jules, we need to find you someone. You're so wound up, you need a little action."

I let it slide and said nothing and kept us speed-walking toward the gym. It was the kind of place where I'd once been so at home. The quiet peace of fire in my muscles, the breaths that rushed out like gale winds when I pushed through a final set. The satisfying clank of the bars dropping back into their hooks when I was done. But being with Freddie and the Fullbrook football guys obliterated the dream.

At first he let me be, but after the first few sets, he kept circling back, hovering like a goddamn shadow, spinning around me no matter which way I walked.

"Girls don't like nice guys," he said. "They don't like quiet guys who never make the first move. Know why?"

"Freddie, I don't need this."

"Could have fooled me. You're out there barking up the wrong tree. Jules? Please."

"I told you about that. I'm not barking up any tree."

"That's what I mean. You pretend like you don't want to do the horizontal mambo with her." He gyrated ridiculously next to the bench I was using. "You're so afraid, you lie to yourself. Girls can smell that fear a mile away. The shit stinks. Nobody scores out of pity, bro."

"Give me a break." I finished my third set of bicep curls and dropped the dumbbells on the mat between us, hoping he'd give me some space. It didn't faze him.

"Moody, brooding, all arty and shit," he continued. "Fine. That works too. Girls think you have your finger on some hidden pulse of the universe. Like you're *misunderstood*." He made air quotes. "Like Hackett, that wannabe musician. Guy can barely play guitar. He just owns one so he can look sensitive. So many girls that get all giggly around the floppy-haired bastard."

I pushed past him. "I don't see you holding hands with anyone."

"Exactly, dude. Ex-act-ly. I'm all about getting laid and being free."

I stared at him. Right then, I realized Freddie was a complete and total jackass. I'd had enough of him. Never mind the girls and the fact that he talked about them like they were from a different frigging planet. He was so cocky and so used to having no one call him on his shit, I had a hard time pretending to be nice to him anymore. I had thought I missed the whole team-spirit feeling, but it actually disgusted me now.

"Man," I said, moving over to the squat machine. I rolled the bar onto my shoulders and forced up the first rep. "I'm with Hackett," I growled, powering through another one. "You sound like an idiot. You don't know shit."

"Oh, yeah, just look up at my window every couple of weeks. I'm stacking pucks, one for every—well, you know." He smirked and bobbed his head like he was on a TV show and was about to get someone fired, or voted off the island, or shunned by the rest of the house—he was all smug like top dog. What a joke. Except it wasn't.

He knew I didn't believe him, but he went on anyway. "For

real. The whole team. We're all doing it. We'll see who has the most pucks stacked by the end of the year. You can't let us call you Puckless." He laughed at his own joke. "You already have a nickname, Buckeye."

I moaned as the bar rolled off my shoulders and back into the rack. "Do you ever shut up?"

He laughed again. "I know you're getting uptight, but you got it all wrong. Girls are down too, bro. You just have to know which ones. Like, I'll give you an easy one. The Viking. Easy. That party Hackett's throwing. Set you up. Easy."

Hackett and a bunch of other guys had been secretly preparing for a huge party up at Horn Rock. They'd been collecting booze and stashing it in the woods around the bluff. Nobody was supposed to know about it, but of course we all did.

Freddie followed me to the bench press. He had the dumbbells in his hands and he started a halfhearted set. "No need," I said, as I lay down on the bench.

"Forget Jules, dude."

I put the bar back up on the rests after only two reps and sat up. Around the room there were more girls now, mostly on the cardio machines, headphones on, pumping away on the treadmills and ellipticals, but some were lifting weights just like I was. "I'm done," I said. "I'm hitting the showers."

"Nobody likes a quitter," Freddie said to my back as I walked toward the locker rooms. "Especially girls, dude!" he added, just to harass me.

I had the awful urge to pop the guy in the face when he came around to use the showers too. The adrenaline surge was back, flooding my limbs and head like helium, lifting me up, dizzy-up, ready to swing. But I couldn't do that. One move like that and I was gone. Scholarship kid. I had to behave. I had to hang with Freddie, despite how I felt about him.

He came into the showers, talking as if I hadn't walked away from him before. "I mean, you had a girl back in Buckeyesville, right?" He wasn't even looking at me, just talking up to the mildew-stained tiles above us. "What was her name?"

"Yeah, I had a girlfriend."

"Why are you holding back? Show me some photos. I gotta see what you were scoring back home so I can connect you here. You should see the photos some guys sent me from last year's Senior Send-Off. Brrrro! Real time. Unbelievable."

"I'm not showing you any photos."

"I can't find you on Insta. You have some creepy ghost account?"

I couldn't get away from him fast enough. I had to get out of there. Stop talking.

"I shut down my account," I said, turning off my shower. "I don't have one anymore."

"Bro," Freddie said, finally looking at me through the steam. "You have secrets."

Yeah, I did. Secrets that smoldered so deep within me, I could almost pretend they weren't there, but they shifted, a wind blew, somebody whispered, a memory flickered, and the coals rolled and glowed again to let me know I couldn't forget what I'd done. Yeah, I did have secrets. But not what he was thinking. I could break someone, as Heather had said, and if I wasn't careful, I was going to lose it and break him. And I couldn't afford to do that at all.

CHAPTER 12

JULES DEVEREUX

"**B**ack home, they still think I might become a priest," Javi said. "They're holding out for it, like it is an actual, *actual!* possibility."

"No!"

He breathed heavily through his nose. "Jules, they still really have no idea. Or it's something even worse."

We had snuck onto the wooded path behind the sports fields, walked down to the boathouse, and slipped in without anyone noticing. There was something about the shells of the eight-oar boats, dry-docked and stored for the off-season, that felt peaceful to me. As if it was okay to rest sometimes, to not always act, think, perform. Just to hang there like a boat, useless, absolutely still. We sat on the bench and stared out the window at the slim beach and the river beyond.

The whole way over, he'd been telling me about his last conversation with his pain-in-the-ass grandfather, the one who, even at eighty-two, still called all the shots for the whole family.

Javi was always morose after speaking with his family. Wealthy, old-money, Cuban, Miami, parties with his sister: he loved them. It was, as I understood it, the Catholic part that did him in. Only his sister made going home worth it. "Seriously," Javi said. "She spoils me, I know. It makes me feel so guilty. Javi this, Javi that."

"My mom spoils me too, but I hate it." I had one of the flags coaches used from the shore to send signals to the boats on the water. I twirled the flag handle on the ground between my feet.

Javi had his vaporizer in his hand, and he looked at it for a second before he hit it. He nodded. "Always better," he croaked after he exhaled.

"But it's not even about me. She spoils me in public," I said. "Everything's all about being public. It's like there's a Hollywood soft-light haze around her. Like she's always hovering in the doorway of the bar in *Casablanca* and she's about to deliver her line. 'Kiss me. Kiss me as if it were the last time.'"

"And who's she saying that to?"

"Anybody. Or no, not anybody. It's like she's always just waiting for the right guy. But that guy could be anybody, for all I know."

"She's lonely, Jules. Cut her some slack."

"Yeah, well, aren't we all."

I hadn't meant it to sound so self-pitying. It wasn't even what I really meant.

"Yeah, well," he mocked, "you don't have to be."

I stood up and walked to the window, speaking to him over my shoulder. "Javi, I really mean it. I'm not into that this year. It's like this. I want something real—I want to know people have my back, and to know I'm spending time with people because they want to spend time with me, not because they want something from me."

"You want everything but the sex?"

I spun around, and he was grinning at me, just like I knew he was.

"Ahhh! Not just the sex—'the sex,' it sounds so clinical. I just want to spend time with people who like me and not just my body."

"You say that like they are two different things."

I walked over to him and put a hand on his shoulder. "Yeah, I know, and that is exactly what I feel like right now."

"Fine. I get it." He held his hands in the air in defeat. "I hear you. Anyway, just because you're alone doesn't mean the rest of us have to be."

I grinned.

He turned away, suddenly coy. "Some of us aren't choosing to be alone."

"What?"

"Let's just say when a little cute finds a little cute, well, the world doesn't look half bad. You know what I'm saying?"

"Oh my God, just say it. Who?"

"It's just texts, Jules, never mind." But he couldn't hold back his smile. Javi. The model with the nonplussed face. The *yeah, you think I might care* kind of look. But not then. There was something like a ten-year-old's giggle bouncing deep within him.

"Come on," I said, punching his shoulder. "Who? Who? Who?"

"All right, calm down, owl girl."

I grabbed his arm and yanked him toward me. "You're killing me. Come on. Who have you been texting with this past month? I've seen you. I know it. It's that junior. What's his name? Charlie? The kid from California?"

He shook his head. Remained tight-lipped. Tossed his eyes over his shoulder.

"Javi!"

"Max Burke," he said, snapping back. "But if you tell anyone, I'll put Nair in your shampoo."

"Max. He's megahot."

"I know."

"I didn't even know he liked boys."

"Yes you did."

"No."

"Well, I knew." He grinned. "I want a little bit of that ginger now."

His happiness was there, oozing all over the place in the boathouse, seeping through the cracks and out into the sand, and for a moment, there we were again, Jules and Javi—the dynamic duo up against everything Fullbrook had to throw at us, and getting by it all. But the moment passed as quickly as it had come. Just as I was about to squeeze him in a hug, we heard tires crunching in the gravel outside the boathouse.

It was definitely the slow, heavy roll of a car. The gray front hood nosed up near the front door. At first we just sat there. Silent. Frozen. But when one of Fullbrook's little green campus security golf carts came zipping up beside it, we bolted.

We dashed back through the rows of boats, crouched behind a

giant crate of life vests and buoys, and wedged ourselves between the crate and a giant plastic barge. It smelled like the bottom of a pond, with little hints of bleach here and there. I almost gagged, but couldn't because I was holding my breath. Nobody ever came down to the boathouse in the fall or winter, which is why Javi and I used it as a place to escape. Shoulder to shoulder, we hid with our backs against the wooden slats and our knees tucked to our chests.

"Yo," Javi said. "Who the hell?"

I shushed him. "Don't even speak," I whispered.

He'd smoked a vaporizer, which never stank very much, but we were inside, not outside, and without the breeze it had left a little something lingering in the air. I just hoped whoever had come here didn't have a clue. Or didn't want to have a clue. That, truthfully, was what you could count on a little more at Fullbrook. Teachers wanted to talk about chemistry, or the transcendental movement in literature; coaches could help you perfect your butterfly stroke. They didn't want to get caught up in this. Drugs. Sex. Those things just made them uncomfortable. Or most of them. You always had to look out for the ones who wouldn't let anything slide.

The door to the boathouse squeaked open. The warped wood stuck and then popped free of the jamb, just as it had for us, and I felt the vibration shudder down into the pit of my stomach. Two men were speaking to each other. I recognized Cray-Cray, but not the other.

"It's that it should be locked," Cray-Cray was saying. "Hey!" he bellowed. "Anybody in here?"

We sat as still as possible.

"It stinks in here," he continued.

"It always stinks in here," the other guy said.

"No. Like weed."

"I wouldn't know about that."

"Oh, give me a break."

They got closer.

"I'm not here to inspect anything," the other man said. "I just need the gear." As he walked through the boathouse, I realized it wasn't one of the swim coaches or crew coaches. It was O'Leary, Mr. Hockey.

"If they see us," Javi whispered, "I'm going to kiss you."

"Just be quiet," I said. "Don't talk."

"It's the only way they'll let us go."

"Shut up."

"It just drives me nuts," Cray-Cray went on. "I'm not their father. I'm not their cool uncle. I'm here to keep them safe. Here to protect them. Even if it's from themselves. Anybody here?" he shouted again.

They were much closer, only a few steps away now. If they stopped talking and listened carefully, I worried they could hear my heart banging in my chest. I understood Javi's plan. If they poked their heads over the crate and saw us, and we were kissing, groping, sticking our hands down into each other's clothes, we'd embarrass the hell out of Cray-Cray and O'Leary. Maybe they'd be so weirded out, they'd just ask us to leave and shuffle us along.

O'Leary and Cray-Cray stopped moving. They stood by the

cabinets at the foot of the barge. "I'm just here to get the bungee cords," O'Leary said.

"If no one's here now, they've been here," Cray-Cray said, ignoring him. "I swear, my days are like a never-ending game of whack-a-mole with these kids. Think they can get away with everything."

The metal locker slammed shut. "Not my guys. I keep my guys in line. They know. That's the benefit of a five-thirty a.m. practice." O'Leary laughed. "Those boys are too damn tired to go looking for trouble."

"Are you crazy or kidding? I can't tell."

"That's what the kids all call you, Donald. Not me."

He laughed again and both men walked away. They hovered by the door, inspecting the lock, Cray-Cray jingling his massive all-campus key ring that always hung from his belt like some kind of medieval weapon. We hadn't even noticed the lock when we'd come. The boathouse was always open. I'd always been able to get in. But the dead bolt flipped with a thud when they left.

"Hey," Javi said. He cleared his throat. "That was close."

"Yeah."

"But we made it."

"Yup." I rolled out from behind the crate and stretched.

"Hey," he said. He stood and followed me back to the bench. I sat and he sat beside me. Putting a little space between us.

I was also feeling awkward.

And Javi knew.

"I wasn't trying to be weird," he continued. "I mean, I'd have kissed you just so we wouldn't get in trouble."

"No, I know."

"I mean, there are some girls who'd be into that." He tried a half smile, and I knew he was kidding. But not really. There were. I'd been all into that our first year. "But for real. The look on your face, when I said that? Jules, I'm sorry."

"No, I'm sorry."

"No. You're right." He smiled that beautiful smile again.

"Yeah." It was hard not to wonder what it would have been like if Javi wasn't gay, if he and I had stayed together. Sometimes I let myself stray and think about how we'd be the perfect couple for each other, but I always circled back. The Javi I loved wouldn't be the Javi I loved now if he wasn't who he was. We were perfect for each other now—perfect friends.

"But what about Max? That boy can kiss?" I teased.

"I don't know yet, but I'll know soon."

"Oh my God, what if your first kiss had been here, like that, all forced and crazy. What a story you'd have for your first kiss!"

He let out a little sniffle of a laugh and I nudged him with my elbow. "What?"

"But that's just it, right?"

"What?"

"If Max and I had been here, and if Max and I had been making out, it would have been different. It just would have."

I nodded.

"I never feel nervous about it. I'll kiss a boy out in the academic quad if he's down. But think about this. If Cray-Cray comes in here and sees me and you making out, maybe he's like, 'Kids, you go on and get,' but if he sees me with Max, and catches me and

Max making out, maybe there's this something else inside him—maybe he says, 'You know what, you boys are trespassing and breaking school rules and I'm writing you up and sending your names to the office.' He'd never say it was because we were two boys kissing, but how can I know? There's just something about it. I feel it."

I nodded again. I wanted to think about that. About what I took for granted. When Javi had come out, he'd been shy about it, but then he'd let that go, and by junior year everything seemed so easy. There were a handful of kids who were openly gay and I just assumed nobody felt any which way about it—or most people anyway. But if I'd been letting my dreams get away from me and dreamed about Javi and me, who's to say other people's thoughts didn't get away from them—but not with affection, with a denigration.

"I'm sorry," I said. "I didn't think about that."

"Cray-Cray? O'Leary?" Javi paused. "They would have strung us up. Stuck us in the stocks." He nodded silently and looked out to the water. "I'm sorry," he finally said. "Because actually, I wouldn't stand out there in the middle of the academic quad. I want to. I mean, you and Hackett last year. I saw you up against the wall in the arts center, or on the stupid steps of the admin building, you know?"

I nodded, trying to hide the blood rushing to my cheeks.

"But let's say I do. Let's say Max is like—what was that *Casablanca* line? 'Kiss me. Kiss me as if it were the last time.' Let's say that happens. Then let's say Fullbrook is sooo liberal they include a photo of it on their website. 'Gay friendly,' the banner reads above that." He stood and folded his arms. "First of all, that is never going to happen and you know it. I've been going to private schools my whole life, and no matter what they say, you *know* I don't get to make out in the halls like you do with Ethan or whoever. Why? And what's more, you know who isn't down with that? Seeing their son as the poster boy for the gay-friendly school?"

He tightened his jaw as he continued. "That's not why they sent me here, or actually, why *he* sent me here. They wanted me away from trouble. Mi Pipo, I'll never forget his old, hairy finger tapping the picture of Fullbrook's admin building in the brochure. *'Un buen elemento,'* Pipo said. Whatever. It's his money. We're all just supposed to fall in line." Javi swiped at the air in front of him with the back of his hand. "Fuck that."

He walked over to the window, sucked another big hit from the vaporizer, and let the cloud swirl around in front of his face as he exhaled. "But no, fuck me, really, because if they catch me and Max playing *Casablanca*, you know who calls up Father Jiménez to speak about an intervention? You know who yanks me out of Fullbrook and sends me back to Belen so they can keep a close eye on me?" He shook his head. "You think that capital campaign donation he gave to Patterson last year doesn't come with some pressure on me too? Hell, he still gives money to Belen—just in case I need a backup. That's how a guy like him works, how he works the whole family. *Un buen elemento*, my ass." He stabbed a finger toward me. "That's the *worse* I'm talking about, Jules. That's the worse I'm always thinking about when I talk to my family."

I got up and walked over to him. I put my hands on my hips and screamed at the window—belted out my loudest and most unhinged. I doubled forward, yelling at the glass, and if I'd been a superhero, the glass would have shattered everywhere and the pine trees on either side of the river would have bent back like they might flip right out of the ground, but I wasn't a superhero and none of that happened, and instead all I did was hurt my throat.

My face tingled like I'd been slapped around. I sat down, exhausted and ready to cry. Why? Why did I have to live on this cracked edge all the time? I closed my eyes.

"What was that?" Javi asked.

"That's all I know to do," I said. "It's so unfair."

He nodded and put his arm around me.

"No," I said. "Like, I want to do something for you, but there's nothing I can do about that. That's fucked."

"Yeah, well." He mustered a smile, and for a moment it hung there, a little lifeless, but then all the energy of his million-dollar flash came back. "You can be happy for me."

"I'm happy for you, you know it," I said to him.

"I know you are."

"I'm happy for him, actually," I said, trying to lighten things up a bit. "I don't think he knows how lucky he is."

"Oh, he might," Javi said, teasing back.

We were quiet for a moment, but then he spoke again.

"I don't know how it works, Jules. I don't think you're going to wake up one day and the clouds will be gone forever. I just think—no, I know. I know it. If I need you, I'm going to call out to you. That's what I need too. To know you'll be there."

"I promise."

"Good." He paused. "But promise me something else."

"Okay."

"Promise me you'll come to me too."

"Javi."

"No. Promise. This is a two-way street, Jules. You're not super-woman and this 'I'm all alone' thing is fine, but you're not all alone. You know what I'm saying?"

"Yes."

"Then let me hear it. Promise me."

"I promise. I promise I'll come to you if I need you."

CHAPTER 13

JAMES BAXTER

The knock on my door shortly after Mr. Hale made his rounds on Friday after lights-out surprised me. It was Javi. I opened it quickly and he snuck in. "Wow," I said, looking him up and down. Skinny jeans. Pale green eye shadow that sparkled in the light. Feet slipped into what looked like two rainbows.

"You have the magic room," he told me, as he moved toward my window. "Come on, I know you're cool, man. Jules said so."

At the mention of her name, I loosened. I should have known it was something the two of them were up to. "Where are you guys going?"

"I tell you what." He grinned. "Want to come with?"

I went to my window. My room was the only one on my floor that had a window that did not face either the main street in front of the dorm or the main backyard. All you had to do was swing your leg over the sill and step down onto the grass. Magic.

"Come on, hurry up," Javi insisted. "Jules and Aileen are waiting for me. You'll make four—it's perfect."

Jules. Working together as we had been, we'd found that a door had opened between us. I'd stepped through it, briefly, and she the other way, and we'd gotten a glimpse into the private rooms within us. It felt safe.

What the hell, I thought. I quickly changed, threw on my coat, and followed Javi outside. We pulled down the window, allowing enough room to pry it open from the outside. We stuck to the shadows as best we could, until we got to Old Main, and then we sprinted down the middle of the street like a pair of dogs let loose in a field. I would have howled, if Javi had.

He led me downhill, away from school, and for a minute I thought we were just leaving the girls behind, until I realized Jules was ahead, leaning against a tree on the shoulder of the road. Aileen was right beside her. Once you were beyond the stretch of street that ran through campus, there weren't many streetlights.

"Okay," Javi said. "I think this is going to work."

"Yeah," Jules said, nodding to me. "And we have room for four?"

"Whatever. He's here now."

Jules pulled out a tube of lipstick and began applying. Her lips turned dark blue, but speckled with starry glitter. "You?" she said, dipping it toward me.

"No thanks."

Aileen smiled. The same blue stars were spread across her face.

"Wow," Javi said. "I don't know if that is amazing or even too weird for me."

Jules socked him on the shoulder and I just stood there,

soaking up the way they always seemed so at ease with each other, as if they'd left their nerves back in the dorms and out here in the world they were just plain free.

Not me. I couldn't help it. "I thought you said you don't get into trouble," I said to Jules.

She puckered her lips and blew me an air-kiss. "What trouble?"

"We're just getting out of here," Javi said. "One night of absolute freedom."

"And your favorite band," Aileen added. "This is on you if it goes south." She glared for a second at Javi, but then relented.

"You can still turn back," he said.

"No," Jules said, pulling us all together. "We all need it. An escape. Forget Fullbrook for one night."

Something in me swelled. It'd been a long time since someone had pulled me into the huddle. The smallest dose of that goes a long way.

"But I don't know." Jules nodded and tossed me a teasing grin. "Can we trust him?"

"What? With sneaking out at night?" I asked. "I don't care."

They all exchanged glances.

Jules reached out and held both my shoulders. "Even if we leave campus?"

"Tonight?"

Javi must have heard the fear in my voice because he laughed. "Yup," he said. "Wendell Phillips College. Their own mini-Ultra." Javi danced ahead of us. "And we're going to it." He spun back around. "All of us."

My voice was trapped in my throat. All I could think of was

Coach O staring at me across his desk if I got caught. What would happen? It just didn't seem fair. None of them had as much to lose as I did.

"Come on," Aileen said, grabbing a handful of my coat. She bounced my ribs with her fist. "Live a little."

Jules smiled as she glanced back and forth between me and Aileen. "Hey, live a little," she echoed.

Aileen and Jules stepped the four of us back out into the street, and I suddenly realized neither of them was wearing pants. They always wore pants; they never wore those fancy cocktail dresses so many of the other girls wore to class every day. Instead, they were both in tights. Jules's were dark. Her coat was unzipped and beneath it she had on a kind of supernova dress of DayGlo swirls and stars. Her hair was gathered in a bunch of floppy horns, sprouting from parti-colored scrunchies. Aileen wasn't in her usual goth-black. Instead, she was in neon green tights and a shimmering silver trench coat.

"Am I underdressed?"

"Just be yourself," she said. Despite the costume, she was the same old Aileen, with the same spray of freckles rising up her cheeks when she smiled.

I followed them down the road to the farm stand, closed and shuttered for the season. It stood at Old Main's junction with the narrow, single-lane Route 17, and one dull, squash-colored light hummed atop a pole in the parking lot. Everywhere else—the fields along the road, the woods behind the farm stand, the street in both directions—was shadows, dim outlines fingering out of a darker background, until a pair of headlights drifted toward us.

The black sedan pulled into the parking lot and stopped beside us. The driver's window sank. "Ms. Devereux?" he asked skeptically, when he caught sight of her glittering makeup.

The three of them sat in the back, chatting away, and they stuck me, Long Legs, up front. The sedan slipped past the farms around Fullbrook and swung up onto the larger highway. I'd never been to a live show. I'd never been to a college party. I'd never been to a college campus, even. Sure, I was supposed to be in college, but it wasn't about that. I felt like I barely knew how to talk. I couldn't get a thought together in class, where I was supposed to think and speak—how could I ever say anything coherent at a college party?

Before long, we turned off and took the exit to Wendell Phillips College. We passed another long stretch of farmland before finally coming to the gate, where Javi instructed the driver to drop us off.

The party, the concert, the show, whatever it was, turned out to be in one of the giant barns off on the side of campus, a gray rickety mess, a giant house of splinters that would have been the perfect set for a horror film if the swirling blue, red, and green lights and the trippy electronica hadn't been bumping out from inside. Javi paid for all four tickets, grabbed Jules by the hand, and ran inside.

They spun in a circle and pushed forward into the crowd. I couldn't move. My feet felt like they were back at Fullbrook, and my head seemed to have drifted into someone else's dream. It was like a circus—just one of a whole other kind. Aileen took me by the hand and led me in.

The stage was against the far side of the barn, and staggered across the enormous dance floor between it and the doors were four huge cages on raised platforms. Men, women, people not much older than me, writhed along with the goofy music. Everywhere people were dressed like Jules, Aileen, and Javi, swirls of their own colors, spinning, grinding, some shirtless, and above them all, disco balls hanging from the weathered crossbeams threw parti-colored diamonds of light across the crowd.

I don't know how long I'd been standing like that, gawking, mouth agape, when Jules suddenly tugged my arm and dragged me into the crowd after her. "Follow my rules," she said to me. "Don't drink anything unless it's bottled water and the cap is sealed. Don't eat anything. And whatever you do, don't get sucked away into the crowd by some older woman. Don't get lost on your own. We're here for us!" She smiled with an open mouth, head cocked to the side, and danced as she dragged me toward Javi.

He was eating a brownie. "What about him?" I yelled.

A light show of green flashes rained down over us. "He has his own rules," Jules said, and laughed.

Javi grinned with a mouthful of brownie. "Zoom, zoom, zoom," he said.

The crowd packed tighter around us. The music dissolved into dreamy shattering of glass, like a thousand chimes blowing gently in the breeze. The lights all went out, and then, in the darkness, an electric keyboard and guitar started weaving a melody between them, and a man's voice that mewled like a cat whined the first lines of song. The lights exploded to life in a hullabaloo around the barn and a thumping beat rattled in my bones. Javi and Jules screamed along with the rest of the crowd.

Although I didn't eat one of the brownies like Javi, the night slipped into a dream. Everyone danced around me, and Jules and Aileen poked me until I started to as well. As the crowd packed tighter, people slipped in between me and Jules and Aileen, and soon we were all dancing with other people. The guy in front of me was dressed in a silvery, skintight jumpsuit, and he dropped and bobbed down at my knees, then slowly inched upward until I felt his hot breath on my nose. He spun and found another guy who would gyrate in unison with him.

Time zipped and slowed. Javi dancing like a grounded bird, wings flapping at the air around him. Aileen rolling in and out of sight and then back beside me.

Jules popped out from a thicket of men and glanced toward me, lunging, smiling, spinning. She slid up between me and Aileen, wiggled once, and then spun back to another group, this time all women, and wove herself into their web of limbs, something like sunlight warming their skin, but from the inside.

Aileen stepped closer. No one could squeeze between us. Like me, she moved more hesitantly, bound tighter. She looked mostly at the floor, to her feet, and when she looked up and raised her arms above her head, she closed her eyes, kept her world private and protected. She spun around behind me, did a butterfly stroke so our backs kissed and released, kissed and released.

I looked up into the rafters above us, wishing I could see the dark roof beams above the mosaic light. I'd felt this way once before. Heather finishing a one-arm handspring in the grass alongside the track, no one else around, the afternoon sunlight glowing in the glass of the gymnasium behind her, smiling to herself, a smile that was for herself, until she turned and offered it to me. I held that smile inside me for months, where it warmed me like a hot coal—until she stopped returning my texts.

Eventually, Jules and Javi found us again and motioned toward the back of the room. We staggered outside and stumbled up the slope of the hill toward the main path to the gates, the music still pounding in my ears. Javi slipped in the grass and laughed as he tumbled to the ground. Jules dove next to him, and even though it felt silly, I crashed down alongside them. Aileen did too. We all rolled onto our backs and looked up into the sky, Javi and I bookending Jules and Aileen. Jules waved her hands in the air above us. She stopped and froze them, palms up to the stars.

"Does it ever feel like it could all just come crashing down on you at any time?" she asked. "Like if you don't hold it up there above you, everything's going to collapse around you."

"Yes," Aileen said. She seemed to withdraw, as if she was scrunching her shoulders in toward her head.

"Awww, man," Javi said. "Let's not go there."

"But it's real," Jules said. "I feel like that sometimes."

"Me too," I said.

"Yeah, right," Javi said. "Mr. Manly Man."

"It does," I said. "It has."

Everyone was quiet for a moment, as if they were waiting for me to say more, but I didn't. I just couldn't. I wished I hadn't said what I'd said.

Javi leapt to his feet. "Get on up here, girl," he said, grabbing

Jules's hands and pulling her up. "On the count of three, I'm going to lift you even higher. Stuff those stars back up in that sky."

Conspiratorial joy lit up her face. "One, two, three." She leapt into his arms.

I turned to Aileen. "You want a boost?"

She sat up. And then, like that, the world stopped moving, at least for me, because the whole world glittered in the corner of her eyes as she looked down at me and smiled. Light from I don't know where played in her eyes, little jewels glinting to let me know they were there.

"Hold me higher," she said.

I crouched like a linebacker at first and Aileen stepped into my hands, and I lifted her into the air. Her shin was pressed against my shoulder, and when I looked up, all I could see was the underside of her chin—her face was pitched to the moon.

"Yes!" Aileen yelled. She glanced toward Jules, wobbled, but regained her balance. "Higher! Send me to the stars!" Aileen yelled down to me.

"Make your legs stiff," I said. She did, and I held her legs and pressed her up. I'd done it before and I knew what I was doing. Heather had taught me.

Jules slid down Javi, and once she was on the ground again, she looked up at Aileen and howled. "Higher, higher!"

"Woooo-hoooo," Javi cheered.

"I'm alive!" Aileen yelled. She teetered. "Am I going to crash?" She laughed nervously. "No, seriously."

She wobbled again and I tried to keep balance for both of us. "Fall right down into me," I said. "I'll catch you. I promise."

She squealed, and then she dropped, and I found myself swooping into motion. Muscle memory. I could have done it with my eyes closed, I realized, my arms cradling her like a hammock.

"All right," Jules said. "Let's get out of here. Your turn, Javi."

He searched his pockets. "Oh shit," he said.

"No," Jules said.

"You don't have yours, do you?" he asked her.

"No! That was the plan. No purse, no nothing for me or Aileen. That was the point. I left mine at home after I called for the car."

"So did I," Aileen said.

"Where's yours?" I asked Javi.

"Gone," he said. He breathed slowly through his nose. "But whatever. I'll just get a new one."

It blew my mind how things like this just never bothered him. Phones, shoes, jewelry, all of it mattered, in that he always needed them, but none of it mattered because everything was replaceable for Javi. It must be nice to be so rich. I still made sure to switch back and forth between my two pairs of non-sneaker shoes every day so I wouldn't wear down the soles too quickly.

"Yeah, but not 'whatever,'" Jules said. "How are we getting home?" She looked at me. "Let's use yours."

"Can't. I need to be on Wi-Fi."

"Why?"

"I can only use it on Wi-Fi. Roaming, I can't."

"Oh Jesus, Bax," Javi said. "Just use your damn phone like a normal person."

But I wasn't a normal person—not normal for Fullbrook. I

had a phone, but a plan with unlimited data was too expensive for my family. "No," I said. "You don't understand. I never use it, not unless I'm in my room or something."

"What?" Javi said. "Who doesn't have his phone with him all the time?"

"Um, you, now," I said.

He shoved me playfully. "But for real?" He looked at Jules.

"This is on you," Jules said to him.

"Fine." Javi shook his head. Then he brightened. "Oh, I know who I'll ask."

He ran back down the hill, and the three of us wandered over to one of the big trees and sat down beneath it, staring toward the barn, which still glowed with the party inside. Jules played with the strings on her coat, twirling them in her fingers and letting them unravel. "I'm glad you came, Bax." She hesitated, then bumped my shoulder with hers. "For real. You're all right. Didn't think I was going to like you. But I do."

She remained leaning against one shoulder, and Aileen slumped into my other one. "Bax sandwich," she said. She laughed at herself quickly. "That was stupid."

"No it wasn't," I said.

They were both quiet as we watched the front door of the barn for Javi. Seconds passed like minutes. A wall of bricks kept getting kicked over in my gut, as Aileen's and Jules's shoulders rose and fell on either side of me, the two of them almost in unison, and I was warmed in the space of their breathing.

I listened for a moment. One of them might have sniffled, or whimpered, or I might have made that all up just straining to hear something in the little bubble of silence around us. My pulse whacked a furious beat in my wrists and ears, I could almost feel my body bouncing as I sat there with my back against the tree.

Javi popped out of the barn and sauntered up the hill toward us, walking alongside one of the guys he'd danced with earlier. We all met down along the street.

"And they say it's too hard to meet a nice guy," Javi said. He glanced coyly at the tall, skinny guy in a loose T-shirt. He had a tattoo of three birds swooping around his arm, like if he pointed to the sky, they'd take off and fly.

"It was already on campus," Birdman said.

"Oh, no," Javi said. "So soon?"

The car crept down the street toward us and Birdman waved it down. He told the driver to take us to Fullbrook. Luckily it wasn't the same driver. It was another car altogether. He looked like he could have been one of our fathers.

"I can't even take your number down," Javi said to Birdman.

"Nope," he said. He smiled. "Why don't you graduate first? Find me then." It wasn't mean. It was tender the way he said it.

"I need to graduate like right now," Javi said. He looked like he was going to go in for a kiss, but Birdman took a step back and waved. He smiled and pointed to the backseat.

"Get in that car," he teased. "And get home safe."

On the way back, we all yawned and nodded off a little. And when the driver dropped us off at the farm stand, he gave us his own version of a lecture. "I should really drop you off at your dorm. I should tell the school about this," he said.

"Please don't," I said drowsily. "These are my only friends." I hadn't meant to say that. It just tumbled out, my sleepy mind having shut down all my filters.

We stumbled out of the car, exhausted. We waited for the driver to pull away, to make sure he didn't trail us up the street. When he was gone, Javi hugged me.

"You're sweet, Bax." He held me out at arm's length. "Yes. Yes, you gentle giant." He grinned. "Yes, we are friends."

Jules wrapped me up from behind, her arms squeezing at my ribs, her tiny hands on my chest—I could feel how cold they were through my shirt—and Aileen pressed in from the side. I stepped back so Jules could slide over between me and Javi, and I wrapped the three of them in a tight hug.

"Don't change," Jules said into the center, to all of us. "Please don't change. This is everything." She paused and yawned. "This is all I have."

"Me too," I said.

PART TWO

THE NIGHT AT HORN ROCK

CHAPTER 14

JULES DEVEREUX

We got there late, and the party was already raging. I almost didn't go, but I told myself I was going for Javi, just in case things didn't work out with Max, which was stupid, because of course it was going to work out for Javi and Max.

I'd seen them speaking to each other in the road outside the student center, laughing, and the way Max looked down and away and then stepped closer to Javi when Javi touched his elbow, it was so obvious they were flirting with each other, but not really, because even though nobody would ever say Fullbrook was a homophobic place, I'd believed Javi when he told me he still felt that hesitation, that inclination to backpedal, when he wanted to tickle a boy in the ribs, hold his hand as they walked into the stands to watch the football game, or kiss the boy he liked right there in the sunlight under the branches of the old elm by the admin building. I believed him, all right, and I knew that with the cover of night, the loose, easygoing air of the party, they would feel free to drop their hesitations and fall all over each other in the moonlight just like the rest of the boys and girls around them.

The cloudless night was a scatter of stars above us, and even though it was the largest party of the year, it was impossible to tell where everyone was, because the party sprawled across the bluffs and into the woods. Somebody had hooked up portable speakers to a phone, and people were dancing all around the base of Horn Rock. It was mostly girls—the boys were all pounding back drinks in the darkness—and as I swallowed the last drops of my own first drink and went to pour another one for me and Aileen, I thought how cool it would have been if none of the boys had shown up and the girls had gotten to rock it alone for once.

Aileen laughed when I shared this thought. "Seriously," she said. "That would be awesome. We never get to do that."

But she wasn't fooling anyone. She wanted boys at the party. One in particular. That was becoming increasingly obvious, and she wasn't very subtle—which made it all the easier to tease her. "That blouse is super cute on you," I told her.

"Really?"

"Is it new?"

"Yeah. Ordered it last week." She smoothed the lines of the shirt where it rested on her belly. "You think?"

I nodded. Took a sip. Took her in slowly. "Absolutely." She hid her smile in another sip from her drink. "I bet Bax will notice."

She darted her eyes away.

"I think it's cool, by the way," I added.

Aileen straightened. "You two aren't . . . Or haven't . . ."

"No. Not at all."

"It's just that I see you hanging out all the time and . . . I don't know."

"No. No way." I held my cup high over my head and announced: "I am officially off boys this fall. No boys. I've got so many better things to think about. Off boys! You heard it here."

Aileen laughed, and I was glad, because I knew where this was going. A couple of the other girls groaned, though, when they heard my pronouncement, but not Aileen. She kept laughing and drinking, and when she held her cup out for another, I didn't pay much attention, because she seemed perfectly fine. I poured her another.

"He hasn't said anything to you about me, has he?" Aileen asked.

"No." I hesitated. He hadn't, but I'd seen the way they looked at each other, and it was cute. He wasn't the kind of guy who opened up easily and talked about it, though. "But that doesn't matter," I went on. "You have to see it too. He's thinking about you."

"Yeah." Aileen toed the dirt with the front of her shoe. She sniffed, and swirled her cup. She let her weight sink back onto one leg. "Cool," she said. She drained her drink and held the cup out again. "Have one with me. You're holding back."

I was glad I'd been pouring tiny amounts of vodka into our cups, because I was already having more than I wanted to and I couldn't believe she was still standing straight. But I followed her instructions, because suddenly that's what it felt like—like she'd given me an order and I was supposed to obey it. I didn't like it.

It was against rule number one of the year for me: the Freedom to Be Me.

I poured the drinks, heavily this time, and clinked with her quickly. "Here's to the party without boys," I said.

She smiled. We sipped. But the hoots and hollers of the boys in the woods behind us rushed ahead of them like ghosts clearing the path before an army.

CHAPTER 15

JAMES BAXTER

The problem with this party was that everybody was going. Nobody was supposed to talk about it, but everyone had been whispering about it for days. I was worried the teachers knew about it too and we were all going to get busted. "We've been doing this forever at Fullbrook," Hackett kept telling me. "It happens every year. Everything's going to be fine."

It was tradition. Just like the ties and the motto and the tree and the ivy crawling up the brick front of the admin building. Everything was tradition. Even the fall party at Horn Rock. Hackett had explained it all. He took on the burden of organizing it all for the rest of us. Everything was going to be fine, he said. It always was.

The problem, at least for me, was that Freddie insisted the hockey team head to the party together. "Let's face it," he said. "We suck at football. Hockey's our game. Let's hit the party like champions."

He was saying it again as he held out his Solo cup for me to clink. "To the championship."

I nodded and tapped cups.

Most of the hockey team was around us. Despite how I felt about Freddie, the team mattered. The game mattered. They all cheered as Freddie knocked back his drink, but I looked out to the clearing beyond us. Lit by the pale glow from the nearly full moon, Horn Rock rose like a giant gray tusk from the edge of the bluff and jutted up into the night sky.

Music was playing, and someone had lit candles and stuffed them in divots around the rock, but they weren't strong enough to provide much light. It was almost impossible to tell who was who from a short distance, except, as I continued to look out from the woods, I recognized two silhouettes in the clearing, and smiled.

I started to walk away, but Freddie called me back. "Hey. You ghosting already?"

"Nah," I said, trying to sound casual. "Party time."

I left them all doing shots in the darkness behind me and made my way to Aileen and Jules. They didn't recognize me at first, and I called out, so I wouldn't be some creeper just popping up silently behind them. Javi and Max heard me and walked over too. We stood in a tight circle, so we could see each other, and as we did, I couldn't help thinking about how there were five of us—just one more and we would have made a team out on the ice. But I was glad no one else was around and it was only us. We were our own kind of team, and I wished we could have peeled away, had our own party, like at Wendell.

But it didn't last long. We all clinked glasses and Aileen was about to say something, when Hackett broke into our circle. Javi gave him a stink eye, but he didn't notice. Hackett had already dug up most of the bottles he'd hidden around the clearing and he was passing out cups and pouring shots of vodka as he walked around. "Refills?" he asked us. He smiled goofily, and I wondered how many he'd had himself by then. He poured out a drink for Javi and Max and then propped his pouring hand and bottle on Javi's shoulder.

"Easy," Javi said. He steadied Hackett. "Why don't I play bartender for a while?"

"Be my guest," Hackett said, handing Javi the bottle.

"Where's Gillian?" Jules asked him.

"Not drinking," Hackett said, clearly annoyed.

"Maybe you should go find her?" Jules said.

"Yeah," he said. "Maybe." He bobbed his head, a little too long, not tracking his movements. Then he smiled. "That's still the coolest T-shirt at Fullbrook," he said, nodding to Jules. Her hoodie was unzipped, so the yellow Happy Daze T-shirt was visible.

"Those days are over," Jules said quickly.

He nodded, then turned to Aileen. "You too," he said. "You look great tonight."

Before she responded, he winked at me like she wasn't even really there. I'd seen it in other guys' eyes all year and just ignored it. Or maybe even felt like I deserved it. Condescension. That knowing look of superiority. I was less than them and they let me know it—even with only a glance.

"Go find Gillian," Jules said again.

"Yeah," Hackett said, pulling back. "All the fun she's having." He stumbled toward the crowd dancing on the other side of Horn Rock.

"Guess we have some catching up to do," Javi said, trying to laugh it all off. He poured himself and Max another shot. I pulled my cup away so they wouldn't pour me more. I'd pretended to knock back a shot with the hockey team too. Nobody else seemed to care, but I was still worried about getting caught. I'd convinced myself that if the party was busted and I could prove I hadn't been drinking, it wouldn't be so bad. Coach might let it slide. Breaking curfew, being in the woods at night, those weren't offenses for the review board. Drinking was. No matter how much I wanted to hang with this new team, there was no way in hell I was getting kicked off the team I'd been bought and paid for to keep pucks out of a net.

CHAPTER 16

JULES DEVEREUX

L ike usual, Javi was livening the party. He scrambled up Horn Rock and took command immediately. I shrugged and gave him my best *whatever will you do now* pose. "Look who's on top of the world," he said down to me.

The spot he'd chosen was too perfect. From where I stood, the moon bloomed like a giant elephant ear off the side of his head. "Step to the right," I said. I wasn't paying attention to anything else—just trying to set the tableaux—and when Javi finally shuffled into position, the whole moon glowed behind him, casting a pale corona around his head.

"Perfect!" I shouted. "Now you are the man in the moon!" I held my cup up and tried to rally a few of the people around me. "To the man in the moon," I cheered. "May he reign in the sky forever!"

"Hear, hear!" he shouted back, stirring a low rumble of cheers in the crowd around the rock. And Javi and I went back and forth, calling out toasts, invoking the sky, celebrating nonsense with nonsense until we had everybody cheering. He sprayed us with vodka, and even though there were little screams of delight all around us, I heard a sigh, and I knew it was Bax behind me. Luckily Javi noticed it too.

"And for my second decree," Javi yelled, "I demand that our very own James Baxter wipe that look of gloom from his face."

I agreed. Fun. One break. One night of everything working out okay. A small piece of the peace we found at Wendell, but at Fullbrook for once—that's all I wanted, for all of us.

Someone turned up the music and we started dancing again, and Javi ticked off his fingers in the air, one, two, three, then dropped himself into the crowd and bodysurfed through the hands, which eventually plopped him down in front of me and Max.

"Is this your party or Hackett's?" Max joked.

Javi put his hands on either side of Max's face and stepped close. "Mine," he whisper-shouted. He'd lost the bottle he'd been holding when he was up on the rock, and he held out his empty cup. "Do not go thirsty into that frat-party night!" he yelled, and we dipped back into the crowd to find another bottle.

When we found one, I poured a bit into all three of our cups, but I didn't put much in mine, because I already felt more light-headed than I wanted to, and it felt like the party was only now, finally, getting started.

Max, it turned out, was also much funnier than I realized, and while we sat against the rock, near the edge of the bluff, and looked out at the river and the treetops on the other side of it, he did his amazing impressions of Coach O'Leary. "Hey, foo-bawl. Hey, hey, foo-bawl!" he mumbled. It was syllable for syllable a

Coach O announcement at lunchtime. "We gotta hit that bus early today. Hey, hey, early, you hear? Don't be late."

"Red Hawks," Javi said, trying to sound like Coach O but not even coming close.

"Red Hawks," Max said. "Red Hawks. Red Hawks, RedHawksRedHawksRedHawks!"

"Eeeow." I tried to screech at the end, like what I thought a threatening hawk might sound like, but it didn't sound dangerous at all.

"Oh my God," Max said. "That was perfect. What if people did that every time at the end?"

"Don't they?" I asked.

"Uh, no. Not like that," Max said.

"That was way more like a sexy cat meow than a bird call," Javi said. He and Max laughed.

"You mean like a terrifying fisher-cat call. None of this sexy cat nonsense. I would never want that image in Coach O's head around me."

"No, of course not." Max said.

"I don't know," Javi said. "Coach O could be kind of sexy," he joked.

"Ugh!" Max said. "If you think a decomposing bag of moldy peas is sexy."

Javi picked up some leaves beside him and threw them at Max. "I'm more an *eau de forêt* kind of guy." He smudged a few more in Max's shirt, did a backward somersault, and pressed himself up to his feet quickly. Max swung around and followed him, and I did too, because I was swept up in all the silliness. We wove through the dancing crowd, then out past the rock and into the darkness of the woods along the ridge of the bluff. After a few minutes, Max actually caught Javi and held him in a bear hug. When he put him down, Javi spun in his arms so they were face-to-face and kissed him. They paused, staring at each other. Then they kissed again, more slowly, Javi reaching up to Max's face and brushing it with his fingertips. They kissed and kissed, paused for air only for a moment, and kissed again.

They breathed each other in and out. Javi's strong arm held Max to him like he was terrified a wind was about to blow them apart. Tears beaded at the corners of my eyes, and at first I thought maybe there was a wind and it was drying out my eyes, but that wasn't it, I wasn't crying for them, I was crying for me. I couldn't explain it. I didn't want to be wrapped up in someone's arms like they were, but I didn't want to be lonely, either. I just wanted to feel a sense of being on my own and not alone at the same time.

And I would have stood there all night like that if Javi hadn't leaned over and said, "Hey, Jules, a little privacy, please."

I slunk away, not even finding a voice to say I was sorry. I wasn't sure where to go. I realized we'd all kind of abandoned Bax and Aileen too. It struck me that they might have found each other, which, in an odd way, made me feel left out. I felt a little gutted, and I wove through the trees, listening to the noise coming from Horn Rock, and I suddenly wished for a fire, or something where no one would accuse me of being weird if I just stared into it silently. Because as the shrieks and howls of the party swooped and echoed around me, I realized that I was exhausted. Exhausted from caring too much and having to care too much about all the Fullbrook sexist bullshit, because the nor-malization campaign had fizzled out, and even if I did finish the designs for all the posters I wanted to put up, who would stop to read them? Who would stop to see them? So terribly few. I was exhausted from trying to change things and exhausted from rallying myself again and again to keep thinking I could. I was exhausted just listening to the boys' laughter booming and roll-ing out over Horn Rock like thunder. *One more year.* God. Could I actually make it another seven months? *Just seven months, just six months.* I was exhausted. This urge all year to be alone felt so much like that final mile in a run, when you kind of want to give up because your legs hurt so much, but you push through it and the pain starts to fade again, and you feel the surge of pride for not giving up. That's what I wanted. That surge of pride. Me, on my own, doing everything I damn well pleased and getting into college and getting the hell away from everyone and all their expectations, getting to where I could start from scratch and live the life I wanted to live.

CHAPTER 17

JAMES BAXTER

"Cheers," Aileen said, knocking her cup against mine. We'd lost Javi and Max and Jules somewhere in the woods behind us, and it occurred to me that Aileen and I had never really been alone, just the two of us. I was glad for it, but I couldn't still the jitters bouncing in my stomach.

"I've come to this party every year," she said, staring toward the crowd dancing ahead of us. "It's cool. It's kind of weird to think it will be my last one."

"And it's my first," I said. "I can't believe we can all get away with it."

"I know." She paused and took a drink, her face and blond-white hair all so pale in the moonlight. "But the teachers. They don't want to know. I think they'd rather not think about it."

"It's easier to believe we're all tucked into bed safe and sound."

"Exactly."

"But we're not."

She glanced at me quickly, then looked away, toward the rock.

"Tucked into bed?" was the line I was going to say next—almost felt like the line I was supposed to say next, like we were playing at a script and we both knew what I would say. I'd been at these kinds of parties before too. Not at Horn Rock, but in the barn at the Dolphy brothers' house, or in Jenna Trudeau's basement, or elsewhere. By the time I was a junior, I was pretty damn sure in the first few minutes of talking to a girl if we were going to end up in the closet making out, or in the woodshed, peeling off some of our clothes. It's so weird like that. Knowing. I got nervous every time all the same, but still. You could just feel it coming.

But that was a while back. Because once Heather and I got together, there wasn't anyone else. And once Heather was gone, there was just no one at all. I didn't know shit after that.

"You want a refill?" I finally asked.

"Sure."

Hackett had told me he'd hidden bottles in crevices all around the base of Horn Rock, and we wandered over to the far side, where no one else was around. We found a bottle under a couple of smaller rocks and dug it out. The moonlight played on the glass as I poured out a little into each of our cups, and I liked the way the reflections wrapped around our hands, too, like a long, pale scarf.

We clicked cups and sipped. Aileen leaned back against the rough slope of the horn. Two girls squealed in the shadows behind me. I jumped and Aileen laughed. The girls sprang out from behind a tree, chased by one of the guys on the hockey team.

"Are you scared?" Aileen asked me.

"No."

She laughed again. She finished the little bit I'd poured in her cup and asked for more. I wasn't sure how many drinks she'd had already.

"You sure?"

"What? Are you watching me?" She pulled herself forward from the rock and held her cup toward me. "Please?"

I poured her a little more and set the bottle back down in the little hole in the ground. When I stood back up, she leaned into me, one hand resting on my hip.

"The Buckeye," she said softly. "Do you like that nickname?"

"No."

"What would you rather be called?"

"Bax."

"Is that what they called you back home?"

"Yes," I lied.

"Did your girlfriend make that up?"

I didn't say anything—just let the silence hold us for a moment.

Aileen pouted and her blue eyes floated, glistening as she looked up at me. She bit part of her bottom lip and nudged me with her shoulder. "You're as big as a tree, Bax."

This pulled me out of my daze and made me smile.

"Oh," she said. "He's alive after all."

"I'm alive," I said. I liked being there with her. It felt good to feel another body so close to mine again, the jitters in my stomach popping out into my limbs, working their way down to my fingertips. But I also knew I didn't want this to continue. Or, rather, I did and I didn't. I wanted it. It. But not now. There was a difference, and it was suddenly clear to me. My hands trembled. Not here. Not now. It didn't seem right—even if she wanted me.

I leaned back and she had to catch herself from falling forward. She took a step toward me again and I held her at the elbow. "Maybe we should go find everyone else?" I was blunt and stupid, but I didn't mind because something about being alone with her now didn't sit right in my gut. She stumbled, and I tried again. "Yeah, let's go find everyone else."

Aileen gave me a puzzled look. "You want to go find people. Who?"

"You know, our friends."

She nodded. "Oh," she said, and smiled. "Wait a second." She took my hand and pulled it around her back. "You're scared," she continued.

"No. That's not it."

But there it was. Those hands. Those hands Heather had stared at, hands that could break someone. It felt like I needed to tell Aileen. I'd been hiding it from her, from all of them, really, Jules and Javi, too. If they were my friends, I needed to be honest with them.

She reached around with her other arm and pulled us together. Squeezed. Before I could speak, she kissed me. I pulled back, but she remained close and locked around me. "Don't worry, Bax," she said. "I like you too, you know."

"What?"

She giggled. As she did, I noticed something shift from the corner of my eye. A shape or shadow leaned against a tree at the edge of the clearing. Aileen giggled again, because she didn't notice. With her fingers she gently turned my face back to hers. Then the woods exploded behind us.

"Hell, yes!"

Two guys from the hockey team came blasting out from behind a tree, snapping branches and kicking rocks as they came at us. "The Buckeye and the Viking—getting it on!"

"Jesus, guys," I said. "Take it easy."

They rushed me and bounced me with their fists. I could smell the sourness in their sweat. They were wasted. Tucker and Zak. Tucker turned and whistled, and another two guys from the team came stumbling out. "Oh," one of them said, eyeing Aileen. "Just us and the Viking?" He grinned.

"Fuck off," Aileen told him.

"Guys," I said, trying to keep things as calm as possible. "I'll catch up with you later."

Tucker whistled again. "Yeah, right, you need a little privacy." He laughed.

"Or," Zak said, "I mean, we are a team, right?" He shrugged, and the other guys laughed.

I shoved him back into the guys behind him. "The hell's the matter with you?"

Aileen slipped behind me, sliding along the rock toward the little path that led around to where the rest of the party was happening. I reached for her hand but she batted it back. "These are your boys?" she snapped. "Give me a break."

She stormed off, making her way toward the party. Zak called to her again, but she ignored him, and I stood in the path, blocking their way. They could have circled around me, but no one did. "Seriously," I said to them. "Try me. Just try me."

"Yo, Buckeye has some fight up in him," Tucker said. He threw a shadowboxing punch in the air between us, and I almost took him up on it. I had to clench a fist just to let out some steam.

Tucker relaxed. "Sorry, man. Didn't mean to bust in on you. I mean, I didn't think she'd take off like that. We were only joking."

"Fooled me," I said. He heard the venom in my voice. These guys were so damn Fullbrook. They fucked around as they pleased and just said sorry after, but only if someone took offense. They wiped their hands and kept it moving. Never a damn care in the world.

"Let's go," Zak said. "We're out of vodka. Come on, Buckeye. Take one with us, before you go find the Viking. She'll forgive you, don't worry."

"Zak," I said. "Stop calling her that."

"Oh shit," Zak said. "He actually likes her." He laughed. "She's not a girl for liking, man. She's, well . . ." He nodded his chin at me. "You know."

I was about to lose it, but Tucker stepped in the way. He nodded to me like he was doing me a favor. Maybe he was. At a place like Fullbrook, the smallest, most insignificant gestures passed for actual concern.

"Let's go," Tucker said to the guys, leading them back the way they'd come—in the other direction, not after Aileen, so I stomped off into the woods to find her.

CHAPTER 18

JULES DEVEREUX

All I wanted was to figure out how to get down from the ridge without having to nose-dive the steep slope, or walk past anybody on my way to the easy path back to the boathouse, but it seemed like that was just going to be impossible. Two hockey players were having a literal pissing contest to see who could hit higher up a tree; another guy was giving a girl a piggyback ride up the path while she whacked his chest like a jockey on a horse. I almost plopped down next to two girls I saw huddled under a tree, whispering, but when one of them pulled out her phone and the screen lit their faces, I realized it was Gillian and Shriya, and I backed away silently. I wanted nothing to do with *them* especially.

Another set of footsteps crashed down the path toward me, and I almost hid behind a tree, until I recognized the outline—it was Bax. He looked frantic, nervous, eyes scanning, and when he noticed it was me, he paused. "Did Aileen come this way?"

"No. Why?"

He let out a breath and looked back the direction he came.

"Bax. I was kinda thinking I was supposed to leave the two of you alone. Is everything okay?"

"No, no," he said. "It's good. It's just." His shoulders slumped. He paused. "I feel like I need to tell her something first. But I couldn't." He nodded at me. "Actually, I feel like I need to tell all of you. Javi, too. It's been burning up inside me all year."

He took a deep breath, leaned back, and let it go into the air above him. "I mean ever since last year, I've just been trying to figure out how."

I was a little scared by the seriousness in his voice. "Is this like a confession, Bax?"

"No. No, it's different. It's just, I feel like if I don't tell you, then I'm not being fully honest. And I want to. Be honest. Do the frigging right thing. Especially after what happened last year."

His expression changed and he looked like he drifted away a little, lost in the memory.

"You know how I used to play football? There was this kid named Vinny Dawson. A friend of mine. There was an accident. It was my fault."

As he told me the story, we stood there on the path with the voices of the party circling like bats, never landing, never appearing, just looming in the darkness around us. I took his hand as he told me about the ambulance pulling away from the football field. "That's just it," he said, turning his hand in mine, but letting me still hold it, so we were both staring down at his palm. "That's what Heather said. 'Those hands could break somebody.'"

For a moment, we just stood there, and I tried to smile and

let him know I was glad he'd told me, glad that he could, but I didn't know if he could even see it. I nodded and was about to say something, anything, to let him know I cared, when I heard someone laugh behind me.

"Aw, Bax. Now, I thought you said you weren't barking up that tree?"

Bax pulled his hand out of mine and the fist he made so quickly actually did frighten me. I turned, and Freddie Watts elbowed one of the guys next to him. There were three of them, and Freddie was holding a bottle of vodka. "I was looking for you, to come share it with you and Aileen. Heard you two were together." He laughed. "But then I find you with Jules. Fine with me. I don't care." He held the bottle up. "Shots for the road, kids?"

Bax stepped toward Freddie, his massive shoulders like a wall between me and the other guys. I was too damn tired for all this. All this macho nonsense. All the senseless teasing. I was exhausted. I didn't need to stick around for the cockfight. I was pretty sure, after what he had just told me, choking back the tears, that Bax didn't want to get into any fights. He was a mess inside. But the violence didn't even have to be physical. Freddie's tongue could still lash out any string of words that would slip around and bite me. I wanted to stick by Bax, but I couldn't. I was too raw for any more that night.

I felt bad, but as Bax stood his ground telling Freddie and the guys to go back the way they came, I snuck away down the path toward the last clearing.

The tree was still there. My tree. The tree out on the edge of the bluff, still clinging, not letting go. One day it would fall, or the ground would crumble beneath it, but for as long as I'd been at Fullbrook, it had been just as it was now—tenacious, determined, leaning like a body into the breeze, bare branches extended toward the sky. The trunk twisted like the arm of a dancer, and below, on the lip of dirt, the base widened. I curled up into it like it was a lap. I'd never needed to get high here. I'd taken breaths as big as I could and just held them until they burned, and then watched the cool air mist like smoke when I exhaled. And even tonight, even with the shrieks and the screams and the laughter that all cut and swooped through the night like invisible birds, there was a momentary lull and silence, I was alone, and the moonlight was enough to hold me.

If I could have wrapped the curl of tree trunk around me, I would have, because after only a few moments alone, I heard someone stumbling from the path into the clearing, and I didn't have to look to know who it was. I could tell by the way his weight fell with each step. I knew the rhythm of his steps sober, I knew them drunk, and in truth, I still knew the outline of his body in my hands, and I could have drawn it in the dirt with my fingertip.

"Hey," he said, wiping his hand through his hair. "It's you."

He hid his surprise the way he always did, with that lazy squint, that retreat into quiet, his sleepy smile, the way he waited for a girl to speak to him first so he could play with her. I wished it wasn't me.

"Your party's a success," I said. "No need to look so mopey."

"It isn't raining," he said. "That was my only worry. Now ..."

He stepped back and waved his hand out in the general direction of everybody huddled around Horn Rock behind us. Some whiny emo music echoed from the other side. There was something so much cockier about him this year, even the way he stood and walked, like there was more weight in his gait—he never hurried anymore. "I promised everyone," he continued, "this year's party is going to be so much better than last year's."

That he'd smuggled bottles in his own bags from home didn't surprise me, but that he'd found a way to have even more mailed to him right on campus did. I'd seen guys mail themselves marijuana from back home, which was already crazy, and Ethan had done it too, but he never worried about any of that, it was all a game to him and he was confident he'd always win. That was what I was thinking about, actually, when he brought up the party from the year before. That confidence. Confidence doesn't have to be cocky. It hadn't been last year, when he'd lit the joint right there in front of everyone and passed it to me. What I'd really wanted when our fingers rubbed each other's as I took the joint from him, when I'd smoked it and stared straight into the crowd of seniors, was that same sense of confidence. I'm not afraid: That's really all I wanted to be able to say, and to say it without posturing. He seemed to say it all the time, even when he merely wiped his long hair back over his head like a rock star and remained silent.

He dripped with it, always, just as he did as he stood there by my tree. His sapphire eyes settled on me and stayed there. "I mean, last year was awesome too," he said.

"Yeah," I said, standing. And a small part of me went zipping back a year when, stoned and sloppy, we'd first kissed.

But that was history. It was too easy to remember the good stuff like that and forget about the boredom and annoyance and about realizing that without the weed, we had a hard time talking to each other, not to mention the hard time I had listening to him spout off in class, or worse, when we were all hanging out for lunch or something. It's just hard to take a guy seriously when he talks about his family pulling themselves up by their bootstraps while he's wearing his own five-hundred-dollar pair of shoes.

He stumbled over one of the bulging roots, and out of habit, instinct, I reached for him and caught him. He smiled. "I'm fine," he said.

"I don't think so."

"I am." He paused, his head wobbling slightly. "You know earlier? I wasn't kidding." He pointed at my chest. "I love that shirt on you."

He hadn't touched me, but it felt like he had. I zipped up my sweatshirt all the way. "Come on," I said, stepping away. "Let's get you back to someone else."

"But hold up," he said.

I ignored him, and then he slumped again, sliding partway down the tree. I turned and lifted him up again.

"It's like you were just waiting here for me. At our tree," he said softly.

And it was that easy, wasn't it—the way he could just take it like that and call it "ours." His arm was around me tightly in an instant, and I stood as straight as I could so he wouldn't loom too much over me.

"It's so funny."

"What is?" I said, trying to get out from under his arm.

He bent close, and I shifted to the side so that he rested against the tree, not me. "You and me, here, again."

"No. It's not."

"But this is our tree."

"All right, enough. Let's get you back to Gillian. You're her responsibility now. Not mine."

I tried to walk away, but he held my hand and pulled me back alongside the tree. "Hey," he said quietly, his hair swinging down in front of his eyes. "Look at that. We're all alone out here."

"No we're not. Come on. Let's go."

"No. We are."

"Ethan."

"But this is our tree."

CHAPTER 19

JAMES BAXTER

By the time I'd gotten Freddie and the guys to clear out, Jules was gone and I was on my own again, so I went looking for Aileen. I was only two feet into the darkness when I nearly tripped over Gillian and Shriya, who were both giggling as they scrolled through a couple of photos on one of their phones. They were sitting at the base of a tree.

Shriya looked up first. "Buckeye?"

"Yeah."

"I could tell by your outline."

I realized I was standing between them and the moonlight.

"Or you could be a bear," she continued.

"Thanks."

"What are you doing?" Gillian asked.

"What are *you* doing?"

"By yourself, I mean."

"Looking for someone."

"Oh, did she actually come?" Gillian said, without missing a beat. "She's gone a little crazy this year."

"Jesus. I meant Aileen. But you don't have to go after Jules all the time either."

"Oh, don't get all grumpy," Gillian continued. "You haven't been here for all of it. You have no idea."

"You're dating her ex-boyfriend. It's not rocket science."

"No. See, that's just it," Gillian said. "That's not the whole story. I told her I liked him. I told her I was going to tell him, and then next thing I know they are totally scoring."

"Wait," I said. "I'm confused."

"Oh, for God's sake," Shriya said. "Why don't you eat a bunch of speed and try to keep up with the rest of us?"

"Stuff it, Shriya."

Her phone buzzed in her hand and she swiped at the image. "Oh my God," she said, eyes wide. She showed her phone to Gillian. "Looks like your buddy Javi is the one doing the scoring now," she said to me. She and Gillian laughed. Shriya held up her phone. I squinted at the screen. In the grainy darkness, I could make out Javi and Max kissing. Comments scrolled under the video, laughing faces, people making fun of them. I wanted to grab Shriya's phone and smash it on the ground, but what was the point? All those comments. The video was everywhere. It was already in everyone's pocket.

Shriya shrugged her shoulders. "Whoops," she said with smarmy, fake concern.

Everything about this night was starting to piss me off. Everyone, too. Even myself. I hated that I was a guy standing there in the middle of a situation like this.

"Who the hell are you?" I said to both of them.

"Oh, lighten up, Buckeye. People are just having fun. It's okay. You don't have to be so serious all the time."

I left them without saying another word and wandered back into the woods. There was something like a tornado whirling within me, drilling down into the pit of me. I felt sick. I'd had almost no vodka—not like what I'd had at the parties I'd gone to junior year—but still, I threw my cup down and crushed it under my foot. I could hear people laughing in the distance, squeals, yelps that weren't fear but pretended to be.

Back then, back when I was normal, back when I didn't care about anything and it seemed like there was nothing to care about and it felt like the world was solidly beneath my feet, I had been one of those voices. I had been one of the kids chasing another kid, pinching a girl in the soft flesh above her hip as she casually danced away from me, not trying to get away, just trying to keep the tease going, because it was the tease that made us feel alive.

Someone laughed nearby, and two girls, both juniors, ran out of a thicket of trees. One of the hockey players was chasing them, growling, hands in the air as if he was a bear. I walked back toward the main clearing, done with it all. I just wanted to climb down, find the path again, and head home to bed. But as I made my way closer to the clearing, I noticed two people by the edge of the ridge that loomed over the path below.

"Get out of here." It was Aileen speaking.

"Come on. You serious?"

"Go away."

Aileen was sitting on a narrow tree that had fallen and was propped up by two other trees. I knew she was drunk, and probably more so than when I'd last seen her, and I was worried she might stand too quickly and tumble back over it, down the steep slope to the path. Bushes and brambles would slow her fall, but who knows what she might break along the way.

"I knew the guy was a wimp. Hilarious."

It was Freddie. All the anger I thought I'd blown out of me came rushing back. But Aileen had it in her too.

She jumped up. "Stop saying that. You're an asshole. You're all assholes!"

As I came toward them, she tried to step past Freddie, but he grabbed her arm and swung her around.

"I'm not afraid," he said. "How about a little sumpin' sumpin' for old times' sake?" He brought his fist up to his face and poked his cheek out with his tongue.

Aileen broke free of his grip. "Asshole!" she repeated.

"Hey," I said, coming close to them. "I'll give you something to laugh about."

Freddie turned quickly and lost his footing. He stumbled, but he caught himself on the fallen tree.

In my mind's eye, I could see my fist connecting. I could see the blood spurt. I could see his black eye and swollen jaw the next day. I could see me sitting in the admin building, back in the same chair I'd sat in when I met with the admissions team, and I could see them saying, "We did our best, but you blew it. You're out of here. Enjoy your useless life."

I could see all of that as I squatted and shuffled forward, readying my punch, but Aileen beat me to it.

"The Viking likes a closer," Freddie began, but as soon as he said her nickname, she pounced and shoved him in the shoulders. His back bent more than I thought possible, and then his feet went up and over the log, and he disappeared from sight, sliding into the thorny mess of darkness down the slope. He didn't even make a sound, or anything we could hear over the crash of his body through the bramble.

"Oh shit," I said.

"Oh shit," Aileen repeated.

Then, with all the meanness still in me, I laughed, and Aileen laughed too. We heard a groan far below. "Asshole?" Aileen called out. "That you?"

He groaned again, and it wasn't something that sounded like shrieking pain.

Aileen smiled, and I could tell immediately that she was smashed. Her eyes looked wild and she couldn't focus on me at all.

"You showed him," I said.

"I showed him," she repeated. She tried to walk forward, away from the log, further up the slope and back toward the heart of the party, but she slipped and went down into the dirt and the leaves. "Oops," she said, still face-first.

I helped her up.

"You are still an asshole."

"Yes," I said. "I agree."

We sat on the log, and I made sure there was a foot or so of space between us. I didn't want to say anything, because I didn't really know what to say, but Aileen wavered on the log, and I put a hand behind her back to brace her. "I'm really sorry," I finally said.

"I know you are, but what am I?" She giggled. At first, I

thought she might be flirting again. She was drunk, but it wasn't flirting at all, I realized. She just didn't know what to say. Actually, it kind of made sense. I didn't know what she was: Angry? Sad? Sorry, too? Embarrassed? Why not all of these feelings at once? Seems weird to think of emotions happening one at a time like playing cards being dealt out. They kind of swarmed all at once in confusion, like a cloud of bees busted loose from their hive.

We heard Freddie, but it was the sound of him breaking through brush again, freeing himself from a bush. "I think we should get out of here," I said. "Or . . ." I hesitated. "We should see if he is okay—like no broken bones and all that."

"No," Aileen said. "Asshole."

"Okay." I stood up and she followed, but stumbled again. I noticed the empty bottle by her feet. "Is that all you?"

She nodded.

"Oh, man."

She squinted. "I want to go home."

"I'll get you there," I said, not sure, exactly, how I was going to do that. Freddie yelled something unintelligible up the slope, and if it had been only me there, I might have waited for him to climb, just so I could knock him down again. But I wasn't alone, and worse, I feared he was waiting for us on the path below. We couldn't climb straight down, and we couldn't take the more gradual slope that led down close to the boathouse, because we'd still come across him. We needed to head back the way I had just come.

"I want to go home," Aileen repeated.

"I got you."

I threw her arm over my neck and waddled her through the

woods to the path back to the small clearing at the far end of the bluff. The moon had risen higher since she and I had been by the horn, and the light coming from it wasn't as bright. As we stumbled forward together, I could hear her breath close to my neck.

"Come on, Aileen," I said, bolstering her again with an arm around the waist. "Help me out here. Keep walking, please."

"Please," she repeated.

"Yes. Please."

"Please," she said again.

"Please what?"

"Please just get me home." She paused. "Safe."

"Don't worry. He won't bother you."

"No. Please." She sniffed. "Just get me home safe."

I suddenly understood she was talking about me. What had I done to make her feel so scared? I was about to tell her not to worry, that of all the people to be with right now, I was the one who would keep her the most safe, when I realized that I couldn't say that. She swayed. In her mind, what the hell was the difference between me and Freddie? For once I felt so certain that I knew what the right thing to do was—get Aileen home safe—but I couldn't do it alone, not if I was actually trying to help her. I didn't know what to do, and I breathed a sigh of relief when Shriya came up the path from the far end of the bluff.

"Hey," Aileen said. "Hey, help."

Shriya stopped and stared at us.

"She's wasted," I said.

"I can see that."

"Help."

Shriya seemed a little shaken herself. "What is going on here?"

"Help," Aileen said again, lunging forward, reaching for Shriya.

"Seriously," I said. "I will explain everything, but right now we need to get her home. And away from Freddie as fast as possible."

Shriya held her ground, not moving. "Freddie?"

"Shriya," I begged. "For real. This is serious."

"Whatever," she said, sidling up on the other side of Aileen, taking her other arm. "This party is a bust anyway," she said. "Everyone is wasted and acting like idiots."

"Not me," I said.

"You're an idiot too," Shriya said.

"Asshole," Aileen half whispered.

"Well, I'm the only sober one here at least," I said.

"Wrong again," Shriya said.

We hobbled with Aileen to the fork in the path. "Don't go that way," Shriya said, nodding toward the small clearing. "Major fight between King and Queen. Gillian is in hell-raiser mode over there."

Aileen moaned. She gagged and gagged.

"Oh, no," Shriya said, and Aileen sank again. This time we let her down to her knees. I held her up at one shoulder, and Shriya held the two braids in her hand to keep them from swinging forward, and Aileen let it all go. She sprayed the dirt, but got it all over her clothes, too.

When she was finished, we looked around for something to clean her up with, but she just wiped her mouth with the sleeve of her shirt instead. Shriya curled her lip in disgust, I thought she might start puking too, but she didn't. Instead, she held Aileen's head and spoke right at her.

"We need you to help us get you home."

Aileen nodded, but said nothing. Her eyelids were heavy and barely able to lift open. Then she bolted awake and gagged again, and after a few dry heaves, she finally crawled forward, away from the mess, and curled into a ball.

"How much did she have?" Shriya asked.

"I have no idea. I stumbled in on Freddie giving her a hard time and then she pushed him down the hill."

"Really?"

"I would have, if she hadn't."

"This is a shitshow."

I wasn't sure if she was talking about Aileen or me or the whole party, but it was clear that we couldn't leave Aileen in the fetal position in the middle of the woods in the middle of the night. There was still the noise of some people back at the party, but not as many, and we heard some others on the path below.

"How the hell are they not all going to get caught?" I asked. "They sound like a parade heading home."

"I don't know," Shriya said. "Maybe this time they will be. But I doubt it." She shook her head. "We just need everyone to show up for Sunday sit-down dinner, and everything will be fine."

If we waited any longer, Aileen would be dead asleep, and Shriya and I both knew it, so we devised a plan: We'd put her on my back, and I'd crawl backward down the slope so we wouldn't tumble, and Shriya would crawl down alongside and help me hoist Aileen onto my back every time she slipped off. It was a great plan, but mostly it was a frigging disaster, and after Shriya and I slipped and slid and tried to keep Aileen from falling while her stanky shirt made me want to puke, I finally just spun around on my butt and shuffled down the rest of the slope with Aileen in my arms and lap.

When we got to the bottom, I tried to give Aileen a piggyback but she was too tired and jelly-limbed to stay on, so I hoisted her onto my shoulder like I was a soldier hauling the wounded out of battle. I crept along the path, Shriya beside me keeping an eye out for whatever we needed to keep an eye out for. Despite her near certainty that we wouldn't get in trouble, I was worried. The key to Shriya's belief was getting back into the dorm without being caught by Cray-Cray. If he, rather than anyone else, saw us, we'd be goners. Our teachers didn't want to play parent or security guard, but that was his actual job.

Shriya stopped us when we got to the end of the path. We crouched in the tree line as she scanned the academic quad, looking for Cray-Cray. "Nothing," she finally said, when she was satisfied the coast was clear.

We made it across the quad, risked the beeline across the wide middle of the lawn to take the shorter route back to the admin building, and then hustled down the road, across Old Main Street, and along the back loop to Mary Lyon. Tomorrow would be another day, but for now we were fine.

I slumped down underneath the bathroom window and dropped Aileen, who was mostly awake from the jostling of the run, but still droopy-eyed and unstable. Shriya climbed in first, checked the hall, and then poked her head back out the window.

"Okay," she said.

"What do I do? Just push her up and over to you?"

Aileen moaned. "I can do it." She tried to climb but couldn't, so I lifted her most of the way and Shriya eased her down on the other end.

Shriya got up to close the window, but I stopped her. "Hey," I said, holding the window up. "Have you ever dealt with someone this drunk?"

"Yeah, of course." She tried to push the window down. "Get out of the way, Buckeye. We got all the way back. We can't get caught now."

"Don't let her go to sleep alone," I said. I heard my father's voice in mine. Something that had worked to get me to straighten up and listen all the years of my life until last year, when nothing could. "Don't let her sleep alone or on her back or on her face. I'm serious."

"That's crazy."

"Stay in her room," I said.

Shriya looked at me like I had four heads.

"For God's sake. Just take care of her."

She nodded. "I get it, Bax," she said. "I promise." I let go of the window and Shriya eased it closed, and in a matter of a few minutes she had Aileen out the door and into the hall and out of sight.

I slumped against the wall below the window, my muscles jittering and finally catching up with the adrenaline that had gotten me there. I smelled like puke everywhere and I wanted to cry and I thought it was almost worth getting caught right then and there just so I could go home—real home, home to Ohio—where I could crawl back into the lumpy bed I'd left there and never get out of it again. But the feeling passed. It wasn't all that bad. I trusted Shriya, and I believed she'd take care of Aileen, and at least I got her back to bed in one piece. I didn't want to think in grandiose terms like that, but it was impossible not to, because that night, catching my breath and looking up into the cloudless sky, everything did feel larger than life. At least larger than mine alone, or anything I could really understand.

CHAPTER 20

JULES DEVEREUX

The noises from the rest of the party were gone and all I could hear was Ethan's breath against my neck. "We're all alone," he kept saying. "Come on, for old times' sake." He grabbed my waist and kissed me.

"No."

"It's okay." His face was close to mine. He was smiling, and he brought his hand to my cheek.

"No, Ethan."

He kissed me and pressed down against me. I tried to push him but he was too strong. "Come on. We used to have so much fun."

"No."

"Don't worry. Nobody has to know."

"Please stop. I said no."

"We are all alone," he said again, as he grabbed my chest and squeezed. "We had more fun, you and me."

"You're hurting me."

"Stop worrying."

His hand went down my pants and into my underwear. His hands were everywhere and I couldn't move, pinned by his weight. I couldn't see anything because it was so dark, and my breath squeezed from my lungs. I couldn't breathe, and everything hurt, and I tried to choke out the word "stop." But it was barely a whisper. I didn't know if he could hear me. "Please." I was crushed, all the air pushed out of me, and I couldn't feel anything. I began blacking out into nothingness.

"Hey!"

Everything eased for a second, and I felt my vision refocusing, air stinging my lungs as it rushed back in.

"What the hell is going on here?"

"Nothing," I heard him say, speaking away from me, moving away from me.

I slipped to the ground, and when I hit the dirt I felt all the pain in my body come pouring back, a fire breaking through a wall and blowing through me.

"What are you two doing?"

"Nothing. Calm down. Jules, tell her. Tell her nothing was happening. I'm just drunk. She was helping me so I wouldn't puke."

"What?"

"Come on, Jules." His hand was on me again, pulling me to my feet. I couldn't stand. When he let go of me, I fell back down. "The hell."

"I saw you." It was Gillian. Through my tears, I could see her yelling.

"No," Ethan said. "What? No. There was nothing to see."

"Oh my God."

My throat was raw. I couldn't speak, but at that moment I was so grateful that Gillian had interrupted before he'd gone any further. I couldn't think. My pants were still on, I knew that. Or mostly. The top button was undone. The zipper was down. I still couldn't speak. I swallowed.

She'd seen it. She knew. I wasn't alone. We hadn't been alone. Gillian had been there. She'd seen what Ethan had done.

But she was stomping off and Ethan was chasing her now. Then they were gone and I was alone again. Me and my tree. I needed to get to my feet. I looked up but everything felt like it was spinning, the sky, the stars, my tree, me, everything was spinning and falling.

PART THREE

AFTER

CHAPTER 21

JAMES BAXTER

There was going to be a lot of fallout from the party at Horn Rock, and I wanted to avoid it all, so I laced up my shoes and went for a run. It was about the only thing I could focus on and do. I went out much further down Route 17 than usual and tried to keep my legs at a faster pace, but that's the thing about alcohol—it saps the potassium from your body and the next day your muscles are tighter than they should be because lactic acid has built up and you just need to stretch it out.

All this was stuff I'd heard Coach Ellerly say back home a hundred times, which is why he always hollered about not drinking alcohol at parties. It would affect our game and if we wanted to party we could be his guest and we could also get the hell off his team. If that was a choice we were prepared to make, he wasn't going to pass any judgment, we just had to know he wasn't going to feel bad for us if we were out of work and struggling to hold down a job years later, because people who acted without any thoughts about the consequences of their actions were children and he wasn't a goddamn babysitter, he was a coach who worked with young men—not children, young men. Men. He'd repeat that so many times. *You want to be a man? Get the job done. You want to be a man? Make pain your friend. You want to be a man? You dig your cleats in the dirt and you push those lineman dummies up that field harder and faster than you did the last time or they'll come back to haunt you later this week when they are real people and all they want to do is bury you in the ground and walk all over your grave.*

When I first made varsity, one of the upperclassmen put it like this: Coach Ellerly blows a whistle like the devil calling souls down to hell. That same year, we were on the bus on the way to Dayton. When we pulled into the parking lot, he made us sit on the bus until some of the staff from the other team came out to make sure we were still coming in. Then he stood at the front of the bus and said, "We're going to someone else's house today. What do we do when we get to someone else's house, men?" He didn't wait for us to respond. "We bust down the door and stab the dog. Hoo-rah. Hoo-rah!" We chanted and yelled along with him and he swung open the bus door and we ran off the bus screaming and holding our bags over our heads like soldiers, making a break for the locker room, running past the parents and staff from the other team, scaring them to all hell. By the time the game started, we were so hopped up on adrenaline that in the first play of the game, I knocked a kid on the other team so hard in the stomach he had to sit out most of the first quarter just to catch his breath. He was useless the rest of the night.

But all those memories were also making me think about Freddie and Hackett and how, if I wanted to, I could make them sit out for a while. Thing was, I wasn't just mad at them, I was mad at everyone, and myself, too. It wasn't that I could barely read what I'd been assigned, barely form a complete sentence in classroom conversations most days—it was more how everyone acted. Like cruelty was currency, and the meaner you were, the richer you were. Just when I thought I'd found a few who weren't, that got all messed up too. I couldn't believe Jules had gotten back together with Hackett. People were talking about it. Jules and Hackett scoring again. Jules seduced Hackett under the tree. Told him to come back to her. Told him not to leave her alone. I wanted to say it didn't surprise me. People slide back to exes all the time. I'd seen so many people do that throughout high school: break up, get back together, break up again, sneak away at a party, pretend they're not hooking up, while really knowing that's exactly what they are about to do. But Jules had been so adamant. No boys. And of all the boys, she chose Hackett (again). It felt like everything she'd said before wasn't true. All that stuff about principles and empowerment. That had all made sense to me. So what was she doing now?

I thought I had finally figured things out, but after the previous night, I felt as confused as I had when I arrived at Fullbrook.

I dug in, lifted my knees high, and pumped as hard as I could to get back up the hill into campus, trying to put all the people from Fullbrook out of my mind.

But when I turned into the street with our dorms, I saw Javi sitting on the ground beneath one of the trees in front of Jules's dorm. I hadn't seen him since I'd left the party, and I didn't know if he'd seen the video or not, but it became clear as soon as I sat down next to him.

"You stink," he said to me. He wasn't teasing me or egging me on. He was dull and flat, like a teacher offering a prayer before sit-down dinner. He leaned his head back against the tree and stared up to the second floor of Mary Lyon Hall. "Usually," he went on, "after a party, after anything, really, Jules comes down here and we do a recap—we run through the highlights reel of the night before. Make sure neither of us missed anything. Make sure we both know as much about everything and everyone as possible. She won't come out today."

I nodded and wiped the sweat from my eyes. "Yeah, well, maybe she's embarrassed," I said.

Javi looked at me. "Oh God, you saw it? Has everyone seen it? Everyone's seen it, of course."

I hadn't been talking about the video.

"Max won't even talk to me. He saw it last night, while we were still out there, and he pushed me away. I tried to tell him it didn't mean anything but he was a mess."

"It doesn't mean anything," I said. "It's something a twelve-year-old would do, or care about."

"But it does mean something! It is a big deal! It was his first kiss—with a boy, I mean." He paused. "You finally get to feel something, feel something that has been spinning inside you but you just didn't really know, you finally feel it, coming out all over your skin, like your sweat is just saying yes, but you've never felt that way before, and all you want to do is explore, understand, feel more, but suddenly you're naked in front of the whole world. The whole world, you know?"

He clenched his jaw, and I knew he was fighting back tears. "Who would do that?" he asked. "Why? Why would you sit there in the dark, laughing, doing that?"

"It's so stupid."

"How many people have made out somewhere on campus this year? But how many of them were filmed? Filmed so someone could say, Look how weird that is. But it isn't. There's nothing about it that's any different from every other motherfucker making out this year." His hands trembled and he balled them into fists and hit the ground. "Mother. Fuckers," he growled. "You can't know this, Bax. You can't know what it is like for people to look at you, and sometimes, you see the way their eyes fall away, and you know they are afraid to look you in the eye. Then they get this video and they're all wide-eyed and shocked, like they're watching animals at the zoo."

"I'm sorry," I said. "I saw it last night." I told him about Gillian and Shriya giggling when they showed it to me. "But it was as much a surprise to them as it was to me, so it wasn't them who filmed it."

"It doesn't even matter," Javi said. "It's like it was everyone."

"Do you want to find out who did it?"

"I'm not even sure. Yeah, I guess," he said, but he didn't sound like he did. "It's not even me. I'm not that worried about me. But Max . . ." He trailed off.

My first kiss was during a game of truth or dare in seventh grade, when someone dared me to kiss Kendra Witticker. I didn't know what I was doing and I drooled all over her chin, and she mine, and when it was over she was so grossed out, she told everyone there they couldn't say anything to anyone about it, and I felt about two feet tall. I could remember that so clearly, and I knew Max had gone out with two girls while he'd been at Fullbrook, and he had his memories of girls too, but then, when he finally got to kiss another boy, the thing I think he really wanted most, it was the opposite of being told to forget it. Javi was right. It did mean something.

"Should we go find Max?" I asked.

"No. No way. He really made it clear. 'Stay away.'" He looked back up at the second floor. "I just wish Jules would come down. I know she's in there. I saw her."

I wanted to talk to her too. It wasn't any of my business, I knew, but I still felt like asking her. What the hell? That guy? I didn't bring it up with Javi, though, because Javi had no love for Hackett, and I didn't feel like making his day even worse. And besides, as he and I were sitting there, I saw Freddie walking up the street, coming from the main campus. Even from a distance, I could see the bandages and stiffened gait of a guy in a lot of pain. As he got closer, all the small scrapes became apparent too—he looked like someone with chicken pox, almost. Even his face was cut up.

The current that rushed through me was terrible and electric. Everything in me was charging me to get up, run after him, and knock him down in the way I couldn't have the night before. I might have been actually getting up, I'm not sure, but Javi sensed it, and whether it was for me or for him, or for some other reason, he simply stuck out his hand and grabbed my forearm. He squeezed. And his eyes stayed me.

Freddie glanced at us but said nothing. He didn't wave or even nod. I didn't either. As he passed us, Javi went on a whispering tirade about how much he hated Freddie, how much Freddie was the kind of guy who ruined people's days because he needed them to be as miserable as he was, but I couldn't help thinking that as much as I agreed with Javi, I was going to have to figure out a way to still talk to Freddie. Hang out with him. Freddie was the captain of the hockey team. That was the only reason I was there—hockey. Hockey, hockey, hockey.

This felt all the more true at sit-down dinner that night, because although I didn't have to sit with Freddie, I had to sit with a couple of the other guys on the hockey team, and although we were sitting in our chairs, as we spoke to each other it felt a lot more like we were circling each other, not letting our guard down, boxers light on their feet feigning jabs before a fight. I ate as quickly as I could and left them to tackle clean-up duty. Jules and Javi had both skipped dinner, but as I was leaving I saw Aileen ahead of me. We were moving at the same pace, and unless one of us suddenly doubled back and bolted into the dining hall, the exiting crowd would draw us closer together. She flinched as I walked up to her.

"Hey."

She kept walking, and spoke to me while looking at the ground. "Hey."

We stepped out into the night, and as we descended the steps, the crowd fanned out around us. We walked a few paces in silence.

"I'm glad you're okay," I said when we were pretty much on our own.

"Oh my God, can we not talk about it? I don't remember any of the night. It's all a blur."

"Wait a sec," I said. I was actually surprised how quickly she was walking. It was like the top half of her body was motionless and her legs fluttered on their own separate motor. "I'm really being serious. When I saw you just now, I was super glad. I mean, I didn't know if Shriya would take care of you or not."

"She did."

"Good."

"I mean, she went all out." She paused. "It's super embarrassing, though, you know. Someone wiping your face with a cloth. Please," Aileen continued. "I mean the whole night. Can we just forget it ever happened? All of it?"

"Aileen. I am sorry. I have nothing to do with that bullshit the guys tried to pull. Freddie, he thinks he can do whatever the hell he likes and get away with it—like we're all toys he uses and throws away when he's bored. I'd have punched him in the face for what he did to you—and me—if you hadn't already thrown him down the hill." I smiled. "That was seriously badass. Have you seen him today?"

Aileen allowed herself the slightest half grin. "Looks like he stuck his face in a paper shredder. Wish he had."

"For real."

She nodded and gave a little one-breath laugh. "I don't know what he has said about me, but not all of it is true. He likes to exaggerate."

"In other words, he's a liar."

"Yes."

"That's why I never listen to anything he says."

"Good."

"Hey, would you mind if I walked you the rest of the way home?"

"I guess it's more fun to talk than carry me home, right?"

We walked and talked about other things going on, like the announcement that the Winter Ball assignments were coming out later that month, and how awkward the whole tradition seemed, and how strange it must be for the teachers who were there to chaperone, but had to stand around and watch what was going on, and the few who ignored all the students and just danced way off to the side to kill the hours—the ones who were probably right in the middle of the dance floor when they were our age. We thought about teachers who might have been goth, or punk, or hippie when they were in high school, and wondered what it was that had drained them of all their flavor and fun.

"Maybe they still have it?" Aileen said, when we were standing outside her dorm. "Maybe they just have to hide it?"

"Like, the teachers have their own secret parties, or concert trips, or Ultra?"

"Camp counselors do."

"I'm not sure I want to imagine what the teacher parties are like."

"You think they talk about us as much as we talk about them?"

"Oh, man," I said. "I hope not. I bet they want to think about anything other than us, whenever they can."

"Maybe," Aileen said. She got contemplative. "I wonder how much they know about us, about the lives we live outside of class, about who we are on our own."

"I wonder how much they want to know," I said.

"They're not our parents," Aileen said. "We raise ourselves here, don't we?"

"I guess so."

"I hope we do a good job."

There was something so sad about the way she said it, a lump formed in my throat. I had no clue. I didn't feel like I was doing much of a job taking care of myself, let alone anyone else.

"Catch you later," I said as she walked up the steps.

"Yeah," she said, turning and looking down at me. "That'd be cool, you know."

She was in half profile, the porch light beside the door warming her face. She smiled, and I swear it wasn't cute, it wasn't pretty, it wasn't playful, it wasn't anything other than brave, and that smile bobbed like a buoy in the pit of me.

"That would be cool," I told her.

CHAPTER 22

JULES DEVEREUX

hid from everyone Sunday, which was easy for most of the day, except for sit-down dinner, which I skipped, and when Mrs. Attison, who was the dorm proctor, knocked on my door to check on me that night, I just said I wasn't feeling well. I wouldn't let her in.

"Please see me tomorrow, just to check in," she said.

I could still hear her out in the hall, or feel her, really, that presence hovering and breathing outside my door. It would have been one thing if she had been a guard, but she wasn't, she was like a fox or a raccoon, prowling the porch, not afraid of the people in the house, skulking, sniffing around, closer and closer to the door.

"You sure you're okay?"

"Yes. Just need sleep."

"Okay."

And then she was gone and so was one fear, that she'd come in and see me trembling, a washed-out mess, but that fear was replaced by another, one that told me I shouldn't be alone—even though I couldn't bear to see anyone. I felt so certain I'd done something terribly wrong, and it was all my fault. I hated myself for thinking it, but I did.

I couldn't sleep. I skipped breakfast on Monday. I wanted to let the hours pass, and zombie out for the day, in the hope that whatever semi-nauseous feeling I had swirling in my gut would go away before I had to face the world—but I couldn't continue to hide out, because the longer I remained a hermit, the more questions people would have for me. And the idea that I might have to answer people's questions began to scare me even more. What exactly would I say?

It was fear that finally got me out of bed, Monday afternoon. Fear that got me into the shower. I had to move quickly. I couldn't miss another class that day. I was afraid of getting found out. But about what? What did I do?

"Jules!"

I almost broke into a run when I heard my name called out behind me, but it was Javi, and when I turned to him I felt a sudden rush, something warming in my chest. "Jules," he said again. "I was looking all over for you yesterday. I was waiting outside for you."

Javi, I thought. He wrapped his arms around me, and when he pulled back, his face was pale. He had bags under his eyes like I had. The urge to shout everything I wanted to say about Ethan rose within me, cold sweats, like I was about to puke.

"I really needed you," he said. He tugged me forward toward Main Street. "I know you saw the video, and it's all crazy. I want to knock on every door and steal every phone, and shout at everyone in the face."

He went on, and I half listened, but if he could see my own need to speak, he didn't notice or say anything. I felt something collapsing inside me, sticks snapping, logs on fire splitting and falling, and I suddenly felt so ashamed.

"It's like the whole world was watching us make out, Jules."

The whole world watching me and Ethan. *How did I let it happen?* I thought. *Why did I let it happen?* Javi kept tugging me and talking, drawing me across the street. The branches of the old elm outside the admin building waved at us as a gust pushed at our backs. We wound around into the academic quad, and all I could think about was how much Javi didn't like Ethan and how stupid I'd been to let myself be alone with him. Javi was still talking about Max and the video, but all I kept hearing in my head was my own voice, getting louder and louder: *Why?*

"Why?" I said it aloud.

Javi glared at me. "What? Are you even listening to me?"

"Yes. Of course. It's so messed up." I took a deep breath, tried to look up, not hide so much inside myself. "There are so many assholes," I began, but he looked away, toward the language building.

"Oh, wait," he said, stepping ahead. "There he is. If I can catch him before class . . ." He sprinted ahead. "Lunch," he yelled over his shoulder as he ran. Max hadn't seen him coming yet. He was still outside, speaking with a teacher on the steps, but as soon as he noticed Javi, he began to lead the conversation into the building.

I spun away and curled back alongside the admin building. My hands shook, and I flexed fists to try to calm them, but my fingers wouldn't stay still. Nothing made sense, and I felt more alone than I had the entire year—like I might suddenly burst into tears if the wind picked up again and blew too hard in my face. Screw Politics in Prose class. I could skip it. I had to see Ms. Taggart. I needed to speak. I couldn't talk to anyone until I said what I really needed to say. Everything else just felt like a lie.

I cut back across the academic quad toward the health center. I was barely in dress code: I had on a skirt, a long one at that, but it was denim—no one I know had tried that. I only owned it because I'd used it for a costume the year before. I'd hated it. Until now. Now it felt like a cocoon swaddling me. It covered the laces of my boots when I stood. I'd thrown on my hoodie over my shirt so I could block out the world and not even see if people were looking at me. I could hear them all whispering behind my back as I walked down the diagonal path. *Slut. Whore. Skank.* Not literally, but their voices as I heard them in my head hurt just as much as if I'd really heard them all around me.

I pushed open the glass door and walked right past the reception desk without saying hello. It wasn't like me, and I know I looked weird, but I'd been there so many times I figured they'd let me slide by this once.

"Julianna!"

I didn't stop at first. I couldn't talk to Mrs. Nichols at the front desk. I needed to get to the back office. Even if I could just nap on the couch, like other girls did. A cup of tea. A voice I could trust.

"Julianna, I'm sorry. Ms. Taggart isn't here today."

I knew what I'd heard, but I tried Ms. Taggart's outer office door anyway. It was locked. Never mind the couch. I couldn't even get into the waiting room. Couldn't see the plant I'd picked out. The posters I'd hung. Even get a cup of water from the cooler. *Please*, I thought. *I can't do this today. I can't pretend.* I felt so dry in my throat, all through me, like I'd been hollowed by the wind.

"Julianna, I'm sorry." Mrs. Nichols had come out from behind the desk. Her scarf, a riot of colors, was a tropical bird slowly flapping toward me. "She's out for the next couple days."

"Why?"

I must have snapped at her. Mrs. Nichols stopped moving. Her head tilted to the side, she was all glasses and helmet of blond curls that never grew or shrank, remaining exactly the same like so many other things during the decades she'd worked at Fullbrook. "She's home today. Her son is very sick. Actually, she had to take him to the doctor."

I felt dizzy, my head squeezed by invisible hands. I was slipping away, or breaking away, like a crumbling glacier cracking from the continent and drifting out to sea.

"Julianna, are you okay?"

"I was just trying to stop by and see Ms. Taggart."

"Shouldn't you be in class?"

"I thought I might ..." I couldn't finish. There was a flood in my head drowning all the words. So much flooding. My lip trembled. I sucked in air and tried to hold myself rigid. "So sorry. I must have my days mixed up."

"Do you need to see Dr. Hammersmith?"

"No. Thanks," I said as sweetly as possible. I might have only squeaked it. "I really just have the wrong day. When is she back, again?"

"Wednesday."

"Thanks so much."

I took in air in little sniffs as I walked past her, and as I walked all the way back across the quad to class. I was late, but only by a few minutes, and Mr. Hale let it slide. I was one of the best students in class. He frowned as I slipped in, but kept on with his lecture. "Lucifer," he was saying. "The name is from the Latin. 'Light-bringing.' 'Morning star.' More literally, 'bearer of light.' What a strange name for the character we attribute as the root of all evil. Some have argued that it's a mistranslation in the bible. But that came later. The word had all those meanings for Milton."

Everything was a cloud. Snapshots of Mr. Hale sitting on the corner of his desk, someone bending in her chair to dig out another pen from her book bag on the floor. Incomplete sentences. A phrase. Words. I'd read the Milton twice already, but I couldn't keep a thought steady long enough to know what it was. Mr. Hale called on me and all I did was shake my head to indicate I had nothing to add, nothing to say. I couldn't trust what might come out if I opened my mouth.

I must have spooked him, because he ignored me for the rest of class, only glancing at me from the corner of his eye like everyone else was. Gillian, the hockey guys like Ryan Tucker, were they thinking *slut, ho, skank*? Bax and Aileen, too. They weren't really looking at me at all, only at each other, nervously, like they knew. Bax tried to catch me after class, but I couldn't bear him saying those things to me. I could see it. The hardness in his eyes. He looked more Fullbrook than he had all year. I was partway across the quad, and I peeked back—four guys from the hockey team had surrounded him at the foot of the stairs behind David Hall, sucking him into their swarm.

I grabbed my lunch to go and ducked into the stairwell beneath the sit-down dining hall, and I remembered Gillian and Ethan in the same stairwell on the first day of school, where we'd all eyed each other uneasily and then agreed: *We're all cool.*

We weren't, and for the forty thousandth time in the last two days, I went over it all again. I didn't really do anything at the party. Nothing really happened. In fact, if anyone would know what had happened, it was Gillian, and even though she hated my guts, we had been friends once, close enough friends, and even though it felt like she was avoiding me as much as I was avoiding her, maybe she was the only person who could help me get my mind straight. And I'd see her again in my last class of the day.

I slumped into calc after her, not making any eye contact at all, and taking a seat at the back of the class, so Gillian couldn't even look at me from behind. Even though I had showered that morning, I felt a tacky film slicking my arms and legs. It was in my hair too—a matted mess of oily ropes. Maybe I was molting. Maybe I was transforming into some gruesome, slithering stage of weird. Or maybe they could all just kiss my ass and stare at the graphs Mrs. Attison had drawn on the SMART Board at the front of the room.

"Julianna," she said to me after the bell rang. She couldn't hide the puzzled look on her face. "Why don't you come up here and show us how you solved the first homework problem." She stepped forward, gesturing to me with the SMART Board pen.

"Nope," I said.

"Excuse me?"

"I'm sorry," I managed. "I mean, I can't. I didn't do it."

Mrs. Attison stared at me. "What?" She couldn't say any-thing else. She just stood there in shock. Which I understood. That didn't happen at a place like Fullbrook. Everyone did their homework—all the time. Even if I was in English class and writing about whatever the hell I wanted to, instead of the assignment, I was still doing something I could turn in. This was a first, even for an outlier like me.

"I'm sorry," I repeated.

"You had all weekend to do it. And yesterday's study group?"

I just shook my head. I had skipped that, too, of course.

Mrs. Attison glared at me and then moved on. "Gillian?"

Gillian got up and walked to the front of the room quietly. She looked at her notebook, then clutched it to her chest and began graphing her answer on the board. Standing in front of class, checking and double-checking her notes, she looked much more hesitant than usual, not the queen out front, leading the field hockey team on their run, not poised like a boardroom executive at a table in the student center, doling out jobs for the Winter Ball committee. She pulled in her lips, as if she was going to chew them, and she looked so much younger. Like at the end of our first year, when we became friends, talking about our moms totally trying to act younger than they were and how weird it made us feel that they spoke like us and texted with emojis more than we did.

Gillian paused. She stared at her notes for a few moments,

brought the pen to the board, made a mark, then got flustered and made some notations in the white space beyond the graph, and tried again. She sighed, loudly, through her nostrils. She knew she was off track.

Freddie snickered in the corner. He had bandages poking out from under his shirt collar. He moved with stiff, robotic jerks and swivels. The left side of his face was swollen, like he'd swallowed a balloon and it still floated beneath the skin. I hadn't seen him all day. He was a mess.

"Mr. Watts," Mrs. Attison said. For some reason she'd called him that when she'd scolded him on the first day of class, and it had stuck. Mr. Watts. "I know you're in pain today, but I hope the painkillers aren't affecting your judgment. There's no need to laugh. She's doing well."

"I know," he said. He straightened in his chair and stretched back, making a giant W with an arm up on either side of his head. "It's just that we went over this in the study group yesterday. So I know she knows it."

Gillian turned to him and scowled. She glanced at me quickly and then back to him. "I know," she snapped. "I have this."

"Let her finish," Mrs. Attison said.

We all waited, but Gillian was clearly disturbed. I wanted to jump up and help her because I had a vague sense of where I thought she was going wrong, but I couldn't be certain because I hadn't reviewed and I really needed to. None of it stuck unless I went over it a dozen times. Still, I thought I could help her. I raised my hand.

Mrs. Attison shook her head. "You had your chance, Julianna.

You'll have to let today's zero sit there with you for a while. Think about what one simple zero can do for your whole grade."

"I don't need her help," Gillian said. The acid in her voice hung in the air. Even Mrs. Attison knew something was up.

"Okay," she said. "We leave all that personal stuff at the door," she reminded us. "What happened in the study group yesterday?" She waved her hand before anyone could respond. "I don't mean, tell me what you all were doing, because I know you all were doing something, only it had nothing to do with calculus. That's too bad. Because we're less than a week away from our next exam."

"We studied," Freddie said. "Look," he continued, walking to the front of the room. He took the SMART Board pen from Gillian. She stood next to him. Too pissed to let him have the spotlight alone. "We were all trying to solve this quadric the same way, and then I realized we just had to invert the way we were looking at it."

He moved quickly, erased some of Gillian's work, laughed when he took part of the grid out, made some notes in the white space, and reworked the solution. When he finished, he spun around and addressed the class, leaning back on one leg, waving his hands like he was making a speech in the locker room.

"It's all about predictions, right?" He nodded to one of his buddies on the hockey team. "I mean, we can predict a certain amount based on what we know," Freddie continued. "Like, if I had a stack of pucks for every goal I scored."

I couldn't listen to the rest. He was so smug. I knew exactly what he was talking about, and it had nothing to do with what he'd just done on the board. Right there in front of Mrs. Attison. Some people in the room were wide-eyed and quiet, two of his buddies snickered along, but I tried to catch Gillian's eye. I wanted her to know how much I hated what was happening, but when she finally looked back at me, I knew it was me she hated, instead.

After class, even though Gillian tried to rush out ahead of me, I caught her in the hall. "Gillian," I said, holding her by the elbow. "Wait up."

She yanked herself free and ignored me, marching down the hallway and heading for the side door to the path toward the admin building.

"Wait," I said again. She paused. "Where are you even going right now?" I assumed she was heading toward the student center for her committee meeting before hitting the library. "Please. I need to talk to you."

"No you don't. I don't want anything to do with you."

"Gillian, come on." There was something waking in me, some-thing rolling over, lifting its head and beginning to crawl up and out of me. I felt it, a weight rising. A heartbeat. "Please. Listen to me."

"There's nothing you can say that is going to make me feel better. You are such a hypocrite."

"No. It's not what you think."

"Well, actually, you're right." She stuck a finger out in front of my face. "It's what I saw. I saw what happened, Jules. There's no pretending."

"That's what I mean. No one else saw but you. And I really—"

"Yeah, but everybody knows."

I could hear my voice shifting, ripping out of me, like I was fighting for breath. "I didn't want any of that to happen."

"Guess what? It did."

"No." I could feel them, the actual words I wanted to say, shaping. "No, I mean what he did to me."

"Oh God," she said, stepping back. "Don't even try to play it like that. I saw you. The two of you, all over each other. You weren't even hiding. You were right there in the open."

"No."

"Yeah! And what would have happened if I hadn't walked up? Maybe then you would have found somewhere to hide and who knows what else?" Gillian shook her head. "Total slut."

"We didn't have sex."

"Grow up," Gillian said. "You just screwed around with someone else's boyfriend. It doesn't matter that you didn't have sex. You probably would have if I hadn't broken it up." She shifted her weight, put her hands in her coat pockets, and pouted, and I realized she was mimicking me. "'I don't need a boy this year.'" She sniffed. "Please. What an act. You gross me out."

I couldn't speak. I couldn't even find a few words to block what she was saying.

"Here's what I want to know," she went on. "Ethan won't tell me. Plus he thinks he doesn't remember what happened—blackout, he keeps saying—but he does. He knows."

"It's not like that. I didn't want that to happen."

"Here's what I really want to know. How many times?"

"What?"

"How many times have you done this behind my back? The two of you."

"We didn't."

"Yeah, right." Her nose was wrinkled in disgust. "Well, he's all yours again. I'm finished with him."

"You're the one who was cheating with him on me last year," I shot back.

"Here it is. Finally." She glanced around like she was making a speech to an invisible crowd. "This is why you've been a total bitch. You think I was cheating?"

"I know you were."

Her eyes narrowed. "You don't know anything."

"I don't want anything to do with him. He's an asshole."

"Yeah, well, guess you like assholes."

"I hate him, don't you get it?" I pleaded.

"You think you are so smart, Jules. You think you're the smartest person here. So superior. You've got it all figured out. 'We're trapped in the system, man,'" she said in a horrifyingly perfectly exaggerated way. I'd said that to her the year before. "'Lemmings,' you called us."

"No. I didn't mean it like that."

"No. Fuck you, Jules. You're not superior." She took a deep breath and smiled. Just like that, she was a wall of ice. Calm and smooth and collected.

Fullbrook's unspoken motto: This is how to grow up—eat shit and learn how to smile.

CHAPTER 23

JAMES BAXTER

I was dashing out of the sciences building at the end of classes on my way to a hockey meeting, when I saw Jules coming up the path from the language building with her head down and her earbuds in. She nearly bumped right into me. I could have moved—she looked so burrowed into her own little world—but I was sick of us avoiding each other all week after the party. It didn't make any sense. I'd told her what had happened with Vinny, and then she'd promptly ignored me—like she was holding it against me or something.

I stood right in front of her, and she pulled up, then stumbled back, faltering. She squinted at me, and threw her head down, trying to walk around me. I grabbed her arm. "Hey," I said.

She yanked her arm out of my grip and yelled at me. "Get out of my way."

"I just want to talk. This is so weird."

She pulled one earbud out. "I'm not weird. I just have to get going."

"Hold up. What the heck is wrong?"

She glared at my gym bag thrown over my shoulder. "You have a meeting to get to, don't you?" She nodded, and continued before I could say anything. "You're just like the rest of them, Bax, aren't you? Deep down. You really are, huh?"

"What are you talking about? I was going to ask you the same thing. Aren't you now just like the rest of them?"

She pointed at me as she made a wide circle around me. "Just leave me alone." She'd lost the sting in her voice, and I could see her eyes, red rimmed and watery—like she was dehydrated or had just cried it all out for too long. I took a step closer, but she backed away.

"I thought we were friends," I said.

"I thought so too." She'd turned us in a one-eighty, and she spun around and continued up the path toward the admin building. I took a step after her, and it was like she had eyes in the back of her head, because she muttered over her shoulder, barely loud enough for me to hear, "Please don't follow me."

I wanted to, and I wanted to know what the hell was going on, but I suddenly had a shock, thinking about what she'd just said. I was just like who? I remembered a moment like that at the beginning of the year, when she was walking away from Hackett—from all of us, but mostly Hackett—and I wondered if she thought I was like him in some way. What, with Aileen? Screw that. I didn't need to be associated with Hackett, that snake. She was the one who'd hooked up—scored—with him, again. Everyone was talking about it.

But she was right about one thing. I did have a meeting, so I went to it.

Coach O had a midweek meeting for all winter sports athletes and I had to sit there all fake-ass chummy a few feet away from Freddie, nodding along when he got up to address the room as captain of the hockey team. Ethan had to say a few words as the captain of the ski team too. I was glad I didn't have to stand up. It was worse than class. At least there everyone knew I had nothing intelligent to say. Here, in the small bleachers alongside the basketball court, under the glow of the gym lights, I was supposed to be in my element. I was supposed to be at the center of things.

"This is our year too," Ethan shouted. His voice strained. Ethan spoke from his nose and throat. Freddie had learned to bellow from his belly, like a volcano erupting.

"State!" Freddie shouted, as he had earlier. The hockey guys echoed him. "State," we all boomed. "State. State. State." Freddie began a slow clap, and the team followed, chanting along in time, stamping the floor as they sped up. Me too. I wasn't loud, but I mouthed the words. I brought my hands together. What the hell else was I going to do?

Freddie's uproar quieted Ethan, but he remained standing. Coach O paced the floor in front of us, the line of other coaches behind him like a troop of military police on watch. "All right," Ethan continued, when the hockey team was finished. "Let's all just go get what's ours this winter!"

At this, everyone jumped up and cheered, all the boys' and all the girls' teams, and the coaches clapped along, pumping fists and feeding the rally. "Red Hawks! Red Hawks! Red Hawks!" the room roared. Coach O nodded along, and as the room began to settle down, he told the captains to take their teams off to the individual meetings.

Freddie led us out of the gym and down the path to the ice rink. It was basically the same building, but he wanted to parade us through the front door. He pointed out the medals and cups from previous years in the display cases in the lobby outside the rink, took us inside, and then finally led us down to the locker room. I was trying hard to follow along, nod along, look interested, but my mind was elsewhere.

"And that's why the Buckeye is here," Freddie said, pointing down at me. When he'd led us into the locker room, he'd jumped up on one of the benches and huddled the rest of us around him. "Let's hear it for our starting goalie this year!" The guys roared and pushed me around between them. "Come on, Buckeye. Let's hear it for the Red Hawks. Belt it out, man."

I whooped something ridiculously pathetic, and for a second there wasn't much of a response, just a few weak cheers back, but I had to admit that as much as I felt all twisted up inside and as much as I wasn't even sure I wanted to be here, here was incredibly familiar. The humidity of the room and the breathing around me. The stench of sweat and mold in the wood. Flakes of rusted metal on the locker hinges. The low growl of ten guys in a room huffing and bouncing, packed in tight. The hiss of heat and water in the pipes all around us.

I roared like I hadn't in over a year and it felt good and filling and free.

They all yelled and punched my shoulder and rubbed the back of my neck, and I grabbed some guys and slammed them against lockers, and two guys bounced me back, and I pulled them into a headlock, pressed them to my forehead and yelled in their faces, and after we'd slammed one other around for a minute or two, Freddie calmed us all down.

"All right, I have nothing else to add," he said. "Weights and cardio starts tomorrow. We hit the ice next week. First scrimmage is against that public school from Buffalo. Let's kill 'em."

The guys cheered again. As they slowly trickled away, Freddie hopped down and threw an arm over my shoulder. He led me down the aisle to a locker in the far corner. It had a number plate, like all the other lockers, but it was hidden behind strips of masking tape. In shaky permanent marker, someone had written *The Buckeye* on the tape.

"Let's put the shit behind us," Freddie said. "And kick some ass this year."

I nodded.

"You in the back. Me in the front. This is going to be the shit." He was almost drunk with excitement. "Northeastern? Boston College? I've always wanted to play for the Kings, man. Think about it. You play ice hockey, but in LA?"

I nodded again. Gave him my best game face. The one I'd always given Coach Drucker back home.

Freddie pulled a puck out of his back pocket and slapped it down in my palm. "Seriously. Bros before hos, man."

I swallowed. And smiled. "Yeah, man," I got out. I almost asked, "What's this for?" but didn't, because I realized exactly what it was for, and I didn't want to talk about it.

He slapped me on the back. "I see you working it."

I stuck around and claimed I wanted to get my head in the space, claimed I had some preseason ritual, which they all bought, filtering out one by one. I needed them to leave so I wouldn't have to keep smiling and nodding like a jackass, which I knew I was going to have to do—but for how long?

I sat on the bench trying to imagine the year ahead, but I didn't have that kind of foresight. I couldn't anticipate; I could only react. That's all I was good at. Catching pucks. Taking shots to the chest. Leveling a bastard who took a swipe at me. I turned the puck over in my hands. There'd been a time long ago when the Mi'kmaq people of Newfoundland played hockey with frozen rotten apples. Europeans witnessed, watched, and wrote about it in the 1600s. Later they swapped the apples for wood, and the Irish immigrants who played called the disk a *poc*—the word for punch or strike a blow. Coach Drucker had told me that. He'd thought it was perfect. Just punch it past the other guy. Or take a punch, was how I thought of it as goalie. But as I squeezed the stiff rubber in my hand, I thought of how fitting that word was now. *Poc.*

I noticed a line of graffiti scratched onto the locker two doors from mine. There was a ton of scratch graffiti all over the locker room, etched in over who knows how many years of guys down here strutting around in towels, finding tools like cavemen to mark their walls. I'd done it more times than I could count back home. But this one stopped me. It was big enough to read it from the bench.

Best deep throat of the year: The Viking.

How many bathrooms, locker rooms, camp cabins, and dorm rooms had I been in and seen graffiti like this? But how many times had I seen graffiti about me? Never.

Poc. Puck. How fucking fitting. How fitting and so wrong.

CHAPTER 24

JULES DEVEREUX

What had me the most confused was how people saw things the way they wanted to. Bax thought I was getting back together with Ethan. Gillian thought I was getting back together with Ethan. I had to keep going over it in my mind so I didn't go crazy. I didn't want to get back together with him—but what had actually happened?

My jeans had never come off. Open, but not off. And his jeans had stayed on. I know, I could still feel them pressed against me, like I was being crushed by a stone wall. We'd done everything together before. We'd had sex whenever we could for at least three months. Why couldn't I even find the words to describe it all now? Everything had once felt so natural, like a language of the body—the rocking of hips, two hands up to his face when I kissed him, the way I sank into the V of his hooked arm like it was a hammock. Now, even the sight of his hands repulsed me. To think of any of it made my skin crawl.

"Finger." The word just sounded so medical, mechanical. So dead.

I had spent too many days making it too easy for him. I resolved to say something to him. He had to look me in the eye, acknowledge me, acknowledge what he did. It wouldn't make it better. Nothing and no one could make it better—but at least I could take some control.

I'd see Ethan in our Modern Chinese History class, and since I'd had my head down, nose tilted into the spine of my notebook, all week, I thought I'd surprise him by staring at him from across the class. Today, when I wasn't firing face-frying laser beams that he occasionally caught and that made him look away, I was answering as many of Mr. Dyer's questions as he'd let me answer.

"My goodness, Jules," Mr. Dyer said at one point. "Yes. That's the spirit. Exactly. A Maoist embrace of capitalism was essential for the party to keep control." He smiled. "Looks like you're back."

"Oh, yes," I said. "And better than before."

"Well, look out," he joked. I didn't appreciate the laughter around the room. If any of them knew and still laughed, I'd be coming for them next.

But right now, my target was Ethan. Gillian may have tossed him aside, but he didn't look rattled. Instead, after he caught me glaring at him again, he leaned back and put his hands behind his head. The back of his chair rested against the old radiator Mr. Dyer never turned on because it clanked and banged like the sound of pylons being driven into concrete. Ethan rocked the chair with only one foot on the floor.

"Taking it easy, Ethan?"

"No. No, Mr. Dyer. Sorry. No disrespect. I was just wondering. All that quota stuff. Certain number of women in each level of office. You think that would fly here?"

"I'm not sure."

"Would it make our society better?"

"I'm not sure, but it would certainly be more equitable."

"But that's what I'm wondering," Ethan said, dropping his chair down and leaning forward across the table. "Is equity really the end goal we want? We say we do, but do we really? To be equitable, some folks have to give up some of what they have. I just don't see that happening."

Mr. Dyer went into another long lecture about the different way of viewing the world from the perspective of a culture that thought more communally than the highly individualistic United States. "On balance, I'd actually argue the US veers more individualistic than any other culture in the world. Most of the rest of the world tilts at least a little bit more collective in its thinking than we do." He concluded and seemed enamored with his own thoughts, but tapped his finger on the table and pointed to Ethan. "You've given us all something to consider, especially as we think about our next paper topics. After all, our next papers have to be about the economy."

But Ethan was just taking up class time to say fuck you to me. He knew me well enough to know I was coming for him finally, but he'd maneuvered class so that the last five minutes were all about him and his brilliance. People nodded, some made notes. Ethan didn't even have his notebook out. He was up and on his way to the door before I could get my bag packed.

I had to bump past a few people in the hall, run down the back stairs, and chase him down on the path around the academic center. "Hey," I said, grabbing his arm. "We need to talk."

"Sorry," he said. "I have a ski meeting."

"No. I'm serious." He began to walk away, but I held him tight and yanked him back. "This is about last week."

"I can't be late, Jules. Later, okay?"

"No. Now."

He knocked my hand away. "Look, I can see you are pissed, but I'm pissed too, okay?"

"You're pissed?"

"Yeah. Gillian won't even speak to me. Really? Not even speak to me? That's so stupid. But whatever. Everything is just so messed up, and I don't have time to deal with all this because I have to get ready for the ski season."

"This is about me, Ethan."

"Oh, I'm sorry, of course it is. It's always about you."

I could feel my hands begin to shake. I couldn't believe this. "I'm . . . You . . ." I couldn't find the words.

"Oh my God. You're supposed to be Miss Tough Girl. I can't deal with your tears too. Besides, I'm the one who is in pain here," he said. "Gillian won't speak to me. But I was wasted. Why did you even sneak away with me? What did you think was going to happen? It's like routine for us, Jules."

"Excuse me? This is my fault?"

"Stop. Just stop with the innocent act." He put his hands on his hips and blew a frustrated breath into the air above his head. "For God's sake, just admit you've wanted to get back together all year. You know you wanted it. And it. It? I don't even know what happened. I just know Gillian walked in, we were about to get busy, and then we didn't. We didn't! We didn't even do anything. So frankly, I don't know what any of you are so worked up about."

I was speechless. I thought I'd been ready but I could barely find my voice. He started to walk away. "Just leave me alone for a while, Jules. Time heals—isn't that what you said last year when you dumped me?" he said over his shoulder.

He was slipping away. For some reason, it felt like if he got around the corner of the admin building, I'd never be able to mention any of it again. I felt flushed to the bone. "What if I press charges?" I belted out.

He stopped and charged back. I almost thought he was going to hit me. "For what? Because you, *you* were all kinds of drunk and made out with your ex-boyfriend, and now you regret it? The feminazi train is heading out of town, Jules. You're so delusional it's frightening. It's impossible to have a conversation with you. You say one crazy thing, one crazy non sequitur after another, and no matter what I say back, you disagree with it. Get the fuck out of my face. Friends, my ass. You're a frigging liability."

He paced as he spat his rant, but the longer he stayed in front of me the more courage I found. "Stay here," I said. "Look me in the eye and tell me you didn't push me and push me even though I said no."

He hesitated a moment, then kind of snarled at me. "I have a meeting," he said. "You're so crazy you should get some serious help."

"I'm not crazy!"

"Or better yet, go find Bax if you are so lonely. See the two of you around together enough anyway."

"He's just a friend, you jerk."

"Oh, really? I better warn him, then. This is what you do to friends. You get all sloppy drunk with them, make out for a while, and then accuse them of something crazy like you're some wounded victim."

I couldn't say anything back. *I was*, I wanted to say. *I am.*

He took two steps away, then turned back and pointed at me. "Seriously. Think about that. Think about all our history, all we've done. Think about all that weed, and last weekend, all that booze. Think about all the other people involved. I didn't rape you, Jules. Don't blow this all out of proportion." He turned back and jogged off toward the dorms, leaving me standing alone. Unsteady. Stunned.

I hadn't said the word even to myself yet. "Rape." But that was exactly what had happened. That night, after I had said no, he had reached down into my pants and grabbed me, gone inside me, and continued, forcing himself as I repeated "no," again and again. He said it—"rape"—not me, and the word stretched out like my shadow in front of me, staring back at me.

CHAPTER 25

JAMES BAXTER

Each day felt more and more disorienting as I tried to negotiate practice and figure out why Jules wouldn't speak with me. I never saw her with Hackett, either, and Hackett was keeping his distance from me, too. The thing that was most disorienting, but in a good way, was Aileen. She and I had kept our word. Seeing each other more often was cool.

We'd met twice at the student center, just to talk over a plate of fries, where I told her about Vinny, and she nodded along quietly and didn't run out of the room, and on Thursday I had late practice, and it wasn't rink time, it was weights and cardio, so I took a chance and waited outside the arts center, because I knew she had photography last, and more to the point, I knew she'd probably linger after class, because it was her favorite. I didn't know a damn thing about photography, but I liked the enthusiasm in Aileen's voice when she spoke about it.

"Well, look who it is," she said, coming out of the building. She was walking next to Jules, and I smiled at both of them.

"Oh," Jules said. She hesitated. "Did you want to head over to the student center?" she asked Aileen.

Aileen glanced back and forth between us. "What were you doing?" she asked me.

"Just coming to find you. I don't have practice, and I wanted to see what you were up to."

That made Aileen blush, and me too. I couldn't believe I was so straightforward. I didn't even know I could think that quickly and easily. I realized my heart was beating a little faster. "But whatever," I added. "If you two are hanging out, I'll catch you later."

"No, no." She came down a step and waved us all forward. "Let's all go."

"Nah," Jules said. "You know what? I left something upstairs. I'll just meet you over there." She didn't wait to hear what we said next. She disappeared back into the arts center, and didn't even pull the door closed behind her.

"Do you think she's actually coming to join us?" I asked.

"That was a definite 'see you later,'" Aileen said, flashing a peace sign. "As in, not today."

I laughed. "Well, good, then, because let's not go to the student center. I didn't want to go there." I had had the wildest idea in class when I realized I wanted to go find Aileen, and now I took a deep breath and hoped for the best. "Actually, I wanted to show you something. Mind a walk?"

She nodded. "The fries suck anyway." She hiked her bag up onto her shoulder as she came down the rest of the steps.

I led her up the walkway, back toward the admin building, and asked her about class. She was working on her series of superimposed photos, images of tools in the shadows layered over more tools in the shadows. I didn't get it at all, but I really did love the way she spoke about it. She spoke more quickly. The timbre of her voice sang.

"It's like a prism, or like a kaleidoscope, you know, but in all black and white. And the thing is, when you spin it or turn it the patterns change, the crystals shift, and some patterns are just more pleasing than others and you don't know why, and I don't think I want to know why, I just want to find the ones I like."

I nodded along, unable to hide my smile.

"What?" she asked.

"Just go on," I said. "Listening to you is awesome."

We walked all the way to Old Main and I turned us right, down the sidewalk. She stopped. "Are we going off campus?"

"Just down the road. It's not far. I promise."

"Really?" She hesitated. "Oh God, are you taking us someplace to smoke out?"

I laughed. "Jesus, no. I have practice later. Plus, I don't do that shit."

Aileen smiled. "Yeah, right." She took a step forward. "Let's not get lost."

"It's on the road. We're good." I shook my head. " 'Smoke out.' That's hilarious. I haven't heard anyone use that phrase since I was back home."

She nodded. "Maybe it's an 'I'm bored in suburbia' kind of phrase."

"I'm not from suburbia."

"Where the heck *are* you from, Buckeye?" She bumped me

with her shoulder and I felt the thrill of it ripple through me.

"That's exactly what I want to show you."

What I'd figured out about the farm stand when I'd been down there with them before, taking off for Wendell, was where it sat just off the campus map, and since it was already November and the sun was lower in the sky, and the farm stand was angled southwest, I figured we'd get the image I'd been looking for. I hadn't been back there yet since the night of the party, because I wanted to share it with Aileen. I didn't want it all for myself.

I asked her a little more about photography as we walked down Old Main Street. In the day, the trees didn't seem as thickly packed together as they had at night. Sunlight swallowed the feathery branches that had already lost their leaves. "So I looked up that photo of Dorothea Lange and Paul Taylor you mentioned. They're out on some dusty outcrop in California, right?"

"Yeah. And she's looking up at him, but the camera is between them. Like no matter what happens, she can document it."

"What's going to happen, though? It looks friendly. Like they're going over directions."

"Maybe they're lost," Aileen said. "I could imagine that. Middle-of-nowhere kind of thing." She said it just as we came around the last stand of trees and stepped into the empty parking lot of the shuttered up farm stand, closed for the season. A chalkboard sign leaned against the side of the little house, attached to a banister by a chain. I loved the simplicity of it, the trust. I wondered how many years the owners had left the chalkboard out there, knowing no one would take it. Beyond the little house, to the right, the expanse of fields was pale with littered husks and broken stalks.

"Like out there," Aileen said, pointing to the fields.

I chuckled. "That's home for me."

I walked us to the edge of the parking lot, so the house wouldn't block our view. The land undulated in the smallest, barely bubbling hills. Even though it was cold, I could still smell the field dust, the ghosts of corn and pumpkins. A hint of woodsmoke cut through it, invisible, too far away to be seen, but still present.

"Seriously," I said. "This is what I wanted to show you. I'm from a place just like this, or part of me is. I went to school at the edge of Cleveland. Cuyahoga County. But a fifteen-minute drive west and I was here—or something just like it. I miss it. My uncle Earl, he has these twisted gnarled hands, and I help him sometimes, and there's no better place in the whole world."

Aileen smiled. I loved the way she smiled at me. It felt like walking outside and feeling the sunlight on your face for the first time all day. I knew right then that I wanted to send a little warmth her way too. I couldn't believe I wasn't nervous.

"And," I said.

"Yeah?"

"And I was hoping I might share something else with you too."

"Yeah?"

"I'm not so good with words, as you probably know."

"Yeah?"

I couldn't believe how loose I felt. I reached for her hand, and she closed her fingers around mine. "Well, truthfully, I have this crazy crush on you and I just wanted you to know."

She stepped in front of me and put her free arm around me, still holding my hand, like we were about to waltz, but in a lazy way. And that's how I felt as she looked up at me, blue eyes glittering with the tiniest flecks of gold. I felt a sway.

"Can I kiss you?"

"Yeah," she said slowly, so softly, almost a whisper.

She popped up onto the balls of her feet and I held her closer and when we kissed I felt the sun warm and yellow in my hair, softening my neck and shoulders—or maybe that was just her breathing into me.

When I pulled back, she pressed closer. "Let's do that again," she said. And we did.

I debated skipping practice—there was nothing I wanted to do more—but Coach would make my life hell if I did, and hell would make it harder to hang out with Aileen again. We walked back up Old Main Street, holding hands for a while, walking in that awkward way you do when you become a sort of three-legged creature, bodies scrunched close, a comfortable, wobbling stumble-forward. When we didn't speak, Aileen hummed so softly and warmly, I thought of the cicadas and the crickets singing at dusk in the dust and hayseed of Uncle Earl's farm.

When we got to campus, we kissed each other good-bye. Aileen turned up the street toward the dorms, and I watched her go for a minute, kind of stunned by what had just happened, but knowing I'd been wishing for it since she stood on the steps of Mary Lyon looking down at me, telling me that hanging out more would be cool. She was right.

CHAPTER 26

JULES DEVEREUX

It had been a week of stepping and not finding the ground beneath my foot. That was what it felt like. "Unstable" wasn't the word. I was so jittery and anxious it felt like the entire world—the chair I sat in, my desk, the couch in the library, my tray in the lunch line, my computer in my lap, the brick wall I leaned against to catch my breath, everything—vibrated just as uneasily as I did. I couldn't name it. It was like when you lift a rock or a log in the forest and see the ground alive with a writhing mess of bugs and worms. That was me. That was the inside of me. I couldn't hold a glass of water without worrying I'd drop it.

I needed to speak to someone, but every time I tried, something happened. Or, rather, nothing did. Days passed.

"Jules."

Javi stood in the doorway, blocking me. Ethan was the first out the door, but half my Modern Chinese History class lingered in the classroom behind me. Mr. Dyer still fiddled with his laptop and the SMART Board.

"Jules," Javi repeated.

"Excuse us," someone said behind me. Javi wasn't letting anyone out. "Excuse us." Louder. "We're trying to get to lunch."

Mr. Dyer's chair squeaked as he stood. "Everything good, guys?"

Javi stepped to the side, but when I walked out into the hall, he cornered me against the wall. "You're avoiding me," he said. "It hurts."

"No I'm not." I didn't say anything else as my classmates streamed past us. I didn't say what was creeping up around me—a feeling of claustrophobia. I didn't like having my back against the wall. I didn't like Javi so close to me, looking down at me. I didn't like the heat of the humanities building, always too hot when it was cold outside.

Mr. Dyer was the last to leave the room, and he eyed me and Javi in the hall. "You guys going to lunch? Let's head over together." He hovered too. Also too close. Everyone, just back off, I wanted to bark. I didn't know what was wrong with me. I really liked these guys. But I also really needed space.

"Right behind you," Javi told him.

Mr. Dyer nodded, but I could see the skepticism in his eyes. "All right. See you there."

When he left, Javi pulled me back into the classroom. He didn't shut the door, but he led me around the corner to the back nook, the alcove with built-in bookshelves and the standing podium with a giant dictionary that Mr. Dyer sent one of us to every time we came across a word that stumped the class.

"Seriously," Javi said. "I'm not trying to be weird, but I really need to talk to you." I nodded and he continued. "Where the hell have you been, Jules?"

He paused, and I almost collapsed. The clouds spun in my mind, pushing, pressing against the back of my eyes. I was light-headed.

"Javi," I said quietly. "I'm sorry—"

"No." He cut me off. I wasn't finished. I was just getting started and I needed time. I needed his silence, but he went on. "I don't care you hooked up with Ethan again. We all make mistakes. Whatever. No one's really even talking about it, except Gillian. Even Shriya's like, whatever. Who cares about that guy?"

"I shouldn't have let myself be alone with him," I said.

"Well, that's true." Javi leaned back against a bookshelf and looked up at the ceiling. "I can never understand what you see in that guy. Just tell me you won't fall for him all over again. Tell me it was a mistake in judgment, and we're good. You don't have to go crawling back to him."

I was so still, my hands at my side, my bag weighing on my shoulder. "I didn't want it to happen."

"Yeah, well, shit happens," Javi said. He crossed his arms and stared at me. "And then, really terrible shit happens. And this is why I need you to stop avoiding me and just listen. I figured something out. Max doesn't want to talk to me anymore, but I got him to hear me out on this, and he agrees. I'm not crazy. The video of me and Max, it's not some silly thing we can all blow off. Remember how long it took Gillian to get over it when it happened to her?"

"Yes," I said. Then something in me cracked and I snapped

at him. "That's like an assault. Someone ripping into your personal space, taking it away from you. It's assault. That video is an assault on you and Max."

Javi let out a long breath. "God damn. Right? It *is* assault." He had a tear in one eye, and he rubbed it away with a knuckle.

The tears welled up in my eyes too, against my will. I tried to stop them. *No, no, no,* I thought. *Not now. Try to listen to Javi.* The bag dropped from my shoulder and I rested my elbows on the giant dictionary. I couldn't help it—I stared at the seat Ethan had been in all class.

I looked at my hands because they were shaking, but I couldn't feel them, like they'd gone numb, or I was numb. I just nodded. I knew he was looking at me, but I couldn't find a word to say.

"Jules?"

He peeled himself off the shelf and came over to me. A soft hand on my shoulder. I sucked in a breath, and he stepped around, lifting me toward him with one arm. "I know," he said quietly.

"No," I finally said. "I wanted to tell you. I tried." I leaned into him. I needed him, another person, the heat of him listening. "I didn't want it to happen." He remained quiet, squeezing me, holding me. "I didn't want him. He forced it. He forced it on me." I'd said it out loud about Javi; now it didn't feel so foreign. I could use it, say it. "He assaulted me. I didn't want to do anything, but he just pressed me against the tree and did whatever he wanted. I said no. I said no so many times."

I'd finally said it, but it didn't feel like a rush, I didn't feel lighter. I felt paler and sicker and exhausted, like I'd pushed something out of me, and now all I wanted to do was sleep. Damp and sweaty. Throat drier than dust.

We stayed like that for a long while, apologizing to each other for not being there when we'd promised we would. "I could kill him," Javi said.

"Don't do that."

"Don't protect him, Jules."

"I'm not protecting him. If you kill him, I'll lose you. I need you."

Javi pressed his forehead to mine gently. "You're not alone, Jules," he whispered.

We skipped lunch and stayed in Mr. Dyer's room, but moved from the mini-library alcove to a corner of one of the big tables in the room and sat there, mostly holding hands, but going over the play-by-play from the party, like we always went over things, but this time differently, talking about how great things were until they weren't. It felt good to talk about it all, but I also felt like I'd lost something. A part of me wished it wasn't all out in the open, because now that I'd told Javi, it was really real. Still. I didn't have another choice. I had to recognize that this had happened to me, but that feeling I'd once had of possibility, of endless possibility stretching out in front of me was gone.

Everything that had once felt so alive now suddenly felt so dead. That was what I wanted the world to know. Ethan stole something from me. Not my precious virginity—that stupid word you worry so much about until it no longer applies to you, and then you wonder why the word held so much power in the first place. It wasn't that. He stole something else. Something deeper—like the voice inside my head, the thought before my word, the rest before the beat of my heart. He took it, and everywhere I went, I walked as a person with something missing.

I wanted it back.

CHAPTER 27

JAMES BAXTER

Every time Aileen and I were alone, I felt like my stomach was a basket of eggs, and I dropped it every time we were close enough to kiss. We had made out a few more times, hiding in the shade of a tree, or up against the back wall of the science building. Once we even ducked into the darkened theater and hid ourselves behind the latticework of ropes at the fly rail. The one afternoon I had off from hockey practice, Sunday, I asked Aileen to meet me by the ball fields, and when we got there, we made a break down the dirt road toward the beach and the boathouse, to watch the sun set on the river.

It was the only place on campus I knew about where we could get away from everyone else. Fullbrook was so damn claustrophobic, nowhere to go, ever, without the feeling that someone was watching you. Back home it had been so easy. Heather's mom would be at work. Or my parents, both of them would be out, or Mom would be home, but she wouldn't see us as we crept in through the basement door and were silent as we could be in the rec room. But at Fullbrook, everything had to be more elaborate.

I guess that's part of what made it so exciting. It was broad daylight, and it wasn't until we were on the path down close by the boathouse that we slowed and caught our breath—which was pretty hard to do since we were laughing, too. I took her hand, twirled her toward me, and kissed her. I ended up kissing her teeth, she was smiling so wide.

I pulled her around the corner of the boathouse and we sat with our backs against the far wall, facing the woods. Even if someone came, we were well hidden. She sank into my arms and I held her, kissing the top of her head as we watched the light play and shift in the ripples on the river.

After a while, she rolled over in my arms, leaned up, and kissed me, softly at first, then more fully, until we were making out with real abandon. It had been over a year since I'd really been with someone like that, and a crackling chain of micro-explosions fired through me. We were all over each other, chasing after breath and fumbling with our hands and peeling back some of our clothes while the sun sank behind the low rolling Berkshires in the distance.

I was so nervous, I almost forgot I had a condom with me. I pulled it from the key pocket in my jeans and asked her if we should use it. She hesitated. Her mouth was closed, but she moved her lips like there were words in there trying to get out. I waited.

"Yes," she said.

"Okay."

I pushed my pants down a little further, and even though I

was still in my underwear, I bit the edge of the foil and opened it. I was about to continue, when Aileen pulled back and climbed off me. She was still wearing a zip-up hoodie, but we'd managed to get other clothes off underneath, and she scooped them all up and clutched them to her chest. She tucked into a ball and stared at her feet.

"I'm sorry," she said.

"No. No. *I'm* sorry."

"No," she said. "No, I'm sorry. I can't do this."

"It's okay," I said. "I mean, we don't have to. Oh Jesus. I'm so sorry. I wasn't trying to be too fast or . . . I don't know."

"No. I want to, but . . ." She let that hang in the air for a while, and I began to worry she wanted me to finish her sentence, but I didn't. I waited. I put my hand down on the ground between us, palm up. She didn't take it.

"It's too weird," she said.

"Okay. I mean, no, you're right."

"Are you sure it's okay not to?"

"What? Of course."

"You didn't just do all this because you thought I was easy, did you?"

"No. Aileen. Seriously. No."

She was quiet, and I wasn't sure if she was mad or sad or both.

"I mean, have you had sex before?" I asked her.

She laughed bitterly. "Are you serious?"

"Yes."

"Didn't Ethan and Freddie and those guys tell you all about me?"

"Fuck those guys. I don't listen to them."

"Have you?" she pressed.

"Yes."

"Oh my God, were you some asshole player back home?"

"I don't think so. I slept with one girl."

"That's it?"

"Oh, wow. Thanks."

She smiled. "Seriously? Only one?"

I shrugged. "We had a lot of sex, though, me and her. Does that count?"

Aileen laughed so loudly, I thought for sure someone was going to come find us. I didn't understand what had made her bust out.

"Hey," I said. "I'm right here, you know."

"I'm sorry." She collected herself. "You really weren't just being nice to me so we could sleep together?"

I was feeling pretty stupid sitting there talking to her with my pants below my knees, chatting away with her in my boxers, so I pulled up my pants and started getting dressed.

"Are you mad?" she asked.

"No."

"But you didn't answer my question."

"Aileen, do I want to have sex with you? Yes. Yes, I do. Have I been having a ball just goofing around not knowing what the hell is going on between us? Yes. Does that have to end in sex? No. Especially right now? Hell, no." I guess I did sound a little mad as I said it, but I didn't mean to sound so pissed. I was telling her the truth.

She nodded along, listening. "I don't know what I want."

"Plus, it's a little easier for me to figure out what I want," I

said. "I have a smaller brain, right? So less room for possibilities."
I shrugged, did my best sheepish expression.

Aileen relaxed. She didn't say anything, but I could see it in
her body; she unpinned her shoulders from her ears, let go of her
knees. When she held her clothes out in front of her, I turned
around.

"I won't look," I said, burying my face in my hands and pitch-
ing forward into the ground. "I want too, though! Real bad!"

"Don't!" she said, teasing.

I waited until she said it was all right to get up and she was
fully dressed again. While I put on the rest of my clothes, she
walked down to the lip of the water. It was dusk, and I couldn't
tell if there were bats swooping or it was the last run for swallows.
It seemed kind of late in the season for all of them—but nothing
seemed right anymore. It was colder than it would have been
back home, but everything still felt more alive. The ground still
felt soft. There were so many trees, and they wavered in the dim
light, dark shadows against even darker shadows.

I walked down to the river edge and stood beside her. Water
lapped at the rubber tips of her boots. I pointed up to the evening star, and she leaned closer to follow the direction of my finger.
That's all I'd ever called it, but now, after Mr. Hale's literature class,
I knew so much more—Venus. I barely understood half the lines in
Paradise Lost, but I'd learned astronomy. I loved it. I loved knowing
something. It made me feel a part of something larger than myself.

"Have you ever seen the northern lights?" she asked. We
were close enough to kiss again, but I didn't. I stood stone stiff
beside her.

"Yeah, once. On a lake in Minnesota. I was on a camping trip with my family."

"Cool."

"The trip? Actually, it kind of was. We caught pike and small-mouth bass. There were hummingbirds all over the place in the woods around the lake. My dad and I saw these three giant pelicans take a running leap up into the air from the water. You could listen to the loons calling all night. But the northern lights. They were amazing. They were gray, and shimmering, and they stretched and crawled out across the sky. At first we thought they were clouds, but then we realized they were moving toward and away from us—not right to left like the clouds. It was amazing."

"I've heard loons out here before."

"Cool."

She stepped away and dug her hands in her pockets.

"Hey, Aileen?"

"Yeah?"

"Can we hug, or something?" I asked.

She stepped close, gripped me hard, and squeezed. "I'm sorry about all that," she said into my chest. "I just can't do that right now. And not here."

"That's really okay," I said.

"You're not going to go running back to Jules now and try to get with her?"

"Seriously, please stop with that. It's not like that with her."

"Why not?" Aileen pouted.

"It's not about that." I could feel her breath warming my shirt. "Jules and me? We're just friends. Or, we were."

She stayed quiet.

"But what's up? Did I do something?"

"I've been with more people than you. Like, a lot more."

"Okay."

She was quiet again.

"I don't care about that," I told her. "Seriously. Let's not be all judgy. Let's start from like right now."

"I can't do that."

"Why?"

"I feel like you are going to hate me when I tell you, but I don't know, I just have to. Look, I really have been with more guys. Slept with more guys. Whatever."

"It's not a big deal."

"No. It is, because maybe I don't even know if I really wanted to be with all those guys."

"Okay."

"Maybe even the first one didn't even listen to me. He just did what he wanted."

"Oh, no," I said. "Oh Jesus, Aileen."

"I knew you'd be weirded out. I knew it." She stepped away and back up the beach toward the path.

"Wait," I said. "Please. Talk to me."

"Really? You really want to hear all about how some asshole walked me down this same exact path after the Winter Ball my freshman year and told me not to worry and just kept telling me to be quiet. Be quiet and don't worry. Be quiet and don't worry. That's what he said."

"I'm so sorry."

"He ripped my dress, by accident, and then he just bought me a whole new one later. He didn't want me to think less of him. I spent the whole spring semester thanking him for being so nice. That's what I told myself! That he was nice! But then I heard. I found out. I was just his Senior Send-Off. Nothing more. That's it. Like a freebie. Like his graduation prize. And then, like that, he was gone. He changed his number, he blocked me. He graduated, went to Yale, and was gone. I felt so bad, I spent the summer a mess. A serious mess. I had the old dress in a ball on the floor of my closet, the new one hanging right above it. So messed up. But I got out of it, just enough. Just enough to come back to school. And when I got back, something just clicked, and I ate up all those soft boys. I just went after them. The ones who looked a little more scared, the ones who weren't chasing down all the more popular girls. I don't even know why; I just did it at every party—not even at parties, whenever. I did that for two years and then just felt so gross. Now it's senior year. I still have the fucking dress. Both of them."

She walked away from me again, marching up the path back toward school.

"Aileen," I said behind her. "I'm so sorry I brought us here. I didn't know."

She waved me off and kept marching. "How could you? You can't know everything about a person."

"Wait up," I said. I ran up ahead of her and stood in the path looking back at her. "Let me just say this. I spent a year feeling so shitty about myself—I know what that feels like, and I know it enough I don't want to make anyone else feel that shitty. It's awful. I don't want to do that. I'm telling you. I don't hate you. I'm just so sorry. But here's something else. Don't for a minute think anything you said right now changes anything I said back there a few minutes ago. I'm telling you. It's okay for me to like you. If you don't like me, that's another thing. I'll try to deal with that. But I can still like you the way I do."

She stopped walking and stood staring at me with her arms folded.

"I care. That's all I want to say. I want to do something, but I don't know what. I mean, have you talked to anyone else about this?"

"No."

"Like maybe a girl?" I took a deep breath, hoping I was doing the right thing. "Like, I know this is going to sound weird, but what about Jules?"

Aileen shook her head.

"I know. I know. But I believe you a hundred percent. I think she would too."

Aileen nodded. She stepped closer and closer, until she was within my reach. I opened up for a hug and she leaned into my arms. It was so impossible for me to understand what it was like to be afraid like that. To walk afraid. I didn't. Ever.

CHAPTER 28

JULES DEVEREUX

"What do you want to do?"

Her voice hung in the air, hung in my ears, dangling, tinkling like a wind chime in an almost nonexistent breeze. I'd told Ms. Taggart my whole story, start to finish, with my eyes closed, while lying on the couch in her office. She wasn't a psychotherapist exactly, but she was a counselor on staff, and most importantly, she was the only adult in all of Fullbrook who I considered a friend.

"I don't know," I said, opening my eyes. I still didn't look at her directly. I focused on the scuffed tips of my boots propped up higher than my head as they rested on the arm at the other end of the couch.

"You're brave," she said for the third time. "And you're right." She took a breath. "I will help. But what do you want to do?"

"Besides watch him burn in the fiery pits of hell?" I risked a glance at her. She was sitting on the edge of an armchair on the other side of the coffee table, her legs crossed, pitched forward at the waist as if she had a stomachache. She wasn't looking at me either. Chin propped on a woven knot of fingers, elbows digging into her knees, she stared at the spread of magazines on the coffee table.

"Yes," she said absently. "Besides that."

Javi was the one who had suggested I make it a priority to talk to Ms. Taggart. I felt bad, with her son really sick, but Javi was right. Who else did I have to go to? It sucked having only one teacher I felt close enough to talk to like this. Only one adult I could really trust to understand.

"Are you okay?" I asked.

She snapped back to attention, pulling herself upright, blinking, finding a smile out of nowhere. "Yes. Just thinking. Want some tea?"

"Sure."

She got up and flicked the switch on the electric kettle. She knew I wanted pomegranate; I knew she was dropping a bag of green tea into the blue mug her son had glazed at school. But there was so much more stillness in the air than usual.

"Ms. Taggart? Is it all right I told you?"

She turned back around and marched across the room with her arms open wide and I sat up straight into a hug. "Absolutely," she said as she held me. "I'm here with you. I'm here for you. I'm sorry I'm not myself, but, honey, I'm absolutely glad you told me. You can't keep this all bottled up."

We hugged until the water boiled, and then she got up and I stood too, because I was sick of lying there or sitting there—I wanted to do something. Ms. Taggart handed me my mug and

I took it to the mantel over the little fireplace. It didn't work anymore, as far as I knew—Ms. Taggart kept a bunch of candles she never burned in the hearth, instead—but it was a reminder, a symbol of how long the school had been here. Even the health center was in an old colonial building with a stone hearth.

"I do want to do something," I said. "I think we should tell Headmaster Patterson."

"Okay," she said slowly.

"He's always going on about how he will make time for students. Well, now's his chance."

Ms. Taggart warmed, a blush blooming in her cheeks and neck, but not from embarrassment. Her smile filled with excitement. "Good." She set her tea down on her desk and flipped open her calendar. "I have my monthly one-on-one with him in early December, but I wonder."

"Right now."

She looked up at me. There was hope in her eyes, or at least that's what I saw.

"Let's go right now," I repeated. "Even if he's busy, something will clear up at some point. He can't ignore us if we're camped outside his door. He needs to know."

"Okay," she said, more resigned. "I'm with you, Jules. Let's go."

We gathered our things, left our tea cooling in our mugs, turned off the lights, and marched out of the health center. I was nervous, but I felt better walking alongside Ms. Taggart. She had an air of purpose. Her style didn't come from her clothes—leather boots, cracked all over the toes, a fraying shawl and faded sweater she hid under—but rather from the way she stared ahead with resolve. Her style, it swept before her like conviction. It was late afternoon—the sky blue but dark, the sun gone—and there was still enough time to catch Mr. Patterson before dinner. I was bright with the fire within me.

We rounded the corner of the admin building, and I was surprised to see the leaves from the old elm littering the walkway. It was a relief to have one un-manicured moment at Fullbrook. Maybe the maintenance crew had the day off. Maybe they had quietly refused to clean the walkway, had just let it go for one day—their own private rebellion.

Inside, we were shocked at how empty it was. Even Mrs. Packard, his receptionist, was leaving early for the day. He was in a meeting but wouldn't be long. She poked her head into his office to let him know we were waiting before she left. Ms. Taggart and I sat in the outer office, barely able to relax in the overstuffed armchairs, and we didn't speak much. Ms. Taggart only said to let her do most of the talking until I was invited to share—and when I was, to speak my mind as I wished.

"Share any and every detail you want," she said. "I'm not going to tell you to censor the details of your pain." I'd been full of resolve on the walk over, but as I glanced around the room, moving from the vase of improbably brilliant goldenrods and orange roses to the enormous oil paintings of the first headmaster and Mr. Patterson's predecessor on the wall above the bookshelf of yearbooks, I began to feel dwarfed by the sheer magnitude of dark oak and gloomy history. Who was I in the midst of all of this?

"Come on in," Mr. Patterson said to us.

Coach O'Leary stepped into the outer office ahead of him.

He waved awkwardly. "Ladies," he said. He cocked and popped a forefinger-and-thumb gun at me as he passed. "Sure I can't wrangle you into a season of water polo this spring?" he said. "I've seen you in the pool. You're a strong swimmer."

That he had seen me in the pool and I hadn't seen him creeped me out. When was he referring to? Yesterday? Two weeks ago? The beginning of the year? All my years at Fullbrook? I was so stunned by it, I couldn't say anything. I just looked at him and blinked.

He smiled and shrugged at my nonresponse. "Last chance," he added as he walked out the door.

"Come on, Jules," Ms. Taggart said. She was already standing, and she led me by the arm into Mr. Patterson's office.

He offered us water, and poured from a pitcher into two cool highball glasses. He set each one on a felt coaster on his desk in front of the two chairs. He swung back around to his chair on the other side and sat down. He leaned back, kicking his feet up on what might be a partially opened drawer. Then he suddenly thought otherwise and took a more businesslike pose, sitting forward with his hands in his lap.

"Mr. Patterson," Ms. Taggart began. "We have some very serious issues to discuss, and I hope you won't mind if we get straight to it." There was no way I could have done this without her.

"By all means. Please." He gestured for her to go on, the cheer and welcome erased from his face.

She took my hand. "Jules and I are coming to you to report an assault."

He remained silent, glancing slowly back and forth from Ms. Taggart to me.

"Jules has been assaulted."

"My God," he finally said. "I'm so sorry. Are you okay?"

I nodded. "Yes." It wasn't what I wanted to say exactly, but I spoke automatically, like the way we say "How're you doing?" when all we really mean to say is "Hello."

Ms. Taggart squeezed my hand. "Sexually assaulted."

"Oh," Mr. Patterson said. He leaned back, then forward again, and perched his elbows on the desk. He rubbed the knuckles of one hand in the palm of the other. "Oh, this is very serious."

"Yes. And we'd like to file a report and begin the process." She took a sip of water, but never let go of my hand. She cleared her throat. It occurred to me that she'd never done this before, that she and I were both fishing for the right words. "Ethan Hackett sexually assaulted Jules," she said. "We'd like to discuss the ramifications of this with you."

"Okay."

"Okay?" Ms. Taggart stiffened slightly. She let go of my hand. Her tone sharpened. "Yes. So we want to discuss what we are all going to do about this now because . . ." She hesitated. "Well, for instance, we'll have to talk about getting Ethan off campus as soon as possible."

"May I ask a few questions?" Mr. Patterson broke in, and he didn't wait for a response. "This is extremely serious, and first and foremost I'm glad to hear you say you are okay, Jules. I want you to know that's my first concern."

"Thank you." It came out of my mouth, but it didn't sound like me. Who was speaking?

"And you're in your final year here, only a few months left, really. I hope you feel well enough to see it through. To finish with us."

"Wait, what?" Ms. Taggart said.

"Yes," I said. "Of course."

"I'm glad." Mr. Patterson smiled, but it didn't feel at all like he was smiling to rally me. He leaned back and folded his hands in front of his belly. "The most important thing is that we secure your path to graduation, and that you carry on and fulfill those dreams of yours." He paused, summoning the kind of starry-eyed reverie of his dining hall speeches. "Because, Jules, you are an amazing young woman with tremendous goals and dreams and energy, and I'm the first to say I want to see you spring out into the world and take those with you, and not let any bump in the road slow you down. You're too good for that."

Ms. Taggart leaned forward and placed her hands on the edge of his desk. "Mr. Patterson."

But before she could say more, he continued. "If you'll allow me to say this again. I'm deeply concerned." He stared at his hands as he went on. "We are diligent in our Title IX compliance. We take this very seriously. There's no room for mistreating people here."

I nodded along, taking it all in. He spoke slowly and methodically, choosing his words carefully. I actually appreciated it—I basically wanted to say as little as I had to too. I didn't want to say anything. I just wanted to be brave enough to look him in the eye once and hope that that conveyed everything—or enough.

"These are delicate situations, and I want to handle it appropriately."

"We understand that," Ms. Taggart said. She tapped the edge of his desk. "I think we need to start talking about Ethan."

"Yes, of course." Mr. Patterson gathered himself. "Exactly. And we know how these things sometimes are. Relationships are always tricky."

Ms. Taggart took a breath, but he continued.

"Now, let's just start at the beginning." He pushed on, adjusting himself in his seat. "You and Ethan. Has he been bothering you?"

"Bothering me?"

"Yes. Is this the first time he"—he paused—"pursued you?"

"No. I mean, we dated all last year."

"Oh," he said. "And this ended, or is it still going on?"

"I don't understand," I said.

"This was in your dorm? Where are you? Mary Lyon?"

"No, by the river. In the woods."

"Oh," he said. The moment hung there. "Off campus. Was this a party?"

"Yes."

He shook his head. "There was alcohol, I assume."

"Everybody was drinking."

"Everybody?"

"Mr. Patterson," Ms. Taggart said. "Let's discuss—"

"No, no," he said, holding up his hand. "Of course. I'm only trying to better understand." He sat back. "These kinds of situations—I need to take all the appropriate steps. Ms. Taggart, you'll help us with this, each and every part of the process?"

"Of course," she said. "I'm here for Jules in every way."

"Exactly," he said. "We'll take a look at the protocol and

proceed accordingly." He leaned toward me. I could feel him without looking at him. "Julianna?"

"Yes?"

His hand appeared on the desk in front of me—where I'd been staring. I looked up. He smiled and sighed through his nose. "We're going to take care of this." There was a long moment of silence. "Julianna?" he said again.

"Thank you." I could barely get it out. I realized I was trembling. I wanted to throw my glass of water across the room. I just wanted it all to end. I also wanted to know he was going after Ethan. He'd seemed to say he was.

"Let's agree to not speak about this widely." Mr. Patterson must have assumed the conversation was ending soon. His voice lilted as if he was in summary mode. "Plan to meet to begin a step-by-step investigation, a community support program, and bring in the legal team, and see what the next steps are."

His chair squeaked, and he gestured to the door.

"I'm glad," Ms. Taggart said. "And if I hear you correctly, we're moving on this immediately."

"Absolutely," he said. "Yes. And we'll be sure we follow every single step of the protocol. We take this very seriously," he said again, stepping around the desk.

I found myself standing. I found his hand on my back. I couldn't tell if he was holding me in a kind of one-handed hug, or giving me a gentle nudge out the door. I didn't want his hand anywhere near me, but it was stuck there, glued to the spot where wings would sprout if I had them—I wanted them.

"Julianna," he said again. "I want you to know we'll look into all of this." He said it so sincerely, I thought, so certainly, so assuredly, that I believed him. Before I knew it, I was out the door, back in the lobby, following the ribboning patterns in the carpeting as they led me toward the front door. I tried to breathe, stared up at the vaulted ceiling, the fluted grooves in the richly stained molding, hoping nobody would speak to me more— make me speak.

But like she had back in her office, Ms. Taggart gathered herself. "Okay, Jules," she said. "We're just getting started. We've alerted him. Now we're going to push and pressure him."

She nodded. I could feel her bracing herself, forcing the words out. "You stick by me, Jules," she said. "This isn't the end." But her voice was so weak. "We're going to keep at this," she added, like an afterthought.

CHAPTER 29

JAMES BAXTER

I was surprised how many students came out to watch the first hockey game. It wasn't even an official game—it was a preseason scrimmage—but the stands around the rink, the three quarters designated for Fullbrook fans, were jam-packed. I got out on the ice and sped around a few times, even in my bulky goalie pads, and then hunkered down in the net as the guys slapped practice shots at me. I swapped out and let Greg, our backup goalie, take a few shots. Puck. Puc. *Poc.* The air was charged with the smack and whoosh of slapped pucks. *Poc, poc, poc.* I swapped back in and took a couple dozen more. Freddie was aiming high. One hit me in the grill. Then he snuck one past my shoulder. Another got past me. But those were the only two. Big guys like me move a little slower side to side. We take up more net but can't adjust as quickly. But I had my eyes and my hands and I used them. Babe Ruth on ice. Everything else I stopped. And when the game began, I was in my zone. I did what I always did. No matter how fast the game moved, and at

Fullbrook, the game was moving much faster than I was used to, I slowed my breath. I breathed like I read, slowly, sounding out each word, tasting the vowels, chewing on the consonants. *Poc, poc, poc.* I stopped them all.

As the crowd roared, I felt the rumble deep inside. It felt so damn good to be good at something. At the end of the first period, we were up one–nil. Freddie sped over and threw an arm around me. He slammed our face masks together. "Hell, yeah, Buckeye! Hell, yeah!" His voice was hot and wet in the air over the ice. "Kick that Buffalo ass!"

The Fullbrook fans stomped and clapped as we began the second period, and Freddie took another two shots in the first three minutes. He was spectacular. I'd never seen anyone who could skate as fast, stop as quickly, turn and swivel like he was planting a cleat in the grass, not stabbing the ice with his skate. Buffalo was slower but fierce. They rocked us against the boards. Freddie took an elbow to the back of the head that turned his legs to rubber. He was pulled off the ice, but was back on a few minutes later, and when he was he went straight for Number Four, the big guy who'd knocked him down. Freddie pinned him against the boards twice. He snuck in an uppercut with the nub of his stick and Number Four crashed to his knees. *Poc, poc, poc.* I kept stopping them. Caught a few hits myself. One of the guys from Buffalo crashed into me, then got locked up in my pads. Whistles blew. "Do it again," I told him as we untangled. "I'll knock your teeth into your pants." He did it again—took a swipe at my leg, clipped me on the back of my calf. A few minutes later he stole the puck and charged toward me, one-on-one. At first

I crouched in position. But then I sprang forward and surprised him. Never a good idea, but I risked it, slid out beyond the safety circle, caught the shot, and dove, shoulder first, into the guy's face mask, taking him out like a linebacker. *Eat you for breakfast,* I heard in the back of my mind, and it shook me.

The roar from the crowd was almost deafening. The only other thing I could hear was Freddie barking over my shoulder. "Yes, yes, yes. That's how we do. That's how we do, Buckeye." He held his stick in the air and egged on the crowd again. "Number one!" he shouted. "Number one!" I didn't know if he meant me, because that was my number, or if he was talking about the team, us making it all the way to State that year, but he got the crowd going again, and they all chanted along. "Number one! Number one!"

The guy from Buffalo slumped off the ice. "Please come back," I whispered.

Coach pulled me, too. "Take a breather," he said. "Not a smart move, but one hell of a stop." He laughed. "You keep doing what you're doing out there, Buckeye." He'd picked it up from the guys. He slapped me on my shoulder. "Good work!"

Freddie scored again and we were up two–nil. The period ended, and Coach wanted to leave Greg in there to get him some more time. Early in the third period, Buffalo scored. It was a scuffle in front of the net and Number Four snuck it through. Buffalo and their small crowd cheered.

Behind me another chant rose up out of the Fullbrook stands. "That's all right, that's okay, you're gonna work for us someday!" They repeated and repeated, drowning out whatever the small group on the other side of the rink said.

The Fullbrook fans kept chanting and chanting, growing louder and louder, and one of the guys from the other team took his glove off and gave all of us the middle finger. This got Freddie and another guy hopped up and they hit him out of play. Whistles blew, but an all-out brawl started as all the players on the ice went after each other. People in the stands went crazy, screaming and yelling, not in fear, but cheering on the fight like we were watching a boxing match. I couldn't think straight. I saw the fight slowly breaking up. I heard the crazy things some of the guys on the bench beside me yelled. Even people in the stands behind us shouted monstrous, foamy-mouthed curses at the team in from Buffalo. But what stuck in my head was that chant.

"That's all right, that's okay, you're gonna work for us someday!"

I couldn't believe I was playing for a team that had a chant like that. It didn't matter that I was on the bench and not yelling along with them all. I was right there in the thick of it—wearing my Red Hawks uniform—if anybody had taken a picture from the ice up into the stands, they'd have assumed I was part of the mob. It made me sick. Fifty thousand dollar kid. Scholarship kid. Sucker.

Play was about to resume. "Goddamnit," Coach yelled. He turned to me. "Buckeye, you're back in. Don't let them score another one for the rest of the game. Show 'em who's boss."

Something in me broke. I couldn't find my breath. The game whirled around me. Bodies slammed against the boards. Freddie scored again. Pandemonium in the stands. I stopped two more shots. I stopped a third. Automatic. Caught it in my glove. But that chant rang in my ears. All I could think about was the guys back home, guys I played with, guys who didn't make it to college, or who did but struggled to make rent while there. The kid with a wheeze all last year because his family didn't have health care. There were too many of us. Us. Was I still part of that us?

One of the smallest guys on Buffalo got around the back side of the net, bumped my leg, and I went limp. I just gave it to him. I slumped into the net and let the puck gently follow me over the line. It might have been tapped in by a toe.

The chant went up again. "That's all right. That's okay. You're gonna work for us someday!" And I almost took off my glove to give the finger to my own school. But the whistle blew, the game was over, and we'd won 3–2.

Back in the locker room, Freddie bumped me before I'd even gotten my skates off. "What the hell was that? You went dead out there."

I shook my head and ignored him.

"Seriously," Freddie said. He grabbed my shoulder pad and was about to say something else, but I swung around, ripped out of his grip, and pushed him against the locker. The guys around us froze. I had Freddie pinned face-first into the locker, with one arm twisted behind his back.

"Hey," Coach yelled behind me. "Don't be pissed at him."

I let go, and it was Coach's turn to grip me. He pushed me back onto a bench, held me by my shoulder pads, and growled in my face. "Don't let me ever see you pull that shit again. You hear me, Buckeye? You folded out there. You think that's playing? That's some girlie shit, folding like that. Don't let me ever see you do that again."

I nodded.

"What's the matter with you?"

"Nothing," I mumbled.

"I want to see hustle. It's your first game back, but that's no excuse. That's all I want to see all day and all night. Some goddamn hustle." He still held me by the shoulder pads, but he stood back up and addressed the whole team. "I want to see the guy who gets to the gym early, the guy who jogs to his meeting so he's five minutes early, not on time, the guy who doesn't say 'Are we done for the day?' but instead, 'What else do you need me to do?'"

"I got you," I said.

"What?" He leaned back down in my face.

"Yes."

"Where's your voice, Buckeye?"

"Yes!" I shouted, but not loud enough to be heard over the guys around me shouting louder.

"You ready for the big league?"

"YES!"

He let go and stomped off, and the rest of the team grumbled and peeled off their uniforms, getting ready for the showers. But Freddie remained right next to me. He flexed his arm. I hadn't realized how tightly I'd held him. He rotated and swung his arm in a circle. "I don't know," he said. "Are you actually ready for this? Are you actually as good as they say?"

"I am," I said, looking at the locker in front of me, staring at my name in the tape.

"Really?"

I didn't answer him.

Freddie stepped closer, and leaned down next to my ear. "Keep your head in the game, Buckeye. I don't care what you think about me. You and me? We're a team. We're the ones carrying us to State. We're the ones bringing all the recruiters here. I don't give a shit what you think about me, you and I are a team. On the ice we're one."

I turned to him and said nothing. Over his shoulder, I could see the graffiti about Aileen etched in the nearby locker. It took everything I had not to pummel him to the floor.

"You're lucky to be here," he said. "If it wasn't you, it'd be some goalie from Michigan or Maine or Wisconsin or wherever. It didn't have to be you. Remember how lucky you are to be here."

He stepped back and curled around the line of lockers to the next aisle, where his was. I sat there trying not to explode. If I'd taken my glove off and popped one of the guys from Buffalo in the face, torn his mask off and given him a bloody nose, I'd have been a hero that day.

I hated myself.

I was the last one in the shower and the last one out, and I let the steam swell and curl around me, hoping I'd sweat and spit and snot all the bitterness out of me, but none of it worked. I was at Fullbrook on scholarship. The fifty thousand dollars they could have gotten from a full-paying student they'd invested in me instead. I was there to work for it. To work for them. It was impossible for me to not think about that all the time. What was I really worth? Was I worth fifty thousand dollars? More? Less? It was a pretty shitty way to think about yourself, especially since fifty grand was chump change for so many of the families who sent their children to Fullbrook. Fifty grand: meaningless.

Where I came from, fifty thousand dollars was a lot of money. Like the guys from Buffalo we'd been playing against that day. Guys I felt like I knew. Buffalo was only two hundred miles up the coast of Lake Erie from where I grew up, and I knew damn well that fifty thousand dollars meant as much to me as it did to almost any one of those guys sitting on the bus back to Buffalo.

The previous spring, I'd been on the back porch wondering if I could just move over to Uncle Earl's when I graduated, when Mom called me into the house. She and Dad were standing by the sink in the kitchen. She clutched a letter from an opened package that sat on the kitchen table. She beamed with delirious mania.

"It happened," she whispered, nodding at me.

"Thank God," Dad said.

Coach Drucker had made it sound inevitable, but I still hadn't believed it was possible. How could a school like that accept me? How could I go there?

She waved the letter. "You're in," she said, her voice quiet and warbling. Dad nodded beside her. He made a face I couldn't read, a forced smile with squished, sad eyes, as if he felt bad for me. I knew it wasn't easy for them. The whole year had been one disappointment after another—more so for them than for me, even.

"You're going to Fullbrook."

That's what he said. Those were the words, but it sure as hell sounded more like *just don't screw up—please, whatever you do, don't screw up.* He had the weakest smile, like he really didn't have the strength or the will to break the blank stare and make his face match the words that came out of his mouth.

"You can do this."

But why did it sound like he was saying I couldn't?

"Why can't I just work with Uncle Earl?"

They made faces at each other. "What kind of son . . ." He paused. "I didn't work my ass off so you could just throw your hands up and not try to make something of yourself. You have to get out there, son. What the hell are you afraid of? Man up. You're going."

"Honey," my mother said, leaning closer, wrapping her arms around my shoulders, "we're all counting on you. This is an opportunity no one gets. We don't have to pay for it. This is the gift of a lifetime. You have to go."

"Oh, stop babying him. He's nearly an adult." Dad stepped toward the table and pointed at me. "You're going." He paused and rubbed his face like he was exhausted, even though all he ever did was wander around the hardware store, waiting for someone to buy something, or sit around our kitchen and drink coffee. When he looked back down at me, he wasn't smiling. "This is your only shot at a future. Don't screw it up."

By the time I got back upstairs, the stands had emptied and the lights had been dimmed to night mode, a pale green glow over the ice, a few yellowed globes along the walls. I stood by the boards in the little driveway the Zamboni took to get out onto the ice, and found myself getting lost in the cuts and grooves the skates had left everywhere. I felt a little too old to feel this emotional, so broken up, I had no words to describe the fissure I felt widening inside me—but I also felt like, why? Or rather, why the hell not? What was so damn wrong with wanting to cry sometimes? Hadn't it felt good to cry with Jules that night at the pep rally? Hadn't it felt good to wash out whatever nameless storm swept through me? In the arena, all alone, I heard the echo of one loud sob double back to me, and it was weirdly comforting, as if there was one other person crying along with me.

The door to the main lobby opened and banged close. Instinct kicked in, and I wiped away my tears as fast as I could. I hawked a loogie in the driveway and tried to fix my face, brace myself, get back on guard. I thought it might be Coach, and he was the last person I needed to see me like this. It was shattering how much I wanted someone there with me, but almost no one at all from Fullbrook.

Almost. Javi came around the corner of the stands and leaned on one of the scaffolding pipes holding them up. "Oh, man," he said. "You don't look good."

I let out a laugh I'd never heard come out of me. It was like a bird calling in the forest—the kind of laugh that picked up and soared after a good cry. "You're the last person I thought I'd see here."

"Nope. That'd be Jules. She'd never be caught dead in here. I like coming to the games, actually."

"Really?"

"No. I'm just playing. I thought Max was coming to the game." He shrugged. "Guess I thought if he saw me, maybe we could talk."

"He didn't come."

"Nope. But then I thought I'd stick around for you. Seriously, once I started watching the game? Man. Now I know what the hype is all about. You're a monster out there."

"Thanks." I knew he was kidding but it stung a little anyway. He was right.

"I think you have to be to play this game."

"Maybe."

"Anyway, I waited for you because I thought you'd want to hear from someone who knows nothing about the game, other than it kind of looks like the most violent ballet on ice, that you were great."

"Aw, thanks," I teased. "It means so much to hear that from someone who doesn't know what the hell he's talking about."

"Oh, yeah," Javi said, coming toward me now. "Anytime. You want to hear some really meaningless pats on the back, just come to me."

I shrugged. He was close enough now that I was sure he could see I'd been crying. I wondered if he'd heard me too.

He stepped closer, put a hand on each of my shoulders. "You really do look like shit."

"Exactly how I feel."

He pulled me into a hug. "I think we both need one of these."

And he was right. The weirdest thing was that I couldn't remember ever hugging a man that long. Not my father, for sure. He could barely get through a mutual pat on the back. Not any friend or teammate. It'd always been girls. Why? How ridiculous.

I squeezed him as tight as I could, and when I finally let him go, we both started walking toward the lobby. Then I paused. "Hey," I said as an idea came to me. "Follow me."

I led him back around to the locker room entrance and then

down the stairs with the same sense of spirit I'd had knowing I had to get Aileen back home from Horn Rock. The overnight lights cast a jaundiced glow over the room, and the whole place still smelled like sweaty socks and bile. I led Javi around to my aisle.

"How do you stand any time at all in this hell pit?"

"It's just normal for me," I said.

"Your normal is disgusting."

"Agreed."

"Why did you bring me down here?"

"For this," I said, pointing to the graffiti about Aileen.

"Sorry, man. I know you two have been scoring, but this stuff is all over the place. It's not just in locker rooms."

"Yeah, I know. But this is the only place I have to come to every single day. Besides, it's not just her. You know how many girls' names are down here?" I went over to my locker, opened it, and dug out my skates. I handed one to Javi.

"Oh, hell, no," he said, handing it back. "I'm not touching that. I'll get like twelve diseases if I hold it for too long."

"It's the best tool I have," I said. "Are you with me?"

"What are you talking about?"

I handed him the skate again and walked over to the locker with the scratch graffiti about Aileen. I held the skate edge and scraped it against the locker, over the words, and in a few seconds it was a barren waste of squiggles.

"Let's wipe them all clean."

"What? There must be dozens, tens of dozens of lines like that all over the place."

"Well, they don't need to be here."

"I know you don't like seeing your girlfriend or whatever disparaged like that, but these guys have been doing this for years. That graffiti was probably from last year or before."

"It doesn't matter. This is my locker room too. This shit," I said, pointing to another line of graffiti about a girl I didn't know, a number to text her something dirty, "this shit doesn't stand. Not in my locker room."

Javi smiled. "You're insane. I am so in."

We bisected the locker room, each to a side, and went at it. It took us more than an hour, but we got it all, or at least everything we could find. At the end, he carried my skate back over to my locker and pointed to my nickname. "We ripping that off too?"

"No," I said. "I'll deal with that later."

He nodded. "You know they're going to know it was you," he said.

"I know. I won't tell them you helped."

"I don't care."

He handed me my skate and I wiped the paint chips from the blade. "But thanks," I said. "I mean it. It helps to know someone has your back."

Javi nodded. "You know who needs someone to have her back right now? Jules."

"She won't talk to me."

"Try again. She needs to know you care." He paused. "If you care."

"You know I do."

"Well, let her know."

"I will," I said, because I knew he was right, and I had to, but I just had to figure out exactly how.

CHAPTER 30

JULES DEVEREUX

I was back in Mrs. Attison's class, trying to pay attention but thinking instead about how exactly I was going to skip the Winter Ball. I didn't want to just opt out, or play sick, or cross my name off the organizers' matchmaking list. I wanted to send a message. It was demented and archaic. Seniors took first years to the dance—that was the annual tradition? There was nothing cute about it. It was a setup for disaster.

Everybody in the administration was sick of me. They were sick of my pleas for more dietary flexibility. They were sick of my demands for racial affinity support groups and more body image counseling for girls. What had Mrs. Attison once said to me? *When will you run out of things to complain about?*

Now Mr. Patterson had me bogged down in some kind of investigation, and I wasn't supposed to talk about anything until he had outlined the clearest course of action. What he didn't say but what was now perfectly clear to me and Ms. Taggart was that that meant nonaction.

"Ms. Devereux?"

"Huh?"

The whole class was looking at me, and I suddenly feared I'd been talking to myself aloud, that I'd really lost it and Mrs. Attison was telling me to leave class and go to the health center.

"Ms. Devereux, I'm asking you to redeem yourself and solve this problem for us on the board."

She never called me that: Ms. Devereux. Some of the guys got referred to as Mr. So-and-So, but never the girls. Never me. There was something so grounding in it. Something inspiring. I was about to say I hadn't done the homework again, when she said it a second time.

"Ms. Devereux, let's see what you have."

I stood, not by command, but through sheer willpower. I walked to the front of the room, knowing everyone was staring at me, but fixating on the problem ahead of me. I hadn't even looked at it. I wasn't sure where we'd gone since the lessons in parabolic ratios the week before. Still, I could begin. I knew enough to begin. And I did.

At the board, I moved as quickly as I could, making my calculations in the white space around the problem and tackling it up to a point. I only paused when I had to, when I didn't know what to do next, the part of solving the problem we'd been doing for the last week when I'd been locked in my mind.

I heard Freddie snicker behind me. I couldn't continue. I was at a loss. Mrs. Attison sighed, and Freddie laughed to someone beside him. I spun around and flung the SMART Board marker at him. I didn't wind up, I just turned, flicked my wrist, and let it fly, the marker tumbling top over bottom like a knife let loose by a knife thrower, and it hit Freddie smack on the forehead.

"What the hell?" he shouted.

The class erupted into chaos. Some people laughed, others were horrified, and nobody knew what to do. Mrs. Attison rushed beside me.

"You sit down right now," she said in my ear.

But I couldn't stop staring at Freddie. "He doesn't get to laugh," I said. "Not at me, not at Gillian, not at any of us."

That stopped Mrs. Attison. She pulled back and stood at the front of the class. "That's true," she said.

"What?" Freddie yelled, as I sat down as far away from him as possible. "Of course you'd take her side."

"No one's taking any sides."

"Yeah, you are."

"If you'd let me finish, Mr. Watts."

"She just whipped a marker at me."

"If you'd let me finish."

"What kind of insane overreaction—"

"Mr. Watts!" She'd never raised her voice like that before, and she sent a static shock through the room. We were all silent. "I don't know what is behind all this, but I've had enough. We're here to do calculus. We're here to work and not act like toddlers let loose at the zoo."

She walked to her desk and sat on the edge. "In fact"—she nodded—"we're going to move the test up a day. That means it's tomorrow." She waited and let that sink in. "The material we were going to cover tomorrow? The review? That's all on your own. Figure it out. I promise there will be at least one problem with the new material in it. I'm not sure which one. Could be problem one, or two, or five, who knows? You want my advice? You work together in study groups today and try to teach each other. See if you think class is a waste of time anymore."

There were a couple of muffled groans.

"But, Mrs. Attison—" Gillian began.

"Enough." She waved her hand out over the class. "Everyone out. Class is over, early."

"But—"

"I said enough! Go." She pointed to the door.

I went back to the seat I'd been sitting in at the beginning of class and stuffed my bag. Gillian and a few other people whispered over my shoulder.

"Thanks a lot."

"Nutjob."

"Happy now?"

I let most of the class walk out ahead of me, and as I turned to leave, Mrs. Attison called me over to her. She waited for the last stragglers to pick up and go, and when we were all alone, she looked at me, not saying a word. Eventually, she lost her patience.

"Don't you have anything to say to me?" she asked.

"I'm sorry."

She sighed.

"I don't know what happened. I just lost it."

"Is something going on between you and him?"

"Freddie? No."

"That all seemed awfully personal."

"I'm just so tired of him. When he walks into a room, I feel some of the air gets pushed out."

Mrs. Attison nodded. "I hear you, but that is never going to be the way to deal with it. Do you understand me?" She stood up and put her hand on my arm. "Honey, there's another way, and I'm not just saying this because I'm your math teacher. You are giving up on this class, Julianna."

"I don't mean to. I'm just . . . I don't know."

"You do not give up."

"I know, but . . ."

"No. You don't understand me. You are not a person who gives up. I have always admired that about you. No matter what, you have never given up."

I nodded. She squeezed my arm.

"You ace that test tomorrow, Jules. You ace that one and the next one. You are a dean's list student, Jules. You stay that way, and you are going to any college you wish. And that's how you deal with the Freddie Wattses of the world."

She hugged me, and I hugged her back, and I had this crazy feeling I was going to say something else to her, something I probably shouldn't but really needed to, because it felt like it had absolutely nothing to do with her class, or calc, or Freddie Watts, but at the same time, it felt like it had to do with everything.

"Now please come back tomorrow prepared."

And with that she stepped away, and began gathering her own stuff and throwing it all in her handbag. I couldn't do much else than thank her and slink away, and that was all I did. But her pep talk shook something loose in me, because I heard my mother's voice in Mrs. Attison's. *You don't give up.* She'd said it to me so many times, but maybe because she'd had to say it to herself and she wanted me to hear it. To know it. To own it. Maybe it had been one of her rules—especially as one of the first women ever to attend Fullbrook. What had she had to do to make it here? First women. They were up against the world.

It was the end of the day, so I knew people were going to start gathering in the library and student center and in the common room back at Mary Lyon, and I didn't want to be any of those places with any of them. I made a beeline for the arts center, ducked inside, and ran upstairs to the photo studio. I was late on that project too, so I figured I'd just take care of it, and then do exactly as Mrs. Attison had directed. Study, so I could nail that test.

The project I was supposed to be working on with Aileen was both digital and film photography, layering old school and new, creating this web collage of busted tools and crumbling bits of architecture, trying to bring back to life the broken. When I got to the darkroom and saw the red light on outside, I almost turned away, but then stopped. Who else would be in there?

I knocked, and after a moment, Aileen poked her head out the door, the black curtain curled around her face like a nun's habit. "Jules?"

"Can I help?"

She narrowed her eyes, giving me one of her nonplussed stares. Then she cracked a grin. "You better."

At first we didn't talk much, just simple stuff about class, and I apologized for not being around, for being an absent partner.

I was stunned by how much she'd accomplished without me. "How did you get all this done?" I said, looking around at the photos hanging on a string at the far side of the room. She'd already cut some of the photos, leaving room for the digital images to slip in.

"What else do I have to do?" she said.

"Uh, I don't know. Hang out with Bax."

I'd seen them hanging out a number of times, but when he wasn't with Aileen, he was always with the hockey team, and I was beginning to worry he was just another meathead after all.

Aileen smiled. "Yeah, him."

"You have been together a lot."

"Not a lot." She turned away and pushed a photo around in one of the chemical trays. "But some, yeah."

She turned around and carried the dripping photo to the string, and I realized that Aileen was the closest girlfriend I had. That wasn't saying much, but it said something. Maybe I was for her, too.

"Aileen?" I said, and I was sure she knew something was wrong, because she wiped her hands on her apron and walked straight over.

"You okay?"

"I just need to talk."

She nodded, and I unloaded. I told her about throwing the pen at Freddie, and we both laughed, but also about him laughing, and all the wild bullshit of the year that was piling up and making me crazy, and suddenly I felt like the animal I had hiding deep inside me, the truth that wanted to break free, was crawling up and out, and I needed to let it loose.

"Also . . . ," I began, and Aileen nodded. She could see the thing coming out of me. Her eyes softened. She reached out and held my hand, because whatever was on my face, it wasn't good, and I told her how fucking awful it all felt with Ethan that night in the woods, and how nobody believed me, that I hadn't wanted anything to do with it.

"Listen," she began. "I believe you." She hugged me for a moment, then pulled back. "Do you know why those boys call me the Viking?"

"I hate that, you know."

"I know."

"But whatever," I went on. "It's so fucked up. People call us sluts, but what about them? What about the boys who sleep around and fuck around with every single girl they can get their stupid hands on? What about all those pucks in Freddie's window, in all those windows?"

"Exactly."

"Exactly."

"But that's not what the name means to me," she said. "They might think it's an insult, but it isn't." She clenched a fist. "I am a Viking. I'm fighting just to get by."

She went on to tell me about what happened to her by the boathouse after the Winter Ball our first year here. The cold, stiff ground. Her legs blue and not working like they should in the night air. She told me how she'd swallowed it all, even the memory of it, like the tiniest bitter pill, and about all the boys she consumed after it just to keep it buried down there.

"I'm fighting," she said again.

"Did you tell anyone?"

"No. Not then." She leaned back against the counter and crossed her arms. "Do you remember Ashley Kramer?"

"Yes," I said. I only barely remembered her. She'd been in our class the first year, but then, near the end of the year, she'd left for health reasons, or so I thought, but given the way Aileen was shaking her head, I was beginning to understand. "So something like that happened to her, too."

She nodded, as if lost in a memory. "She tried to say something, Jules. I don't know what. I don't know to whom, but she did. And then, instead of anything happening, instead of the boy leaving, she left. She wasn't sick. She was terrified of seeing him every day."

I put my arm around her and held her.

"I understand," I said.

"She was smart enough to be afraid," Aileen said. "There I was, thinking Sam Crawford was my boyfriend until he went to Yale." She pulled out of my hug. "I thought he was my boyfriend. How dumb is that?"

"You're not dumb," I told her.

"I just don't want to feel helpless or voiceless anymore."

"I know," I said. "Everyone says, 'Suck it up,' 'That's life,' 'It's not a big deal,' but I want someone to say, 'Hey, this happened to you, it's wrong, you were hurt, and it's not your fault.'"

"I need people to stand there and acknowledge that it happened and not look at me like I have four heads."

"What if we go to the other extreme?" I said.

"What do you mean?"

"What if we scare them for once? Make everyone see something they can't ignore?"

"What do we do?"

In my mind I began my own little mantra, again. Not about college. About right now. It buoyed me. It braced me. It lifted me up. *You do not hear me. You do not see me. But you will.* I just didn't know what I meant by it yet.

CHAPTER 31

JAMES BAXTER

I was having the hardest time keeping a smile off my face, so I remained as silent as possible during the deliberations. We crowded the aisle on the other side of the room from my locker. Freddie sat on the bench, shirtless, hands tucked behind his biceps to make them look bigger than they were.

"Someone comes in here and does this behind our back?" he said. "It's like TP-ing our trees before a game."

Except it wasn't at all.

"Graffiti over graffiti," someone said from the back.

"What's the big deal?" I couldn't hold back anymore. I towered over the guys in front of Freddie, and he looked up at me, a snarl in his upper lip, as if I'd bit him.

"Yeah," Greg said, surprising me. "Who knows? Maybe maintenance came in. Who cares?"

"Someone came into our house and defaced it," Freddie said, staring at me. "Better question is, why would someone do that?"

There hadn't been time to talk about it before practice, but after Coach grilled us and pushed us and punished us for not whipping Buffalo enough, we dragged our exhausted bodies to the locker room and Freddie tried to play Sherlock Holmes. He'd looked for evidence of a tool. He'd searched the room to make sure it had happened everywhere.

"You notice it's only the stuff about girls that's scratched out?" another guy said.

"I did," Freddie said. "Stuff about Hodges, that's still around. Just girls."

"Whack," one of the guys muttered, but Greg and a couple of others peeled away from the group. I followed them, crossing the room to my own locker.

"You think it was one of the girls?" Freddie asked the guys still around him, but he was addressing the whole room. He stood. "Probably Jules. She's always on a tirade."

"All right," I said. "No need to go there."

Freddie glared at me across the room, but I ignored him, wrapped a towel around my waist, and walked over to the showers.

He followed me. "What if it was? What if Jules snuck in here, maybe with one of her friends? Maybe the Viking had a hand in all this? Your locker went untouched."

I closed my eyes and let the water drip all over my face. I was enjoying Freddie's confusion, but his new line of attack was starting to get under my skin. I tried to breathe, find my game-time focus, and let it roll off my shoulders.

"Maybe we should hit something of theirs? Mary Lyon? Raid the bathroom?"

"Or you could just let it go," I said.

Some of the other guys were talking about it, but most of them were talking low or ignoring it. Freddie showered next to me. The silence that walled up between us made everything worse. I was sure others could feel it too. "Hey, Freddie," one of the guys said from the other side of the showers. "Rumor true? You get paired with Margot for the Winter Ball?"

"That little European hottie?"

"Damn, son. Hell of a Senior Send-Off."

"Yeah," Freddie said slowly, turning the water off and walking toward them. "Let's see how she likes my *coq au vin*." The three of them laughed, but only the three of them. Everyone else in the showers was silent. But everyone knew. The Winter Ball came first, then later that night, the Senior Send-Off. Tradition.

"Jesus," Greg muttered next to me.

I took my time washing and letting the water warm all my muscles, and when I finally finished and walked back to my locker, I found Freddie scratching something into one of the lockers near mine. It wasn't his. It was an underclassman's, Tuttle, the only sophomore on the varsity team. Freddie had his arm around him. I tried not to look, but I couldn't help but see the hastily squiggled genitals, and the phrase below: *Jules, come and get it.*

I stopped. Tuttle looked up at me, and I eased him aside. Freddie snickered. "What?" he said. "It was probably her. She's the one who got all hot and horny with Hackett at the party. She's crazy, but like Hackett said, the good kind of crazy." He grinned and slapped Tuttle on the shoulder.

I reached into Tuttle's locker, grabbed his skate, and started scratching out what Freddie had just drawn. "Just don't," I said. "There's no need."

Freddie eyed me. "You've got to be kidding me."

"No. Who cares? Just don't do it," I said.

"It was you."

Some of the other guys began crowding closer. Freddie, Tuttle, and the others were all dressed, but I was still in my towel. Freddie tapped the lockers with the metal pen clip he had used to etch the graffiti.

"I really thought it was her. She's the one running around crying rape because she went crawling back to Hackett and now regrets it. I was sure she was the only one crazy enough to do this. But it wasn't her." He stepped closer to me, pointing the metal clip right at my chest. "It was you."

"What'd you just say?"

Freddie laughed. "Oh my God, you can't lie for shit. You did do it."

I swallowed and tried to keep my temper in check. "No," I said slowly, "what did you just say about Jules?"

"I can't believe you, man. You probably spent the whole night in here scratching this all off." He laughed and backed away, walking toward the center of the room. "This guy's spending all his time with the Viking and Jules. No wonder he's going crazy."

A couple of the guys laughed with him, but not the ones who saw me staring at Freddie's back. "Freddie," I said. "What the hell did you just say about Jules?"

"She's so desperate, man," he said, walking away. "So desperate.

Making such a big deal. Twisting it all out of proportion. Crying rape? So dangerous. Can ruin a guy's life with that word." He was halfway out of the locker room.

"Hackett tell you that?" I yelled after him. He ignored me and left.

I was still in my towel. I handed Tuttle his skate back. "Finish cleaning that off," I told him. I know I sounded like some kind of drill sergeant bully, but I didn't care. I just didn't want that kind of shit in my locker room.

I got dressed as quickly as I could. What did I know? I had to find Jules, or maybe Aileen. She'd know what to do. I couldn't figure out how to deal with the blood racing through me—the storm. I kept trying to still my breathing, but it was impossible. I was on fire.

I thought I was the last one out of the locker room, but as I turned out of my aisle, I saw Greg sitting on a bench, leaning toward Freddie's locker with a key. At first I thought he was scratching something in, but I realized he was using the blunt edge and smudging something out. I didn't even want to know what it was.

Greg nodded at me. "I got you," he said.

"Nice one." I paused. "This is on us, man. We can't just stand around and pretend there's nothing we can do about it."

"I got you," he said again.

"Hey," I said. "You hear that stuff Freddie was saying about Jules?"

He frowned. "I don't know. Couple of the guys were talking about how Hackett was going on about it. Someone was passing around photos of Jules on vacation somewhere last year. Caribbean, I don't know. Calling her a cocktease."

"Freddie?"

"No. A guy on the ski team. Guys in my class. Hackett had shown them the pictures on his phone." He went back to scratching at the graffiti. "He's got everyone calling her crazy. Gillian too. Some of the girls are saying you can't trust a thing she says."

I couldn't hold back. I spun and punched a locker so hard I put a dent in it. I yelled as I did it because I didn't have any words, only the rage welling up and steaming out of me.

Greg didn't flinch. "Yup," he said calmly, still scratching. "I'm with you. It's messed up. I know she's your friend, dude."

I hated myself in that moment, because I knew I hadn't been her friend. I had assumed just like everyone else that she was trying to get back together with Hackett. Javi had been right, and I should have found her yesterday.

As I tore upstairs and out of the hockey arena, I tried to think about where Jules might be, and how to calm down enough so I didn't scare her. Let her know how much I wanted to help. Let her know I was her friend, just like she'd asked me to be, I just hadn't realized how.

It was dark out, and the streetlights along the academic drive in front of the student center and gym barely lit up the street. There was enough light to know there were shadows moving up ahead or behind you, that's all, and though I knew there was a group hanging out on the benches by the student center, I had no idea who they were until I heard one of them yelling my name. "Buckeye! The list is posted. Come check out your date to the ball!"

I blew by them because I couldn't imagine Jules sitting there with them, and as the guys continued to call my name, I didn't bother looking back or answering. I didn't want to turn on them in that moment. There was too much adrenaline in me. I couldn't trust myself and I knew I couldn't start a fight with my own teammates. I didn't know how I was going to avoid it for the next six months. I wanted to rip the student center's glass doors off their hinges and smash them. I wanted to yell—I needed to get something out of me.

By the time I made it to Mary Lyon, I had almost calmed down enough to think about what I might say to Jules, but as I walked up the path toward the front porch, I saw Hackett leaning against the railing, playing guitar and singing to two freshman girls, Lianne and Margot. I lost it.

"Hackett," I hollered, coming up the path.

He stopped and blinked at me as I came into the light.

"Jesus, Buckeye," Hackett said. "What the hell is the matter with you?"

The two girls had been gazing up at him, bobbing their heads along to his song, Lianne so close she was almost leaning against his leg. They were as startled as he was, and Lianne shuffled up against him.

"What are you doing?" I said to Hackett. The fire in my veins still zipped through me, and I wasn't sure I could hide my anger for very long.

"Well, when I find a few expert ski bums like these two, I can't resist sharing my ski song with them." He chuckled. "It's totally dumb, I know."

"No it's not," Lianne said.

Hackett rested his guitar against the porch post behind him. "Lianne's skied some of the best places in the world," he said. "I love it." He smiled down at her and ignored me completely. "But really, which one do you think is better? Cortina d'Ampezzo or Zermatt?"

"Zermatt," she said. "Besides, you can ski into Italy from there, if you want. Ski both countries."

"Love it," Hackett said. He stepped closer. Something about the way he touched her shoulder caught me off guard. She smiled. "I just knew it. That's my favorite too," he said to her.

"Hey," I interrupted. "I need to talk to you. Maybe you two want to get out of here?"

Hackett heard the venom in my voice. I could see the flash of fear on his face. "Damn, Buckeye, no need to start barking orders. Have some manners in front of the ladies here."

I almost sprang forward and tackled him. Instead I took a deep breath.

"Then you come down here and take a walk with me."

He held his own, eyeing me cautiously. "All right," he finally said to the girls. "I'll hit you up later? Lianne?" He smiled at her. "I have to deal with the bear."

"Excuse me?" I said.

Lianne looked back and forth between us.

"No worries," he said to her. "We'll catch up later." She glanced at me again, quickly. *"Sans souci,"* he said to Lianne. "I'll catch up with you after dinner tonight." He stepped away, and even though he kept grinning with that big, carefree smirk of his, he swept up his guitar, sprung down the steps, and headed for the walkway—angling away from me and walking toward our dorm.

I ignored the girls and followed him. He wasn't running, but he was walking as quickly as he could. "Hey," I said, a step behind him. "Where you going?"

He glanced back at me for a second as he headed up the drive toward Tapper. I don't think he knew where he was going. He'd made the wrong move. He should have stayed on the porch with the girls. I grabbed his shoulder from behind and slowed him down.

"You don't waste any time, do you?"

"What?" he said. He lifted his nose. Tried his smirk. It was weak as shit.

"You and Lianne? Seriously? She's like fourteen years old."

"Take it easy."

He broke from my grip, but only briefly. He fought to get free of me, but I backed him up against the wall of Mary Lyon. It was dark, but the girls poked their heads around the corner from the porch steps and could see us.

"I don't feel easy," I said.

"I'm just getting to know my date to the ball," Hackett said. "Relax, man."

"Your date?"

"Yeah." Hackett found a little courage. "Just check the list. You want me to find out who you're going to be paired with? I can do that."

I held my hand up. "Shut up for a second. Tell me what you're saying about Jules." I wasn't sure why I couldn't just come out and say it. I tripped over my words.

"Oh, that's what this is about? You're jealous because she was with me and not you?" He laughed. "That's crazy. Well, she's all yours, Romeo. She's a nutcase."

I kept fighting for words. "No. It's not like that."

"Oh, I think it is." He tried to walk around me, but I blocked him again. Pushed him back against the brick wall. "Just let me by," he snapped. "You can use your left hand if she doesn't want you. It's a free country, dude."

He tried to move again, but I grabbed him by the shoulder and held him in place. "No. It's more like she didn't want to be there," I said.

"Yeah, she says that now." He sniffed. "That's not what she was saying that night."

"She's not a liar."

"Take it easy, Buckeye. Let go of me."

"She's not a liar," I said again.

"So what are you saying? I am?"

"Yes."

"You're out of your league here. I know you think you know, but you don't know anything. You don't know her. You don't know me, and you don't understand anything about life here at Fullbrook. You don't belong here, dude. Why don't you get out of my face and go back to whatever dirty little garage you crawled out of?"

I grabbed him by the front of his shirt and slammed him back against Mary Lyon's wall. He grunted, and then I pressed him up, held him in the air off his feet. He kicked out at me, but I pinned him with my whole body and pressed harder into his chest. My head felt light and electric, like when I was back on the line. All I could hear was Coach Ellerly's voice. *Hit–hit–hit. HIT.*

"I can break you," I spat.

"Hey, stop!" Lianne yelled from the porch. Light suddenly shone through the window above us.

"Yeah," Hackett said, fighting to get his arms around to try to hit me. Useless swats. "That's the kind of thing a kid like you says, because that's all you have, isn't it? Your muscle. Watch how I own you, dipshit."

Someone was leaning out the window above us, shouting for us to break it up. Margot and Lianne shouted too. I could hear them all, but they sounded so far away. I couldn't slow my momentum. I pushed harder, heard him yelp like a whipped puppy, then I dropped him. Just as his feet landed, I socked him in the stomach. He doubled over and coughed, but before he fell to his knees, I caught him and pressed him to the wall again.

I kept him pinned there, catching his breath, but his words had scared me. I pushed harder and he groaned. "I want you to know," I said. "I just want you to remember this. I can break you like you've never been broken. Remember that. Remember when you're walking across campus at night. I'm coming for you."

Despite his obvious pain, he looked me in the eye. He trembled and his voice wavered like I'd never heard it, but he still found a small grin before he spoke. "No. Remember what I can do to you, Buckeye."

I laughed in his face, but he didn't flinch.

"I can ruin you," he continued. "And everyone you care about.

I can sue your ass and sue your family and bankrupt that shitty little hardware store back in Bumfuck Nowhere and ruin you and everyone. I can do that. One call. Remember that, you dumb fuck. That's what I can do. You can't do anything. You're nobody. You'll always be nobody."

I let go and was about to punch him in the face, when I heard my name.

"Bax! Bax! Stop!" Jules shouted. "Jesus, Bax, don't do this! This isn't helping."

My fist shook and I wanted to knock him so hard so bad, but I held back. I stepped back. I let go. Hackett pushed me in the chest, but I knocked his hands away and he didn't try again. He stepped away from the wall.

"Don't!" Jules shouted again. She came running up and stood so we could both see her. "He's not worth it."

"I'm not sure," I said. "It might be worth it to make sure he can never smile again."

"Don't," Jules said. She was terrified and her eyes were wet. "This won't help. Don't do this."

Neither Hackett nor I knew what to say. We stood there catching our breath as Jules continued. "Just let him go. He's not worth it," she said again.

Hackett stepped away from us, and picked up the guitar, which had fallen to the ground. There were some other people coming out of Mary Lyon now, mostly students, but I wasn't sure if Mrs. Attison was there too. Everybody else was in the shadow between the porch and where we were. "Well, there you go, Buckeye from Bumfuck Nowhere," Hackett said. He tried to collect himself as he walked backward, away from us. "And, oh, I'll remember, all right. I'll remember."

Jules grabbed my wrist and I stayed put. I needed to do something. I needed to break something. I needed to break someone, but in the end, all that breaking only breaks yourself—and I knew it, I just couldn't stop myself.

Hackett speed-walked to Tapper, and I turned back to Jules, shaking. I wanted to scream. I wanted to cry. My body wasn't working right.

She held me.

"I'm sorry," I said.

"I need you here, Bax," she said as we hugged. "Please. Please. Please. Don't do that."

"I can't just let him get away with that. I can't let him get away with everything," I said. "I don't understand. I don't know how to fix it."

"Just keep your shit together and stand by me, please," she said. "I need friends, Bax. I don't need friends getting booted from school."

"I was coming to look for you," I said. "That's exactly what I wanted to say. I wanted you to know I was your friend. That guy . . ." I pointed toward Tapper. "That guy . . ." I fought to find the right words. "I'm sorry. I left you hanging. I left you on your own. I didn't know."

"I have a lot to tell you," Jules said.

I hugged her. "I just wanted you to know I was your friend. I wanted you to know I wanted to help."

"You want to help, you stick around, Bax. You stick by me, man."

"I will," I said. "I will."

"I need to know you're my friend, not just when I'm around, but when I'm not in the room, you know? I need to know you're the friend who's sticking up for me, when I'll never hear it."

"I am. I really am."

"And not this way. You don't have to prove anything this way," she said.

I nodded, and we pulled apart. She took my hand. "Besides," she continued, "I'm working on something. I don't know what yet. But something. I need you to not get kicked out of school so you can help."

"Tell me about it," I said as we walked into the shadows beyond Mary Lyon, walking away from everyone who was still lingering out front waiting to see if anything else would happen. Nothing did. Jules and I just skipped dinner and I listened to her tell me everything she had to tell until lights-out at eleven o'clock.

CHAPTER 32

JULES DEVEREUX

Now that the Winter Ball committee had published the list, it was all anybody spoke about, but when I saw the list, and I saw Lianne's name next to Ethan's, all I could think of was how quickly he'd forgotten me. His hands had pushed and kneaded my body as if it was clay, as if there was nothing else inside me, no person, no me at all. If he'd ever seen me, seen the person he once thought of as his girlfriend, how could he have forgotten? Or had he ever really seen me in the first place? What could he do to Lianne?

I tried to catch her in the hall in Mary Lyon, and then again at lunch, but she avoided me. Finally, I found her between classes at the end of the day. She was walking with two other first-year girls, and they hung back when I said hello. Lianne flashed them a scathing look, so I knew something was up.

"Hey," I said to her. "What's going on? You're avoiding me."

"Nothing's up, Jules," she said. She swallowed and continued, staring at the ground and talking to me out of the side of her mouth. "Except you stalking me."

I was so stunned I walked beside her silently until I got to the language building, and Lianne kept going and her friends caught up with her and the three of them huddled together as they walked on to the math building, one of them looking back at me over her shoulder.

The next day, when I was getting a coffee at the student center and I saw her alone at a table with her headphones on, texting with someone, I thought I'd give it one last shot. She was beaming as she thumb-typed away, until she looked up and saw me across the table. Her smile dropped immediately.

"Wow. Did you just appear out of nowhere?" she asked, taking off her headphones.

"Sorry," I said. "You were kind of wrapped up in your own world."

"Yeah." She fidgeted, looking for an escape immediately.

"Hey, I'm just going to come right out and say it. I know you've been talking to Ethan."

Her eyes darted around the room.

"And I am not stalking you. I'm just saying be careful. He's nice, I know, but he's also, I don't know, not nice sometimes." I couldn't understand why I couldn't find the words. Her phone buzzed. "Are you texting with him right now?"

She sighed. "Yes."

"Why?"

"Why not?"

"You don't have to, you know."

"Why wouldn't I? It's fun."

"But is he?"

"Oh my God. He's just being nice. I know the two of you were scoring last year, but like, I'm sorry. It's all set up."

I tried to stay calm. "If it gets weird at any point, you know you can ask me. I mean, I've navigated these guys for the last four years."

"Thanks," she said, although it sure sounded more like *Get out of my face.*

"It's just, they give you all this attention and then they graduate. Older boys, I mean."

"I'm really fine," Lianne said. "In fact, maybe there's something you should know." She looked around and then leaned closer to the table. "Some of the senior girls have already talked to most of us in our grade. They've been super helpful. They've explained why we don't need to get all paranoid." She stopped and looked away.

"Go on."

"Like you. They said. Nobody wants to end up crazy like Jules, they said."

I tried to hold a straight face, but I was sure I wasn't doing a good job.

"I, like, feel bad for you," Lianne went on. "It's really mean, I know, but also, truthfully, you look super pissed all the time. I don't want to be like that."

I could picture Gillian giving this lecture. I could see her waving her hand and dismissing me, calling Aileen a slut and me paranoid. "Please," I said to Lianne, reaching for her. "Don't think I'm crazy. I'm not."

"I don't," Lianne said. She yanked her hand free. "I just think you're super lonely. I'm not going to do that to myself." She smiled and caught someone coming into the center through the doors from the workout rooms. She waved. I could feel the heat of bodies approaching me from behind. "Hey, guys," she said.

I didn't turn around, because I couldn't be sure my face wouldn't crumble.

"What's up, Lianne." It was Freddie. "You do something different with your hair? Looks nice."

"Thanks!"

Freddie and two of his hockey buddies hovered beside me. "Jules, man, you are becoming the most unfriendly person at Fullbrook. What happened to the old Fullbrook hello?" He laughed.

"You're not a stranger, Freddie. You're the same jerk I've known for three and a half years."

"Wow. She's as cold as ice." He half sang it, like the song lyric. "Lianne, you have to be careful around this one. She's toxic."

"Actually," Lianne said, standing and grabbing her phone and headphones, "I was wondering if one of you guys was heading to the dorms. My back is killing me after my workout and I seriously need a hand with my bag. I have like five hours of homework."

"Yeah, we're all heading that way," Freddie said. He stooped, grabbed her bag, and tossed it to one of his buddies. "Let's go."

She giggled and joined them. They all walked away, and even before they got to the front door, I heard a squeal of joy. Lianne had hopped up onto Freddie's hips so he could give her a piggyback ride to the dorm. Nobody else in the room batted an eye. If they noticed it, they didn't care. Everything was normal.

But normal scared me. Normal was the way Lianne had stared me down with a stiff, frozen distance and the way she melted into a soft S when she said hello to Freddie. Normal was Ethan texting her every day in the lead-up to the Winter Ball. I couldn't help but think about what else might be normal. Was Ethan slumped over me against the tree normal? Was it normal how easy it was for him to just forget Gillian, or not care about her, as soon as we were alone and pressed together? Was it normal for him to not think or care about what that would mean to her, or to me?

This wasn't a new normal. It was all the same old normal that had been here for years—the same old normal, just dressed up in a brand-new jacket and tie.

When I stepped outside, it was already starting to get dark. Dinner wasn't for another hour, but I still needed to drop my books and bag back in my room. As I walked down the road toward Old Main, I heard something in the sky, south, by the highway. I looked up and squinted, and saw a black shadow knifing through the dusk light, the blades chopping as it drifted closer, dropping lower and lower as it approached Fullbrook. The helicopter ripped by overhead and the noise it made sucked up all the air around it. Stunned, I watched it hover over the academic quad and slowly sink like a black claw reaching down to the ground from the sky.

Cray-Cray's security cart was parked in the footpath on the far side of the quad, and he rushed over to greet the man in a suit climbing out of the helicopter. They got in the cart and Cray-Cray came zooming up the path around the grass toward the admin building. A squat man in a black suit, head hunched forward like an old dog's, sat in the passenger seat, and even though he was partially obscured by the netting, I could still see who was in the back, his knees hiked up onto the bench because there wasn't enough legroom.

I shouldn't have been so surprised. Ethan's father had arrived at Fullbrook like this before. I'd been there last year when he came for the ceremony of putting the Hackett family name on a plaque on the new wing of the science building, and I'd seen him arrive for a board meeting the year before that. He never stayed for very long. An hour, tops. The helicopter remained on the quad, waiting for him. It would do so again tonight, and as the helicopter lifted him into the sky, its spotlight would cut across the campus.

For some reason, the thought of a helicopter's spotlight slicing through the campus at night spooked me. It was like that feeling you might have walking at night and knowing that someone is watching you but you can't see anyone there, or worse, like there's someone or something in your house and there's nothing you can do about it.

Cray-Cray's cart zoomed around the bend in the path, and for an instant, Ethan's face was lit up by the walkway light overhead. He didn't look toward me; he probably didn't even know I was there. He probably didn't care.

He didn't have to. They were going to see Mr. Patterson. It made me sick to think of the three of them sitting in the office together—just as Ms. Taggart and I had. I suddenly hated him. I hated him as much as I hated Ethan, maybe even more. It was one thing to ignore me, to abandon me, to talk about "looking into things." But it was another to shred my relationship with

Ms. Taggart too. To tear her down in front of me and put her in her place. To turn her into a liar, too—*we're going to keep pushing,* she'd told me, but we hadn't. If Ethan had robbed me of my sense of safety, Mr. Patterson had robbed me of my hope. At a place like Fullbrook, a man could do whatever he wanted to me, to anyone, and get away with it. Ethan. Mr. Patterson. It was built to protect them, not me.

CHAPTER 33

JAMES BAXTER

They put me on probation.

"It wasn't a fight," I told my parents. It was the same thing I'd told Patterson, but he hadn't listened, and now I was on the phone with them and they weren't listening either.

Dad's only bit of advice about my going to Fullbrook lurked in the background—he didn't have to say it, because it was loud enough in my head already. *Don't screw it up. Don't screw it up. Don't screw it up.* I could see them back home, in the kitchen, the burnt-orange afternoon light melting over the chipped table and the faded brown tiles beneath it. They were saying the same things Mr. Patterson and Coach O had told me. How disappointed they were with me. How irresponsible I was, disrespectful I was—how ungrateful, self-sabotaging, undisciplined, unruly, and lazy.

"You're on probation?" They were both on the line, but Dad was always so much louder. "Have you lost your mind?"

"No. I haven't. I'm actually doing well."

"What is the matter with you, Jamie?" he continued, as if he hadn't heard me. "You can't control yourself for half a minute. As soon as it bugs you, you snap. No thinking at all."

"Forethought."

"What?"

"The word you're looking for is 'forethought.' I don't have forethought, you're saying."

"Don't get smart-mouthed with me. Goddamnit, what is wrong with you, son?"

I smiled. I was being a jerk—I knew it. But there was something about being called a smart mouth, the fact that I knew enough about a thing to be sarcastic about it, that made me feel good, too. It wasn't good, but it was honest, and that felt like the world to me.

I wasn't sure why I'd said it, and I apologized, but it didn't matter because he was so angry he yelled more and then told me he was too mad to talk. Apple didn't fall far from the tree. I heard him hit the table at least twice while we were on the phone. He'd never hit me. Really hit me, I mean. With a closed fist. He was shorter than I was, but I still cowered next to him sometimes. Some guys can do that to you. And whatever he was yelling about on the phone, it drove me crazy, because out on the ice everyone went bonkers when a fight broke out in the middle of a game. The fights are why anybody goes to a hockey game, a clerk at Walmart once told me, straight to my face, when I was buying a new pair of gloves. *Control yourself,* Dad always said. It was nuts—everybody wanted me to be two different kinds of people all the time.

When Dad hung up on me, I held the phone so tightly, I thought I might crush it. I wanted to punch a hole in the wall. Instead, I sucked in as much air as I could and breathed it back out. I smiled. "How's that for control?" I said out loud, with no one there to applaud me.

CHAPTER 34

JULES DEVEREUX

I t smelled like snow. Only a few scattered clouds crept across the sky, but the air still felt too crisp, almost burned, like all the moisture was gathering into something solid, something we could feel.

Aileen and Javi were slightly ahead of us, up the path, and Bax was telling me about Coach O giving him the cold shoulder at early morning practice. It was Saturday. He was supposed to have late afternoon practice too.

He walked with his head down, talking to his toes. "A bawling out would have been better," he said. "It would have been normal. All that silence? Made me crazy."

"Meanwhile Ethan's with the ski team, probably taking selfies at the top of Jiminy Peak," I said. "Doesn't seem fair."

"It's not," Bax said. He paused and looked at me. He put a hand on my shoulder, something he was doing a lot now, looking at me with too much pity. It was annoying.

"I was talking about how it's not fair for you," I said. "Not me."

"No. I know," he said. "It isn't. But here's what gets me. So I have most of the team pissed at me right now, like I'm some kind of aberration, like I've disturbed their sense of calm."

"Yeah," I said. It hit home. I knew exactly how that felt.

"But what I'm saying is, no one is giving Hackett a hard time. They're all giving me a hard time for giving him a hard time. Like everybody would be cool if I just ignored it, kept pushing things along like normal, but because I'm not, because I can't do that, they all have a serious problem with me." He hesitated. "Like people all have a serious problem with you. Like if you'd just shut up they'd like you more."

We followed Aileen and Javi off the main path and started up the hill toward Horn Rock. That was exactly it, wasn't it? *What are you making such a big deal out of, Jules? It's not like anything really bad happened.* I'd heard that so many times I was starting to think I was crazy, but the thing was, I wasn't. It was terrifying to think I might be right, and Fullbrook and all the rest of the people there were the crazy ones. Why was it easier for the whole school to let Ethan be Ethan and to tell me to shut up about it, instead?

Well, not everyone. Bax and Javi, and Aileen, who knew truth like sunlight in her eyes—they all held me together. They were mirrors, but not for my face, not for what was on the outside, more like they reflected something back to me that was deep and invisible but real and on the inside. Maybe that was what some people called the soul. Whatever it was, I could feel it looking back at me through them, telling me I wasn't alone.

Javi and Aileen stopped and turned to us. They were further

up the hill, and they waved us on. "Smells funny," Javi shouted down to us. "Hurry."

Bax and I trudged up the hill and joined them. Aileen was out in front, and she led us into the first clearing around Horn Rock. She glanced back at me and nodded, knowing without asking. She pushed us ahead, toward the second clearing, toward my tree.

I'd asked them all to come with me, and all three of them had agreed in an instant. I didn't say, *Hey, want to head to the bluffs?* or *Let's get out of here for a while.* "I need to go to my tree" was all I'd said, and we were on our way.

When we made it to the second clearing, Javi stepped closer to the bluff edge and pointed. Smoke rose into the air in the distance, far downriver. It wasn't insignificant, it was more like a line rippled around the edge of the field, slowly creeping toward the center. There was almost no wind, even up on the bluff, and the smoke curled and wafted upward like a curtain quivering as it shuttled across a stage.

"Should we call someone?" Aileen asked.

"I don't think it's a big deal," Bax said. "It looks like a controlled burn." He gave half a smile when none of us knew what he was talking about. "My uncle Earl," he continued, "he had me help him sometimes. Burn out the weeds and dead stuff after the harvest. We'd do it at the end of the season and we'd do it again in the spring sometimes, depending on which crops were in rotation." He made a visor with his hands and squinted. "Those are the fields behind the farm stand," he added.

Aileen crossed her arms. "Looks a little nuts to me."

"It's pretty tame," Bax said. "It's controlled. We'd use drip torches like Cray-Cray uses at the bonfire. Just burn out the old, and get ready for the new."

"Crazy farm boy," Aileen teased. Bax blushed, and Aileen could barely hold back her smile. She pushed him, but he barely moved, and instead, as she tried to push him again, he pivoted and pulled her into a one-armed hug.

"You know what would be awesome," Javi said. "If we all just skipped everything else this evening and we just watched the fields burn. It's so weird. It's hypnotic watching a fire."

"Even from this distance," Aileen added.

I remained quiet. I wasn't mad, and I didn't really want to make a big deal out of coming up to the bluffs, to my tree, I just wanted them there with me. I didn't even know what I wanted to do—I just knew I had to come back. Face it down. I needed to make it all my own again.

Bax let go of Aileen and walked over to me. "I would," he said to me. I shook my head, but he continued. "No, for real. I want to. It's just, if I do one more thing wrong, if I do anything, they boot me." He rubbed his hands through his hair. He had so much more of it now, curly and wild, nothing like the buzz cut from the beginning of the year. "But I don't know. I don't even know if it's worth it. This place. Fullbrook."

"You know what I wish," Aileen said. "I wish we could do something about this stupid Winter Ball. It's so demented we still do that here."

"Burn out the old," Bax said again. "I can't believe I said that." He looked a little pale. He pointed down to the river. "That's what Hackett and Freddie made me do at the beginning of the year." He glared as if they were actually standing down there. "I just can't believe it."

Javi nodded. "Like this dance. It's like everyone knows but they don't want to know. It's not the knowing that's bad—it's knowing and not doing anything to stop it. To know and do nothing. Senior Send-Off—seriously?"

"We're outcasts," Aileen said. She looked around at all of us. "Nobody else seems to care what can happen."

Senior prank. Senior carpet. Senior couches in the library. The Senior Send-Off. All of it disgusted me. All of it was really about the boys—as if they'd imported us girls here just for them.

I peeled away from the other three and stood where I'd stood the night of the party. Without thinking too much about it, I scratched the word "no" on the side of the tree. I dug and dug, chipping away at the gray bark until the soft brown inside of the tree glowed with the word, like the tree itself was saying it. *No.* Like it was speaking down into me and reminding me that I'd said it, and it meant something and I could say it again and I would probably have to. And not only me. So many others.

No, the tree said to me as I stared at it. As if the tree knew. As if it held all the knowledge, the truth. It was so much better to see that—the tree reminding me what I knew. I knew the truth too. I had lived it.

It wasn't that I just knew the facts. It was so much deeper. To know right from wrong, and to know it so profoundly, was a gift. No matter how much they wanted me to behave, to play by the rules of their little, fake Fullbrook paradise, I didn't have to. I knew too much to play pretend. I knew the real world—and it was mine to live in. They could take so much from me, but not everything. What was left was strong, and they couldn't stop the me I would and could become—how I'd poke up from what they'd torn down, rise from it all, and bloom again, wild and free.

I turned back to the three of them. "Hey," I said. "We can make them care."

"What?" Aileen said. "How?"

"They can only not care if they continue to pretend they don't know." I stepped closer to them. "So we can make them know. All of them. Make it impossible to pretend."

"What are you saying?" Javi asked.

"I'm asking if you're with me. If you won't let me do this all alone."

"We're with you," Bax said.

I looked at him. "Did you say you know how to use one of those things? The drip torch?"

"Yeah," he said.

"Good." I walked out to the bluff edge again. I looked back out to the fire snaking through the dead brush. From this distance it was nothing more than a squiggle of graffiti in the earth. But it was enough. "We'll speak to them in a language they can't ignore."

Burn out the old. Bring in the new.

PART FOUR

THE WINTER BALL

CHAPTER 35

JAMES BAXTER

My probation didn't bar me from playing hockey, of course. Coach would have lost it if I'd been pulled from the game against Hodges. It was in the afternoon, a few hours before the Winter Ball, and the stands shook with what felt like all of Fullbrook cheering as we glided onto the ice. It's impossible not to feel a rush as the noise fills your ears, throbs and swells, pulls you into motion, so you're not flexing your own muscles as much as riding the roar. My body hummed through the warm-ups. Pucks flew at me, one after another, and I stopped them all, or nabbed them out of the air, dipping and moving like I knew where each puck would hit before it was slapped at me.

Hodges hit hard and fast. They'd shown up with their own fleet of fan vans, but no matter how loud they yelled, they were drowned out by our chants. I breathed deep, slowed the game down in my mind to the speed I needed. No matter how fast they moved, how fast they cut and swiveled, how fast the sticks popped back and forth, I slowed everything down and remained focused. It felt good to be back. Not for Fullbrook. Not for Coach O. Not for Freddie and my own team. Not even for the game, as Coach Drucker had once told me. For me. I needed to know. I could do it. Not for the fifty thousand dollars, just for me, for my mind. For clarity.

The first shot was a slap from ten feet out. Just testing me. Easy. Caught it and dropped it for Tucker to take wide left. The next couple were tougher, as they always are when they're closer. Sticks dancing, swerving, keeping the puck in endless razzle-dazzle motion. I stopped one with my shoulder, a little ugly, but anything and everything works, as long as it's a stop. Took another to the leg pads. I almost fell for a fake-out. Hodges's top scorer, Number Seven, broke free. In one-on-ones, advantage is to the shooter, especially if he's as good as this guy. He dipped right, and tried to flick the puck to the corner above my opposite shoulder, but I snapped my head and blocked it off my face mask. By third period, I'd blocked twelve shots. Freddie had scored twice. Our crowd roared, and Hodges's kept trying and trying, but nothing was going their way. Tucker took out Number Seven with a solid hit, but Number Seven took revenge mid-period and flattened Tucker. With him out, my best defender was gone. I was more on my own. In the tenth minute, they hit me with a combo. One, two, three shots on net in a row. I blocked the first two—chopped the first one back down to the ice with my stick, but they got the puck and shot again in an instant, and I blocked it with my shin pads. One of their forwards stole the puck back before I could even get set, and shot, and I nabbed the puck midair, robbing him of the easy goal. In the last minute, with a two-on-one, Hodges shuffled the puck between their forwards, and it was impossible to guess who was going to shoot, but I did a split to stop the last one from sliding beneath me. The buzzer boomed like thunder in my head, and Freddie, despite everything, charged me and knocked me back into the net. He wasn't pissed; he was delirious.

"Buckeye, you bastard!" he yelled. "Number one! Number one!" He got the crowd chanting behind him.

I scrambled out of the net and began a victory lap around the rink, tearing off my glove and holding one finger in the air. I had no idea what was going to happen to me that night, after the showers, after I put on a suit and walked out into the darkness with Jules's plan memorized down to the minute. But before all that, I was here, on the ice, doing what I did best. Nothing and nobody could take that away from me. For one hour and a half, I was the glittering morning star I knew I could be.

Tradition has it that if we win the home game the day of the Winter Ball, everyone pours out onto the ice to congratulate us. That day was no different, and while Hodges's team filed off to the locker room, and their fans slowly exited the arena, the Fullbrook crowd unlocked the doors in the boards and, in a flurry of wool hats and scarves, all Fullbrook maroon, spilled out into the rink, slipping and sliding and tumbling around, a nonsensical pandemonium of discombobulated bodies undulating on the ice.

People roared and cheered around me, teammates slammed and hugged me, even Coach O, who'd donned his own skates for the moment, carved an arc around me, pumping his fist in the air.

But this wasn't the place for me. I could do this. But not here. Everyone had told me Fullbrook was it—the perfect place—but it wasn't. All I had to do was look up into the stands and see Aileen there, on her feet, completely alone except for Jules sitting beside her. Aileen dropped her large coat from her shoulders and stared out over the ice, for all of Fullbrook to see.

I'd thought she was going to wait until that night, at the ball, but that she'd come to the arena instead made so much more sense. I broke free from the crowd and skated over to the Fullbrook team box, stomped in, unlocked the door behind the bench, and still in my skates, stumbled up the stairs until I was next to her.

Together, with Jules on one side and me on the other and Aileen standing tall in the center, we stared down at the rest of Fullbrook. Defiant. Proud. Indefatigable.

CHAPTER 36

JULES DEVEREUX

Even I came out for the game. Watching Bax flop and dive for pucks was like watching grizzly bears catch salmon leaping upstream. It doesn't seem possible until you see it, and you're amazed despite the horror. It was contained within the rink, where it belonged. But what if Freddie checked people off the sidewalks with the force he used to smash the Hodges players into the boards? What if the Hodges guys came swinging into a classroom, whacking people with their sticks the way they did on the ice, and no one in the class was wearing gear?

It was a brutal ballet on ice, exhilarating, breathtaking, but elsewhere, in the real world, it was raw, devastating violence. The bear sinks its teeth into the fish's flesh because it must; it never terrorizes a deer for a night of fun, just because it can.

This was what I was thinking as I sat in the stands next to Aileen. People left space around us. I hadn't realized she was going to wear it to the game, but it was all the more powerful here, out in the open, not only on the dance floor at the Winter

Ball. She sat in the middle tier of benches, a long beige shearling coat wrapped around her. The Fullbrook crowd leapt to its feet every time Bax saved a goal, or every time Freddie scored, or every time it was close. But in the quieter moments, the moments after a whistle stopped the clock, or in between periods, Aileen rose from her seat, shook the coat from her shoulders, and stood for all the rink to see. It barely fit, but that didn't matter. It fit because of where and how it was ripped—the dress she'd worn to the Winter Ball her first year.

I thought people were going to yell at her, make fun of her, call her all the names I'd had rattling around in my mind since the day after the party at Horn Rock—but they didn't. Instead, they tried to avoid it. They looked away. Only some people might have understood at first, but the whispers would travel. Nobody at Fullbrook might have wanted to talk about it, but they couldn't deny seeing it, especially when she got up and walked to the concession stand between second and third period, and again, after the game, when the stands emptied onto the ice and she rose, glowing above us all, her blue sequins sparkling like stars under the halogen light.

They called her the Viking. They had no idea how tough she was.

Bax pounded up the stairs to join us, but none of us could stay long. We all had to get ready. I'd laid out the plan for the night, but I still had to put some of the pieces together. Get the tools in place.

When I stepped back outside, it was snowing. Large, light, cotton ball flakes gently sifted through the air, blanketing the campus in a kind of idyllic innocence. Or so it looked. When Aileen and I walked by the dining hall and saw Gillian and her team stringing lights up under the portico, Aileen dropped the coat off her shoulders again and stared ahead. For a moment, Gillian paused and looked back. Not even the snowfall could hide the violence ripped through the missing fabric across Aileen's body.

CHAPTER 37

JAMES BAXTER

The night of the ball, instead of getting ready in my room like all the other boys, I went upstairs to Javi's room. Firstly, I had no idea how to tie a bow tie. Javi had insisted I get a real one and not a knockoff, prefab bow tie like the ones I'd worn to every prom and semiformal back home—the ones that made the most sense to me, since we all yanked them off and unbuttoned our shirts as soon as we started dancing anyway. But not Javi.

"I'm not going to be seen in a photo with a guy wearing one of those," he said.

"Who cares? This whole thing is a mess anyway."

"Mess or no mess, I'm thinking about that day I look back twenty years from now, and I'm not about to have some rent-a-tux on my arm."

We were standing in front of the full-length mirror on the back of his room's door. He was already spotlessly spiffed up and ready to go. He stood on tiptoes behind me and craned to see over my shoulder as he slipped the black tie around my neck and tied it for me. He was immaculate, everything fit him perfectly, he had the cleanest shave at Fullbrook; he looked as strong and fresh as a tree—he even smelled something like cedar. I sniffed. "What is that?"

"My mother's favorite cologne. I can just hear her reminding me. It's habit."

He handed me my coat and I awkwardly fought to get into it without ripping the seams around the shoulders. When I was sufficiently encased, Javi pinned the boutonniere to my lapel, straightened my collar, and then stood back.

"Let's take a look at you."

"Well, I don't look half as good as you," I said.

"My God, Bax, are you telling me I look good?"

I blushed a hundred shades of maroon.

"Are you?" he teased.

"Yes," I said.

He stepped close, took my hand, then leaned up and kissed me on the cheek. "You too, Bax. You clean up better than I expected."

"Thanks," I said, even though I felt more bagged, tied, and trapped than I did in my everyday Fullbrook uniform.

"Not my type, usually," he said, grinning. "But I'm grateful for the date." He kissed me again.

"You're welcome," I said. "Now, let's do this."

I swung my arm out like a car door and he looped his hand through. We stepped out into the hall and Javi looked at me. "Ready, boys?" he yelled. "Here we come!" We walked down the hall, and then down the stairs and into the common room, locked arm in arm.

As we entered the room, many of the guys averted their eyes, like it was impolite to look or something. I was used to people doing double takes when they saw me, because of my size, but it was weird to be on the other end for once—to be the one they did double takes away from, like they were nervous to make eye contact. I leaned in and squeezed Javi close.

"Don't cut off the circulation in my arm," he teased.

Tapper's freshman boys were lined up in the common room, excited, terrified, maybe looking a little too much like they were going to a funeral instead of getting ready to go pick up their dates. It was crazy. Even though the senior girls were the ones who were calm and practiced and had been to the ball three times before, it was tradition for the boys to walk across the quad, each to his date's assigned dorm, and each to offer his arm to the girl whose corsage matched his boutonniere. Some of the guys twitched and fidgeted like boys half their age trying to hold it and not let it all loose down the pant leg. Poor kids. I actually felt bad for them. They had no clue what was ahead of them.

Meanwhile, the seniors were completely relaxed. Freddie strolled around, asserting his usual authority in the room. He jabbed at a few of the freshmen as he walked by them—especially the smallest ones. "Who knows," he teased, "maybe one of them will make a man out of you tonight." He laughed and glanced over to Hackett, who was perched on the arm of the couch, and who ignored him, too busy scrolling through his phone.

"Hell, yeah," Hackett said, more to himself than anyone else. He grinned and texted something back. He was in his own world, and until Freddie referred to him, nobody had paid him any attention.

Instead, most boys looked at Freddie. The sophomores and juniors were already gone. Tradition went like this: The sophomores and juniors picked up their dates first and went to the dance. Then the senior and freshman boys picked up their dates and paraded to the dining hall. The seniors and freshmen filed in, one couple at a time, alternating between senior boy and freshman girl and senior girl and freshman boy. The names of the freshmen were read aloud—like the induction to some kind of society. Like a debutante ball. Like a *hey, you are on display, and the rest of us are watching you, judging you, sizing you up, deciding where you belong in the hierarchy.*

Freddie turned his attention to us. He shook his head. "It's annoying, you know. You guys having to throw everything off. You won't get announced because neither of you is bringing a freshman."

Javi had explained the whole tradition to me. What did we care? We both thought it was stupid. Or worse. Some of the guys glanced back and forth from Freddie to us.

"Bax is new," Javi said. "He should get introduced." Neither of us cared, of course. He just wanted to egg Freddie on.

Freddie glared at me. "Which one of you is the girl?" he asked.

"Neither of us," I said.

"That's the point, dumbass," Javi added.

Javi and I remained arm in arm, and I kept my eyes fixed on Freddie's. I knew he'd look away, and he did, smirking. "Boys," he said, "here's to making it a night to remember."

And with that, Hackett stood and pocketed his phone. "Okay. Ready?" he asked. There were a few nods and halfhearted hoots.

"What the hell?" Freddie said. "He asked if you are ready. ARE YOU READY?"

Now, like they were all back at the pep rally, they yelled in agreement.

"All right," Hackett said. "Let's go."

He led the freshmen out of the common room and toward the side door, marching out front like the captain of his penguin army, and then Freddie and the other seniors made their way to the other door, closer to Mrs. Attison's dorm proctor suite.

"I guess we make our own way," Javi said to me.

"Good," I said.

I couldn't imagine falling in lockstep with Freddie and the other guys. Of course we had to make our own way, just like Jules and Aileen—the four of us, outcasts mounting our own private and necessary revolution.

Javi nodded. "Ready?" he asked.

"To take on the world?" I said. "Absolutely." But as we walked out, following thirty yards or so behind all the seniors, I was nervous about what I was going to do that night.

It had snowed the day before, and again that afternoon. The fluffy flakes had fallen and fallen for hours, so the whole campus was blanketed in a thick, gleaming whiteness. On any other night, the guys would have been scooping it up by the fistful, making snowballs, and bombarding each other, but not tonight. Tonight, coolly, almost solemnly, they marched to the girls' dorms, deadly serious.

When we got to the dance, Javi could see my nerves, because I positioned us over by the far wall, like some middle school boy at his first dance, and fidgeted like one too, even more than usual. Juniors and sophomores crowded around the punch bowl and snack table, and a few brave theater kids were already out on the dance floor. Once the seniors and freshmen came parading in, I couldn't stop my nerves from getting the better of me, and I began shuffling my weight from foot to foot.

"Is that what you call dancing?" Javi asked.

"No."

"Good, because it isn't."

I stood still—too still, like at attention, but without the salute.

"Are you going to stay there all night?"

"No."

"You're acting a little weird."

"Sorry, man. I just think the whole night is weird." I paused because it wasn't coming out right. "I mean, not this. Not us. Like, that's good. Or. Well. I don't know what I'm trying to say."

Javi laughed. "Let's dance, big boy."

"What?"

"Don't for one minute think you signed up for this and don't have to do any dancing," he said. He laughed again. "Come on. Don't leave me hanging." He dragged me out onto the dance floor and even though it was still early in the ball, and there wasn't real dance music playing, but rather something old, a swinging, bluesy Elvis song, Javi found the beat and started moving to it. We were smack-dab in the middle of the room, and people started turning to us. The juniors and sophomores already on the dance floor moved in a little closer, watching. Javi grabbed my hand and held it in the air. A couple of the dancers cheered. I was out of my league.

The music jumped into the chorus and Javi spun himself around under my hand. The dancers all slid closer, most of them already swing dancing to the tune. As the song moved toward its crescendo, Javi shouted to me, "Come on, Bax. Live, baby, live." And I couldn't hold back anymore. I dropped into it and did my best to keep up with him. He spun me around and we shuffled in tiny circles amid the dancers around us, all cheering.

CHAPTER 38

JULES DEVEREUX

A ileen and I had ditched the system and we let Gillian and her team figure out what to do. Neither of us was around when our dates came to pick us up, and while we felt bad, we also thought it was ridiculous that two seventeen-year-old girls had to sit around and wait for two fourteen-year-old boys to come pick them up. The whole charade was so gross. Instead, we hid out in Aileen's room until everyone else was gone.

We walked arm in arm to the dining hall, entered late, and might have slipped into the ball unnoticed, except for Aileen. The tear along the leg ran from the hem to the waist. The shoulder strap was torn from the back and hung limp and loose on the side, and there was an extra rip under the armpit. Her bra strap was left bare over her shoulder and Aileen had fastened the dress to the bra with a safety pin, just to keep it from sliding down. When she took off her coat, Mrs. Attison and her sixth sense of decorum caught sight of Aileen's dress from across the room. She marched toward us through the crowd.

"Excuse me," she was saying as she approached. "I don't think that's appropriate attire for a formal."

"Brace yourself," I said quietly to Aileen.

"No way. I'm not just going to stand here. Let's dance."

She pulled me forward and we hustled into the throbbing mob near the center of the room, and even though I knew she wanted to say more, once we were in the thick of it, Mrs. Attison didn't pursue us. I'm not sure she even knew why the dress was a mess. Maybe after a moment's thought, she realized she didn't want to find out.

Once we were on the dance floor, I wasn't sure I was seeing what I was seeing. Javi and Bax shaking it together in the center. I could hear the song winding down, and I was worried it would all end, but as the next song kicked in, they kept at it, and more people joined them. I grabbed Aileen by the hand and we jumped in right next to Javi and Bax and swung along with them to the next song. We all turned and turned, and for a brief few minutes, I thought I could spin the rest of the party right out of my mind.

And as if the universe heard me, as if, for one moment, all the feet in the world leapt and landed in time with the song, another body squeezed into our tight circle. It was Max.

Javi eyed him and played it cautious for a moment, but Max tapped Bax on the shoulder, to get him to make room. Bax grinned, backed up, and let Max slide in front of Javi. They yelled at each other over the music.

"I was wrong," Max said. "I was scared."

"Me too," Javi yelled back.

Yes boys, yes, yes boys, yes, yes boys, please, I wanted to chant, but instead all I could manage was a smile and a nod.

"I don't care what they think," Max shouted. "I don't care at all." He stepped closer, pulled Javi toward him, and they moved in unison, bumping and grinding, speaking a language of forgiveness with their hips and smiles.

There had been this perfect moment the night Javi, Bax, Aileen, and I all went to Wendell, this moment in the barn, dancing, this moment feeling like nobody expected anything of me, and I too expected nothing from the world. Expectations. Javi called it my paranoia. But it wasn't. It was more an almost-always-present low-watt fear and worry that hummed somewhere deep inside. But there, dancing in the parti-colored light in the barn at Wendell, sweating and feeling the pulse of music in my stomach, an electricity like my first real kiss howling through my bones, I felt the weightlessness of no worry at all. I felt free.

I was almost there again—a feeling like a thing you can smell but can't see, so you know it's there, but where?—except I was so far away. Bax had stepped away from the dance floor and strode over to the punch bowl. He had Ethan by the arm, and he leaned in close to whisper something in his ear. Aileen was with him, standing between them and Lianne, by the edge of the table, and she got a few more first-year girls to huddle around her. I knew what they were saying—it was all part of the plan.

The music changed. It slowed down, and as Max stepped back from Javi, Javi grabbed him by the wrist.

"Kiss me," he said to Max. "Right here. Right now."

With the crowd all around them watching, they kissed and

kissed again, hesitant at first, and then, with the care and passion that they'd been robbed of back at Horn Rock, they let their mouths close together and breathe each other in.

The next song was a country tune, and for those who knew a box step, it was slow and soft and inviting. Max nestled in close to Javi, and I couldn't hear what they said, but they took each other's hands and fell right in line, stepping into rhythm with the song. *Is that how easy it could be?* I wondered. If only always, and not in these little bubbles, these few faint stars in an otherwise too dark night.

I slipped away, not speaking to anyone. I had to hurry. I looked at the clock. It was almost time.

CHAPTER 39

JAMES BAXTER

Over by the punch bowl, Hackett was leaning in close to Lianne, whispering something in her ear. Her body cocked to the side, and although she gave him a quick smile, she took a step back. He reached for her and held her by the wrist and whispered again in her ear. Then he stepped them both forward, away from the table, and he twirled her beneath his hand.

I watched all this as I hustled toward him without trying to look like I was hustling toward him. The music changed, the lights swirled in a lazy red-and-blue swoop, and Lianne looked to her freshman friends all bouncing on the dance floor nearby. Hackett twirled her again.

"Hey, man," I said to him. He threw me one of those *sans souci* smiles he'd been tossing at me since the beginning of the year. Toothy, wide, confident. When I took him by the arm, he let go of Lianne. He didn't drop the smile. He only glanced over my shoulder. I didn't look. I knew it was Aileen pulling Lianne to the side too.

"You have something to say to me?" he asked.

"No."

"How about you head back to your date, then?"

"No."

He looked over my shoulder again and dropped the smile. "What the hell is she saying to Lianne?"

"No."

"What?"

"No."

Hackett tried to pull his arm out, but I held him tight. "Let go," he said.

"No."

"Stop saying that."

"No."

He struggled again, and I calmly wrapped him in a hug, trying to minimize the scene as much as possible.

"What the hell is the matter with you, man? Let go."

"Are you going to shout for help?" I asked.

"You are a freak of nature, dude. I don't know what kind of game you are playing, but you better let me go right now."

I squeezed as hard as I could, listening to him groan. "No. You hear me? No." And then I released him. I looked over my shoulder. Aileen had led Lianne and Margot and the others away from the punch bowl. At first I couldn't find them. I looked around for Jules and couldn't find her, either. It was a slow song and Javi and Max were dancing close, caught in the soft cone of blue light from above. Then the music switched again and leapt into something fast and galloping, and I saw Lianne and

Margot and a bunch of the other freshman girls dancing. Max and Javi joined them.

"You're insane," Hackett said to me.

I swung back to him and pointed to his face. "I know you heard me."

"You're on probation. You can't touch me. You're dead. You're so dead."

I glanced at my phone. It was nearly time. "No," I said again. "I'm right where I need to be."

The music had everyone swaying and bouncing into each other, and for a moment, I wished I could jump in and join them. For a moment, I thought I could melt back into the fun and forget about everything else, but I'd made Jules a promise and I was going to stick to it. I slipped away and walked briskly toward the bathrooms, and almost slammed into Aileen.

"You okay?" she asked.

"Yes."

"You don't look it."

She could read it all over me. I was so anxious I was starting to feel it in my gut and crawling up and down my skin. "Are you okay?" I asked.

"I think so."

"It's almost time." I looked at my phone again.

"For me too," she said.

I squeezed her arm and took a step toward the stairwell, but she held my hand and pulled me back, the flicker of disco ball light running in from the main hall and flashing on her face. "Can I—" I began, but she interrupted me, stepped close and smashed her mouth against mine, and I felt like I was way up in those stars, getting a glimpse at what it felt like to watch the world spin far below.

And then we were both running across the foyer to the door near the kitchen, and then down the stairs to the basement. The bass beat from the main hall thundered in the stairwell, echoing off the walls and in my head. Aileen pulled rubber gloves from her purse, snapped them over her hands, and ducked below the service window in the basement hallway to the small metal door by the dishwashing room. She was heading toward the circuit breaker. I bolted out the basement door, dashing into the cold, dark snow.

The timing was everything. She couldn't see what we were about to do outside. We just had to trust each other and brace ourselves for all that was about to come.

CHAPTER 40

JULES DEVEREUX

I couldn't grab my coat without raising suspicion so I slipped outside using the stairwell by the bathrooms. It was kind of ironic it was the same place I almost tripped over Ethan and Gillian on the first day of school that year—ironic, or maybe more fitting. I couldn't remember what we said to each other that day, but I knew I had the feeling that he hadn't heard me, that same feeling that haunted me about him now always. He wasn't listening. I was just a prop in the drama of his own mind.

Not anymore.

I couldn't believe how cold it was, and because my dress was long, I had to hike it up so I could run, and my bare arms and neck and legs all had to face the freezing bite in the air. I bolted along the walkway and rounded the academic quad until I came to the huge bushes by the arts center, and then I reached into the thicket, scraping my arms as I pulled out Cray-Cray's drip torch and then another.

I'd broken into his shed earlier and stolen them both, and the pouch he'd used back at the pep rally. I'd found a plastic bag with the little balls he used to fuel the fire, stuffed as many as I could in the satchel, and stashed it all in the bushes by the arts center with a pair of work gloves. Getting caught wasn't my concern. I just wanted to be sure I could go through with it.

When I had the gear, I stood and looked back at the dining hall on the other side of the great lawn. The windows still blinked with the blue-red flash of the dance, and the low bass thumped loud enough to drum out into the night air. I took a deep breath and ran out into the snow.

My ankles stung. I loped like a long-limbed beast across the lawn of the academic quad, swishing my feet through the snow, almost skating, so I would leave footprints behind. I cut one line, then another, and then another, then went back over the same lines with the back of my heel, digging a groove all the way down into the dead grass. And just as I wondered if he was going to join me or not, I saw a lone figure running toward me, an enormous shadow. I wasn't afraid. I was relieved.

He was panting when he reached me. "You ready?" he asked as he tried to catch his breath.

"Yes." I handed him one of the drip torches. "Last chance to duck out, Bax. This is it."

"I'm not backing out," he said, taking it from me. "I'm with you. You're not alone."

He didn't touch me. He just stood there, arms loose by his side, the nozzles of our drip torches gazing at each other. But I still felt held. Held but not trapped. Like he was holding me without embracing me. I was exploding with fear all over, but excitement too. Freedom. Like all my strings were finally clipped. Completely on my own—and not alone. I wasn't abandoned. I was free.

We walked up and down through the trough I'd made. I handed him the little balls from the pouch, and when he placed them on the ground, I doused them with lighter fluid. Beside the last line, we made two sweeping arcs, carving a circle into the ground, and filled it with the kindling as well. I had no idea if it would work. I had no idea if it could be seen clearly and legibly from the windows of the dining hall—but that was all I wanted. The whole party drifting to the windows to see the fire of what I had to say.

When I felt I had done all I could to prepare, I crouched and felt the chill sweep down through me from my teeth to my toes and waited. I didn't have a phone or a watch or anything. I just waited. "Come on, Aileen," I whispered.

And like that, she answered.

The lights cut out. The music stopped, and for a moment there was a peace and calm and quiet that stalled me, that made me wonder if I shouldn't go through with it, but under the moonlight, I could see the shadowy fingers of leafless trees poking up out of one darkness and into another, and if he didn't listen to me that night against the tree at Horn Rock, he would at least have to see it now.

Bax demonstrated first. He lit a few of the balls on fire and showed me how to do it slowly. He began to trace a line of fire along the arc. It was now or never. I ran over to the other letter, dipped the nozzle, flipped the switch, felt the heat steam up through the handle and off the sides of the can, and ignited the first ball. I walked backward, like Bax was doing, like Cray-Cray had done, drawing my line of fire. Flames zipped through the troughs I'd dug. I'd written it the right way, so that when they looked out the windows from the darkened hall, they'd see it ignited in the snow. My flaming script: the word "NO."

I stood for a moment, smoke curling around my legs and around the hem of my dress, watching the word burn down into the grass—a fiery tattoo of the word they'd ignored for too long at Fullbrook. NO. The word flickered and danced as steam rose up like shadowy breaths released from the ground through the snow.

Pandemonium had probably taken over the dining hall, and I could only imagine the currents of fear ripping through the teachers, let alone the students. Bax and I ditched the cans and satchel in the bushes and ran the long way back, in the shadows and darkness in front of the science center, across the footpath near the path to the boathouse, and through the snow up around to the side door to the dining hall. We thought we'd probably get caught, but if we made it back before the lights went on, there was still a chance we might not. Maybe, if we were in the crowd when the lights shot back on, we'd send our message and still be able to stick it out for the year. Maybe.

I was exhausted and leaping with my own kind of fire on the inside, but the rest of me was blue with cold. My feet were soaked. When Bax and I got to the stairwell door, the one I'd exited, I knocked once, and then again, and like air coming into my lungs after I'd held my breath for too long, Aileen opened the door and swept us in.

The lights were still on in the basement, and Aileen stood holding a trash bag and another pair of shoes. For a moment, as I heard the ebb and flow of commotion echoing down the stairs, I held my breath again. I thought about what it would mean if I was able to get away with this—just like Ethan and all the other guys had been able to get away with what they'd done—if we could make our mark of permanence on their minds in the same way I was sure they had left theirs on ours.

NO: an afterimage burned on their retinas, the glow seared forever in their memory. Knowledge of a truth they could no longer avoid.

Ready to take on the world...

JAMES BAXTER

There's a quote a teacher of mine back home used to have up on his wall. I'd looked at it so many times and never really thought about the meaning. "Be kind, for everyone you meet is fighting a hard battle."

There's controversy about who said it first, so in our classroom it was attributed to "anonymous." That seemed fitting. I suppose anybody could have said it. Anybody who'd tried to grow up and sort out what to do and who to become in a world that is too confusing for me to ever understand. You have to use what you have and do the best you can.

It hadn't taken us long to get caught. In fact, it was only a few days, and frankly, I think they knew more about every little detail that happened than we did. That's power—you have all the advantages. The rest of us just live here. The admin team, the faculty, they had all the power. As did the board of trustees.

I was thinking about all this as I sat on the overstuffed couch in the lobby of the admin building, right where I'd sat the day the folks in admissions tried to decide if I was worthy and exceptional enough to join them. Why would I ever want to stay here? The place was full of lies, and maybe the worst lie of all was the one they told themselves. That Fullbrook was some kind of paradise nestled in the hills of New England.

What a relief to walk out into the world and be free of it.

The night of the Winter Ball, it was easy for me and Aileen and Jules to sprint back upstairs to where the power had been cut and, in the darkness, slip back into the crowd as if we'd always been there. Everyone in the room had migrated over to the windows along the wall, and gazed out toward the great lawn in the academic quad. The fire still burned, terrifying and hypnotic.

NO.

Then I heard Javi.

"No." He said it loud and slow, so everyone could hear. "No, no, no, no." He was all alone, no one joined him, and it was like some distant echo from the pep rally. One man chanting by the light of the fire. But then Max joined him. Then someone else. Soon there was a small chorus, only a few voices—but it was enough.

It was hard to see who was who, so I couldn't tell if Hackett was there, or Freddie, looking out the window with everyone else. But when the lights came back on, I spotted them turning away from the windows. Pale and shaken. Freddie didn't look at me, but Hackett did. He saw the word on fire and knew immediately what was going on. He knew I had something to do with it and Jules had something to do with it too. He went to the admin building the next day and told them his suspicions. That was the beginning of the end.

The next day I watched, along with many others, as his father's helicopter circled the air above Fullbrook again, hovering with its deafening noise and menace, and descended slowly to the football field. Cray-Cray drove him and his lawyer up to the admin building. That's when I knew I was finished. Jules, too.

He was the target of terrible bullying, he explained, and he wanted it ended. He was a victim, he told everyone. The victim. As Javi told me, "He just got in front of the narrative, man. That's how it works." And he did. Two days later I was sitting in the admin building lobby with the threat of being expelled under charges of assault and battery and arson. I wore the same stupid suit I wore to my admissions meeting. Heard the subtle undertones of what everybody was saying back then, even though nobody else was in the lobby with me this time. *You do not belong here.*

I leaned forward on the couch and ripped the seam along the back of the jacket. As soon as I heard it, I felt looser, freer. I laughed. I took the coat off and slung it over my knee, rolled my shirt cuffs up my arm, loosened my tie, and freed my neck from the top button. I felt more ready for what I had to do than I had in over a year. I remembered my old man once telling me that every morning, he swung his feet out of bed, planted them on the floor, and reminded himself to smile, because he was about to get up and do everything he had to do, everything he wanted to do, and everything he didn't. He started each day reminding himself he could be proud to be the man he was, and that pride could get him through the day no matter what. It wasn't bravado. He wasn't tough. All he had was integrity, and that was enough.

The door to Headmaster Patterson's office swung open and Jules stepped out. She had on what I knew she called her brave face, the one where she squints ever so slightly and sets her jaw on lockdown.

As she walked away from him and toward me, Headmaster Patterson called to me over her shoulder. "Mr. Baxter," he growled.

Jules curled a smile into one corner of her mouth, and she flung a mischievous side-eye glance at me as she passed. Headmaster Patterson cleared his throat and called me again, but I turned first to watch Jules walk away.

"Bax," she said as she turned toward the front door. She flashed a peace sign over her shoulder as she stepped out of sight.

I felt my feet planted firmly on the floor, and I cracked my own smile as I stood and stepped toward Headmaster Patterson, and I didn't slouch or hang my head, or even look away. I stared him right in the eye to let him know what Baxter pride looked like when it rose to meet the day.

JULES DEVEREUX

It didn't take a forensics team to put two and two together and discover I was part of the duo who tattooed the great lawn with fire. But truthfully, I'd really always known I was going to get caught anyway. I didn't mind. I'd had it with Fullbrook.

Aileen and Javi hadn't done much of anything. There was no reason for them to get in trouble too, and I might have been able to take all the blame if Bax hadn't already been on probation, and hadn't spooked Ethan all over again right before running out to help me, although I loved seeing how terrified Ethan looked after that, scared in the way some girls are when they don't know whose steps they hear behind them on the walkway between buildings at night. I didn't want any of them to get expelled with me—I just needed their help to make sure I could finish what I had set out to do.

When Aileen had thrown out my wet sneakers and the gloves, we all rushed upstairs into the main hall and watched as the rest of the room stared outside. Some people had already drifted away, but most were still watching the flames flicker out on the great lawn, and everyone had to listen to Javi. He was still chanting when I got into the room. It was too dark, he didn't know if I was there or not, and I could hear the strain in his voice, as if he'd been shouting it out for a while. I was surprised no one had stopped him yet.

Obviously, there were teachers running around trying to figure out what was going on. Mr. Hale even bumped into me by the door as he staggered out of the main hall. He didn't apologize, he just stood still for a moment, fear ballooned on his face, openmouthed and unable to find that condescending glare down the slope of his nose he usually found for me.

I couldn't see who was who. I didn't know if Lianne and Ethan and Freddie and the whole damn hockey team were all at the windows watching the word burn into ash and coals in the ground. But I knew they'd know. Everyone would know. They'd have to address it in a new way.

Javi took that on. He knew exactly how to follow up. He wrote an article for the *Red Hawk Chronicle*. He drew up a petition, had it signed by a hundred students, and demanded an all-school training workshop on consent. He didn't disappoint. He could say with a clear conscience that he didn't have anything to do with the fire, because he didn't, and that became abundantly clear when Cray-Cray and a local police detective searched my room the very next day and found my smoky dress, and when they found Cray-Cray's drip torches in the bushes, and they found the footprints and witnesses who said they'd seen me, and they had my track record of being a pain in the ass.

But it was worth it. Aileen shared her story in another

article in the *Red Hawk Chronicle*, and a handful of other girls came forward to share their stories too. And that was only the beginning.

Three days after the fire, Headmaster Patterson had me in his office and he used one form or another of the word "expel" eleven times. I didn't say much at all, especially because I stared at him blankly as he spoke, really thinking about how he wasn't expelling me as much as I'd chosen to do what I did, that leaving Fullbrook was really my choice, he wasn't casting me out, driving me out, as much as I was pushing on and leaving it behind me. I was staring back at him telling him that I was walking out. I was ready to take on the world. I was living.

He might have felt it radiating off me. "Are you listening, Julianna?" he asked me.

"Are you?" I replied.

I liked watching a man finally dumbstruck into stillness and silence before me.

When he recovered, he told me he'd see me when my mother arrived and he would explain everything to her again, in person, although he'd already explained it to her over the phone, and she didn't believe him and she explained that she'd been giving money to the school in one way or another for forty years, but what Patterson didn't say and what I didn't have the heart to say either is that that didn't matter, what she had done, it was nothing compared with the crusty old bald man shuttling into Fullbrook in his helicopter and demanding that Ethan, a man with a future, be protected.

I had to hand it to Bax. I'd never dreamed of getting Ethan booted from Fullbrook, but making him know just how much had to go into protecting him was a nice kind of dig too.

I was just sorry Bax had to go too.

I saw him on my way out of Patterson's office, massive and oafish as always, but unbuttoned, loose, someone I admired because when I asked him to be there he had been. There is an old Italian proverb that goes something like "To find a friend is to find a treasure," and I think that's true. They're as rare and precious as any buried gold.

I gave Bax my little wave of love as I passed him, tried to buoy him on his way in to hear the news he already knew was coming too, and I pushed open the front door to the admin building. In the sunlight, I stared at the old elm tree ahead of me and smiled, because to some degree, Fullbrook had done its job. I did feel ready to take on the world. I already had.

Then a final thought came to me. I leaned against the wall of the admin building and waited for Bax. His meeting wasn't all that long either. He came lumbering out the front door, a crooked smile cracked across his face, and he seemed a little surprised to see me waiting for him.

"Can you do one last thing with me?" I asked him.

He nodded. "Only if you promise me it actually isn't the last."

"I promise."

The administration, the board, the whole community at Fullbrook was already beginning to wipe away the evidence of the flaming script, and within days they would have the lawn dug up, and within months, there'd be new grass spread out and perfectly manicured in a stitched work of green. I wanted to make some mark that would last a little longer, something next year's first years could look up at and think about, and the first years the year after that, too. So that when they were asked to look up at the school motto and reflect on the power of the words, they could see too how their own words should carry the same respect. I wanted them to know that when they spoke they should be heard.

I led Bax over to the old elm. "Hoist me up as high as you can," I said.

I dug out my keys, and with his back braced against the tree he lifted me up along the broad smooth trunk. I held my key like a knife and I scratched. I dug and dug until the soft brown pulp beneath the bark began to glow in the sunlight. Ten feet high in the air, my words were writ large and bold: *I SAID NO.*

Just as I finished, we heard Mr. Patterson out on the steps. "Hey," he yelled. "Hey, what are you doing?"

Bax dropped and caught me like we were doing a pep squad routine. As soon as my feet were on the ground, I grabbed him and began to run. We had no idea where we were going. We were simply sparked, ignited—free to wander hand in hand, all the world before us, not what it was but what it could be, the world to come, the one we made ourselves.

for the time, space, and resources to pursue, write, and edit this novel. I can't thank enough the people at these two institutions— the work they do to bolster the arts is vital. Thank you for all that you do to help the work that artists make see the light of day.

I am incredibly grateful to David Groff, Christa Desir, Randy Ribay, Shaun David Hutchinson, Meg Medina, and Jason Reynolds for taking the time to read and offer their profound advice for this story—thank you for your enormous hearts; so much love to you all.

Nicola Yoon, Amber Smith, Jeff Zenter, Amy Reed, and Kathleen Glasgow's generous and galvanizing early support for this novel means the world to me. I admire you all, and I'm humbled by your words—thank you all!

Thank you to my large and growing family, Heide Lange, John Chaffee, Joshua Chaffee, Garima Prasai, Maryanne Kiely, Tom Kiely, Trish Kiely, Niall Kiely, and Bridget and Leo—I love you all. I am deeply grateful for your love, expert advice, patience, and indefatigable support, and for the many hours you spend hearing me talk about the stories I'm inventing in my mind. Thank you for listening, and for teaching me how to be a better listener, which to me feels like the most important skill to cultivate when trying to live lovingly.

And thank you Jessie Chaffee for inspiring me to try to live as lovingly as possible. Thank you for the integrity of your earnestness, for the wisdom of your thoughtfulness, and for the strength of your love. Thank you for sharing your life with me. I love you all ways and always.

ACKNOWLEDGMENTS

I deeply care about the issues at the heart of *Tradition*, but I wouldn't have had the courage to begin writing this story without the care, counsel, and expert stewardship of my editor, Ruta Rimas, and my agent, Rob Weisbach. They inspired me, spurred me on, and devoted so much of their intelligence, thoughtfulness, and time to the creation of this book. I'm forever grateful to them for this and for everything they do—thank you! Thank you also to Justin Chanda and the entire team at Simon & Schuster for their tireless efforts and nurturing of this book at every level and in every department—thank you to my whole publishing family.

As I began the book, I knew enough to know I knew nothing—Sarah Tarrant Madden and Savannah Whiting helped to give the story shape and heart. Thank you both for your patience, wisdom, and willingness to breathe life into what was at first only an idea. And a special thank-you to Ruby Kinstle for the wisdom, courage, and inspiration you gifted this novel. Jules and I both owe you a debt of gratitude.

Thank you also to everyone at the Lower Manhattan Cultural Council and the New York Public Library's Allen Study Room